How
Wendy Redbird Dancing
Survived the
Dark Ages of Nought

D0144092

LYN
FAIRCHILD
HAWKS

ISBN-10: 0988883724
ISBN-13: 978-0-9888837-2-7

Quotations from:
A Raisin in the Sun by Lorraine Hansberry, Signet edition, pp. 113 and 119. Copyright ©1988 by Robert Nemiroff.
Of Mice and Men by John Steinbeck, Penguin edition, p. 81. Copyright © 1965 by John Steinbeck.
Prayer to St. Michael. Part of the Leonine Prayers of Pope Leo XIII. 1886.

Cover and Formatting: Streetlight Graphics

ACKNOWLEDGMENTS

A first novel is a bit like a first child. Bear with me as I open an album stuffed with photos and make you look. Understand that without the village I'm about to describe, this book wouldn't be here.

This story began when I heard a voice, Wendy's flatline recitation, telling the world how it is, was, and will be. Her first words scrawled themselves into the back of a composition notebook in December 2009, six months after I'd tried to explain to a 12-year-old who Michael Jackson was, the day of his passing. A few days later, I sat down with my friend Teresa and said, "Can I read you some of this story?" She listened, and said she wanted to hear more. Six months later, she agreed to read the whole, rough thing on a train to Baltimore and came home raving. That same summer my writing partner, Jen, realized her eyes needed help when she peered at my fine print (I was trying to save at Kinko's). But she got some glasses and persisted anyway. She had no idea she'd be reading many more versions over the next two years, or how much her advice I try Blake Snyder's *Save the Cat* would change my writing. Stephanie, our other partner, kept pace with every new draft I brought, helping me again and again with her meticulous feedback. She has such warm words and faith in my prose, I am truly grateful.

My sister, Antonia, called me up with great enthusiasm

after she read the first draft and said, "It's YA for Gen X!" This year she read the most recent, said it was "Intense!", and gave more insightful critique. She talks about my characters as if they're real, claiming she's seen Sunny Revere around town.

Also cheering me on since that first draft was Gordon, a fellow author keeping it real on the Left Coast. If I hadn't had him to commiserate with during the crazy query journey, I'm not sure what I would have done. His humor got me through some moments of serious disappointment, never mind the brilliance brimming out of his keyboard.

Bob, my Peaceniks pal since our writers' residency with Doris Betts, not only helped me with thoughtful read-throughs but also kept the praise coming, understanding how important this book is to me. I knew if he was excited, I should start getting excited. He's been a true friend advising me through the realm of publishing. As I've prepared Wendy for her "launch" into the world, Dave, another Peaceniks pal, has been a stout encourager of this self-pub enterprise and a great editor and adviser on everything from back-cover blurbs to cover design. I'm thrilled to join him and Bob in True North Writers' Co-operative, where we're all about *scribere quam videri scribere*—writing, not just seeming to write. We keep the inspiration of Doris with us. She always told the truth with an impeccable sense of humor, challenging us to find our authentic stories.

The term "beta readers" doesn't do justice describing the people who agree to try your manuscript in the early days. These friends are givers and dreamers who cheerlead your work along, no matter how ragged. Thank you, Randy, Delia, Kira, Gwyn, Amanda, and Vince who labored through early drafts. Thank you, Nancy S., for amazing conversations about writing, art, and passion. Thank you to Marcia, who advised me on emotional issues for youth, and to my cousin Elizabeth and my friend Nick, doctors both, who helped me write scenes of cardiac arrest I hated to remove. (Believe me when I say, *They'll be back.*) The Muu Muus—Marcia, Beverly, Susan, Laurie, and Katie—heard various bits and pieces over the last two years at group and gave me pep talks when the journey got tough. And friends at the day job—Elizabeth, Bobbie, Sally, Tracy, Deirdre, and Jean—how often you heard the reports and said, *Stay strong, have faith, hang in.* Nancy P., thanks for your wonderful emails shouting joy and encouragement across the miles. Elizabeth, I appreciate so much the time you took to comb through the book with your keen editor's eye.

Nina and Bonnie of the Wilkes University Creative Writing program called me after the manuscript won the first runner-up award for the James Jones First Novel Fellowship. They said that it was between mine and the winner. That kept me going.

From July 2011 to October 2012, I worked with Sarah, a literary agent, and she challenged me to rip that draft up and start over. I'm happy I took many of these risks, and I'm happy I kept Wendy's soul in the process. Many agents along the path of querying let me know that this book had promise, and I thank them for their kind rejections.

I thank Diane for vetting the manuscript and catching many errors, whether grammatical, mechanical, or logistical, helping the book to make good sense. I'm grateful to Streetlight Graphics for making the cover of my dreams.

Cat lovers will ask if Strike and Retreat is real. Yes, he is. My mewse, Sonny Hawks, knows this book quite well. If he hasn't sniffed, scented, or shed upon it, then it's not an approved draft.

Henry, my stepson, helped me with teen expressions in this book as well as the texting, seeing as I'm a Luddite in the phone department. I'm grateful for his assistance and his thoughtful votes on my cover.

Thank you, Carolina, for reading it twice and for being

so faithful with encouragement. You get my soul buddy wanderings into strange realms of spiritual belief.

Amy, you're my hero. You joke that you're no writer, but to paraphrase Pat Schneider, *You write on air whenever you speak.* Thanks for your wise counsel and great wit. It keeps me going.

My parents, Stephen and Katherine—I'm not sure how many drafts you read. All I know is, I am so loved I can't measure it. I am able to write today because you always gave me hope and space as a child to let creativity flourish. You gifted me with trust that my ideas matter.

Greg Hawks, my partner in artistic faith, you have loved me through all the deadlining—always saying, "Let's do this." Sweetie, it's on. Bless you for getting me to laugh and rest when I take my art waaaaay too seriously.

All these midwives, all these helpers, and now, the birth.

May art heal and help. May it get us to speak of what's hidden. One out of three women; one out of six men. I say it's far more. May we all learn to ask the right questions.

There is no sun without shadow,
and it is essential to know the night.
—Albert Camus, "The Myth of Sisyphus"

WENDY REDBIRD DANCING'S PACT WITH MJ. JUNE 25, 2009. 2:27 P.M.

O St. Michael, prince of heavenly hosts,
thrust into hell this Satan,
who prowls about the world
seeking the ruin of souls.

IF I START TELLING HOW things happened, it must be nothing but the unblinking truth. Every raw, horrific fact must be laid bare.

For nights I've dreamed of cleavers separating his hand from his arm, his head from his neck. But each dream ends with my hands, arms, head flying into outer space.

I'm bad. Hounded by night creatures. Stamped by the smoothest of criminals.

Let truth be told in this old-school journal. Not some tweet-text-IM, spamming everywhere, gone with the next breath. Ink instead, sure as blood. Note the red leather: hardbound. Note the handwriting: cursive. Note the lock and key. Let's do this like monks, like nuns, like girls of old.

If he shows again tonight, or tomorrow, and I must look him in the eye, I will find the strength to say it. Then I will 911 Grandma. I will beg her presence in this house. Show her this tome when terror takes my tongue. No one will hurt me now, because they'll know what's true.

Coming soon: The Big Reveal. This girl will peel back the glittering glove, and she will doff her mask.

CHAPTER 1

W E'RE GETTING HONKED AT YET again in the school drop-off circle because my dear mother, Sunny Revere, has failed to move forward in a timely fashion. Or perhaps they hate us because of her hippie bumper stickers: MATRIOTIC, COEXIST, NATURE IS MY CHURCH.

"4...G...V...N...? Forgiven? Whatever," she says, sneering at the license plate of the silver SUV in front of us. She lurches our car forward, then loops her gray-brown hair into an unsteady knot on the crown of her head. "And look, another John 3:16. Since when did this place go Bible Belt?"

"Since always, Mother," I snap. We're trapped at .000016 miles per hour, disallowed from disembarking till the right fascist moment. I've already counted 15 boys with backward ball caps and 7 girls with 4-inch heels, and neither are workable numbers.

"The ignorance," Sunny mutters, tailgating the SUV. One false move and our rusting 1991 Mitsubishi Mirage Colt will be a pancake beneath it.

"Then why did we come here?" I ask.

We're at a dead stop again, thanks to the fat palm of the good ol' boy officer just ahead, sweating like a hunk of pocked cheese in this swamp heat. "Poor guy, he looks dehydrated," she says.

She rolls down her window and offers him her thermos of

organic goji berry tea. "*As-Salam Alaikum*," she calls cheerily. She's taken up Muslim greetings to protest racial profiling in Southern suburbia.

"No thanks, ma'am." The officer looks spooked.

"You're scaring him." I sink lower in my seat.

"I was not!" She rolls up the window.

"Once upon a time, life was good," I say. "But no, we *had* to leave—"

"Enough with the rants, Wendy!" When Sunny makes a face, her jaw elongates even more, getting lean and horsey. "If I survived this place, you can. You'll get back on stage and all will be well."

"I told you, I'm done with theater! It was my most important play, ever!"

Two, bright red doll spots bloom on her cheeks. "I couldn't take things anymore. You need to understand!"

I am the most understanding 15-year-old she will ever meet. Like when she said I'd be with Cindy for eighth grade in San Francisco, but we suddenly ended up in West Virginia. Or when she went crying back to California three months into my ninth grade year, but then insisted we flee for Idaho at Christmas—only to make us go right back to California in June. And now, May of my tenth grade year, we've made haste for North Carolina. I could put a fist through this window.

Another lurch forward. "It's just..." Her voice trails off.

"Just what? Who is it this time?"

She won't say.

My heart slams my ribcage, and I start counting 4 cracks in the windshield, 4 rust spots on the hood, 4 nicks in the dash—she always has a backup man, every time we've bolted. I know she has a new dude here, which is why she left Jerome, heinous couch-surfing Jerome, with his lean and ragged look and the constant smell of B.O. and clove cigarettes. Narrow eyes always watching me whether Sunny was in the room or not.

Our silence simmers. Only two cars till drop-off.

Sunny explains to the windshield, "You had an understudy. There will be other shows."

"No, there will not. I had the lead—like that's going to happen every day." Viola, in *Twelfth Night*. Cindy, who ruled the stage beside me as the lovely Olivia, said it was a damn shame; then she cried.

Sunny messes with the radio dial. She lands on some oldies station where Elvis croons "Don't Be Cruel." He growls, "Mmm," the way a randy lion might check out an impala's sweet flesh, and she laughs.

"I'm leaving, you know," I say. Now she's singing. "This is it. After London, you'll never see my ass again." On July 24, 2009—my birthday—Cindy and I, proud and rare owners of tickets to see Michael Jackson at the O2 Arena, we shall bow down in the presence of The King of Pop. Grandma's funding it, so Sunny can't do a thing.

"Okay, drama queen," Sunny says with a sigh. "All the world's *your* stage." She inches us forward the last bit. "But this is my home—my roots!—and someday, it'll be yours, too. You'll see."

I grit my teeth.

Right then, I see Deanna Faire stroll by, trailed by minions and flipping salon blond over a shoulder. She who rocks the tiny glitter tee, skintight jeans, and red cowboy boots stars as my latest nemesis. Somehow I've enraged yet another Mean Girl, and it doesn't help she's a local country star with four thousand Facebook fans and a publicist. Now her hate for me is trending. Thank MJ she doesn't notice our rusting carcass spewing white smoke, or Mother's latest outfit.

"Have a beautiful day, my little redbird!" Sunny sings as I get out. Heads turn and faces sneer in crowds nearby—at me and my dear mother too loud in a ratty blue sari and peacock feather earrings. I've only been here 7.2 days of May, but the masses very much know who I am.

The Carolina heat hugs me like hot, bad breath. I plug Michael in my ears and make my entrance, head down and hoodie up.

CHAPTER 2

BAM! A SHOULDER HITS MINE in these factory halls reeking of sickly sweet Lysol, raging hormones, and rank sweat. Too high, that redneck who just bumped me, too many fools and tools swarming to get over, under, around. Drones ogle phones and thumb tiny keyboards, faces stuck to screens.

"Hey, emo screamo!" yells a Skoal-dipping senior with a long-ass drawl. "What's under the hoodie?"

How low can they go? Praise Michael Jackson for filling my ears, King of my Walkman, granting me sanity—*ooh!* I push through the idiocy, the illiteracy, beating and bopping, giving thanks to guitar, praise to bass, bless the drums—*ow! Yee-ha!* Brassy and rhythmic, I dodge these zombies, 8 steps per verse, blocking tongues like razors. Though sweat pools in my pits, though looks slice and dice, it's all right, that's right, do you fools have an anthem?

"Hey, look who's back in black." It's Deanna Faire with her pack of fawning minions, leaning against the wall of the main hall. Mysteriously, inexplicably, she has something to say every freaking day about the black or the hoodie—like her reputation depends on it.

She says to them, "Think she's a lez?"

The drone BFFs giggle. One says: "She's kind of psycho."

"And her mom's a ho," Deanna says. "A hippie ho." This

cracks them up mightily. Then she says, low but so I can still hear it: "What do I pay him for? Wasting time with that skank!"

I pick up the pace. How the hell does she know about Sunny's cross-country manhunts? Pay who what? At least today Deanna's pack doesn't tread on my heels, a beauteous rarity.

Behind me, Deanna's last drawl. "God, somebody needs to clean house. This place has gone goth, ghetto, and Mexican." Cackles from her crew, while I twitch and keep walking.

I see Cindy's stricken face, and I wonder when I became a coward. Just a week ago at dress rehearsal, we sat in front of mirrors with her dark foundation, my light, joking about the three commandments of makeup. Tonight she will speak Shakespeare and light up the stage.

At the intersection of the Math and Science halls, I forget which way English is. So many lemmings swarm from every side, I'm stuck in the middle, pushed by a teen tsunami up against a Unity mural where deformed blacks and whites grin like pumpkins, grasping four-fingered hands.

"Move along, Wendy Redbird Dancing," calls Ms. Washington. She is a tall, older black woman on fearsome heels, wide in her brown silk suit. You can tell she hates white kids from suburbia and my hippie name. I don't blame her. Sunny claims I make this up, but seriously, Ms. Washington looks at me like she knew Grandma in a whites-only kind of way.

I land in AP Lit, bruised, but hoodie still intact; run over, but still breathing. Ms. Teasdale, who looks like a big lanky bird in a tie-dye, passes out books for our AP exam review. Praise MJ, I read all of these back in California: *Adventures of Huckleberry Finn, Uncle Tom's Cabin, The Scarlet Letter.* Hmm, do I choose racist hate, bloody whips, or branded harlots? I flip through *Huck Finn* and see she's blacked out *nigger* on every page.

"What the hell?" I say under my breath. "So we can't handle the truth?"

"I know, right?" says a voice just in front of me, to my left. It's Tanay DeVries. We've never said boo to each other, but she did nod at me yesterday. I like her face because it's heart-shaped with apple cheeks. She also has a nose broad as a barn, like MJ's before the surgeries, and her eyes glow an eerie, bright-crystal green, like she's a demonic chocolate elf. She's wearing fatigues with a tight purple shirt pulled over her curves, but somehow it all works.

"The woman means well," she says, nodding her head at Teasdale, "but it is what it is, know what I'm saying?"

"Yeah, like Mark Twain said: 'Denial ain't just a river in Egypt.'"

Tanay's eyebrows rise. Then her face clears. "Ah, pun. I bet they put that on the exam." She sighs and shakes her head, like Armageddon is on its way.

Andrew Burrell leans forward from where he sits behind me to my right. Like Tanay, he's the only black rep for his gender in the class. "So you say it's okay to use it? You still mad at me?" He's looking at Tanay.

Tanay rolls her eyes. "Do I care what you do?" she says. "Go ahead, use the whole damn dictionary with your boys."

"Come on, girl, it's all about context." He's grinning at her, and he's got a voice that's rich and deep, a chiseled nose and jaw, and a head shaved close—the kind of classic face that starts gastrointestinal fireworks. He glances at me. "Don't mind us, we like to fight."

"I bet you don't say that word in here," Tanay says. "But then you're out there saying it all the time with your boys!"

"Out there, it's a term of endearment," Andrew says.

"It's a racial epalet!" Tanay says.

Epithet, I think, but don't say a word.

"Don't be judging me now. You're all for it in the book," Andrew says. "It's all about who's saying it and why they're saying it."

"Yeah, well, now the rednecks around here think they can do it, too," Tanay snaps. But her lips are on the verge of a smile.

"Fools were racist long before me," Andrew says with a shrug, and settles back in his seat.

"I hate censorship," I say to no one in particular. "But it's not a word I'd say, you know, just to have the right."

"See, she's got sense," Tanay says.

"She's always got to have the last word," Andrew tells me.

Tanay rolls her eyes and snorts. I see I am sitting on a high-voltage line of sexual tension.

Deanna Faire slithers in as the bell rings, beaming and bestowing love on her peeps. She sits her bony ass right in front of me. While Teasdale yaps about the Big AP coming soon to a desk near you, the prominent and preferred Miss Dee swishes her locks, then turns, and gives my garb The Elevator. Up, down, sneer. Last, those Xanax-blue eyes land on my Egyptian eyeliner, worn in honor of one singer who brought us the biggest of all Thrills.

Then she leans over to one of her girls and whispers, "Does she ever shower?" Her pointy nose wrinkles. "Anyone got Febreze?"

Laughs here, there, everywhere except for Tanay and Andrew. My face gets hot; burning waters roil at the edges of my skin. My fists clench, pushing a jagged nail center of my palm, stigmata fierce.

Tanay glares at Deanna and says, "You are one nasty human being."

Deanna smiles at her like an angel. "Sorry, but something smells nasty." More giggles.

Oblivious Teasdale scribbles on the SMART Board, *Connect*

the Dots. "The AP exam wants you to see the big picture," she says. "You need to make connections among all these readings. What's the theme?"

"Prejudice," I say, loudly. "Like some people who say this school's gone, and I quote, 'goth, ghetto, and Mexican.' Unquote." I look straight at Deanna.

It's very quiet. Deanna's face lights up in pink neon. "Who says *that*? It's like 2009! People just elected Obama! Please." Sympathetic murmurs and eye rolls for Deanna's enlightened status. "I mean, I don't see race. I think people who always talk about it are the racists."

"Did you, or did you not say, 'This school's gone goth, ghetto, and Mexican'?" I snap. But my voice is shrill.

Deanna sighs. "I have no idea what you're talking about, but I do know that's *slander.*"

"Watch out, she's got a lawyer," says some white dude in a backward ball cap and a polo with the collar flipped. Everyone chuckles, and Deanna smirks like a satisfied cat.

"Settle down, please!" Teasdale squeaks, running nervous hands through gray, flyaway hair. "Let's get back to connecting dots!"

"I mean, come on, Andrew," Deanna says. "You're class VP and starting quarterback. Like *that's* racist?"

People laugh. Andrew's face shuts down.

"Excuse me," Tanay says, her voice like steel, but I can see her leg jittering beneath her desk. "As long as blacks are seventy percent of the suspensions around here, but less than thirty percent of the population, we've got a ways to go."

Andrew clears his throat. "Yeah, it was in the paper the other day."

"Well, if people get suspended here, it's for violence," Deanna says with a sniff.

"Uh-uh." Tanay shakes her head. "Some people get suspended just for attitude."

"I got two days for starting a fire," the dude in the polo says proudly. Everyone cracks up.

"Keshawn McAdoo got seven for writing on the bathroom wall," Tanay says. "You do the math."

"That can't be true!" Deanna sputters. "He must have a record or whatever. This isn't 1960-something!"

"Excuse me," I say, raising my hand. "I have to vomit."

Around me people recoil. But Tanay shoots me a grin, looking at me like she knew me in another life.

Ms. Teasdale sighs and hands me the big wooden hall pass—a long, phallic symbol of freedom. I race out of the classroom and down the hall, gritting my teeth. I actually do have to vomit. This always happens when my damn period presents itself like an assault, out of nowhere.

Inside the bathroom, which is blessedly empty, I barely have time to count stalls—1-2-3-4, before I can access the absolute, perfect middle of 8, which is half of miraculous 16. I dive into Stall Number 4. Bubbly waves of digestive hell hit me over and over, but I can't puke. *Ucch.* Nothing comes up. I lean my face against the cool wall and pray to die.

"I hate this place!" I groan, and my voice echoes off slimy walls.

I hear the bathroom door bang, and with that, a raucous bark of laughter.

CHAPTER 3

I STARE AT MY DRY UNDERWEAR, say a prayer of thanks I don't have to deal with feminine products just yet, and emerge from the stall, swaying from queasiness.

Tanay stands near the sinks, shaking her head. "I feel you. Told Teasdale I'm sick, too." She drops another two-ton hall pass on the counter.

I say, my voice nasal as Deanna's, "That can't be true."

Tanay leans against a counter. "What the hell was that, 'I don't see race'? She looks at me every day like I'm a damn quota."

Tanay pulls out a pack of cigarettes and lights up with a quick glance above, like there might be cameras. "And she better stop messing with Andrew. Talking like he's the rule, not the damn exception." She takes a drag. "Today we finally gave her some shit back." She looks at me like I helped things along.

I consider the disturbing nature of this fact, that they need the likes of me, as she offers me one of her funny brown cigarettes with an orange stripe.

"No, thanks," I say. "I may puke." My intestines still writhe like a brood of vipers.

"Why, you pregnant?" She grins.

"Not unless it's the Immaculate Conception."

Another laugh, husky prelude to that bark. "Deanna was in here the other day with her man, dry humping with that nasty ass."

"Lovely. Who's her man?"

Tanay snorts, releasing smoke. "Koyt Collins, the firestarter. Girl had him pinned and he was trying to get the hell out. If you've got to convince a man, he's a fag. Why's she after you?"

"I don't know; she's snarled at me since I came. Why ask why?" My voice is light. Better Tanay not know I have the makings of a target or just how big the bull's eye has been, ever since I can remember.

"Where you from again?"

"California."

"Your name, Dancing Bird—what's up with that?"

"According to Mother's mythology, my dad was a Zuni. She went down to the reservation and got the hook-up."

"Are you serious?" Smoke wreathes around us. Then: "Your mom's that hippie."

I nod. Her look says she pities me. There really is nothing more to say.

"Hey." She's giving me that past-life look again, and I get a chill. "I saw you did real good on that practice exam yesterday. So I was thinking...Me and Andrew, we need somebody to help with our project."

I look at her blankly.

"It's that thing Teasdale's making us do after AP exams—twenty-five percent of our grade? Andrew and I want to act some scenes from *A Raisin in the Sun*. We need someone to play the white guy."

My heart hammers, staccato. I swore at Sunny Revere on the drive cross-country I would never, ever take the stage again. I say, "I think I'll just write an essay or make a speech."

"But Teasdale said you acted before. So why not?"

Now I regret oversharing with Teasdale. "I was supposed to be in a Shakespeare play this weekend, but I'm done—"

"Sounds all fancy." Tanay rolls her eyes. "So I guess you

wouldn't care about our little ghetto scene." She gives me a look like I'm Deanna Faire.

"Um, I've read *Raisin*," I say, "and it's one of the best plays, ever. It's just not a good time for me."

"I got to get an A for this," she says. "The bigger I do this thing, the better. Three or four actors, lines memorized, everything. I've got a D in that class and I won't make but a two on the exam." Her stare won't let me look away. "The way I see it, you need something, and I need something." Her eyes have the glint of heavy metal.

"And what do I need?"

"A little help with your girl."

"My girl?" Oh, Deanna Faire. "I'm okay. Have you asked other people?"

"Ten of these fools," Tanay says grimly. "Problem is, *Oklahoma* just got done and everybody who was in it says they're 'too tired.'" Her face gets a hard look. "That was after Deanna Faire went around saying Andrew and me are doing a 'P. Diddy play.'"

Someone hammers on the door. We glance at each other. She crushes her cigarette beneath a chunky wedge heel and electric purple toes and yells, "What?"

Andrew's face peers around the door, looking like he really does not relish this task.

"Teasdale says y'all need to come on back."

"What if I'm puking up my guts?" I demand.

"Oh, oh, I did not need to hear that," he says.

"Why'd she send your ass?" Tanay says. "Sometimes Teasdale just ain't right."

"Trust me, hippies like unisex situations," I tell her.

Tanay cracks up. Then she says, "Come on in, boy." She folds her arms and leans back on the counter with a slinky look. "I think I just got me a recruit for our play."

I say, "Uh, wait a second—"

Andrew says, "All right, all right." He hasn't moved from the doorway. "I got your Walkman."

"Why?" I say.

"Because Miss Thing tried to grab it." He presses the felt pads on the headphones, then holds out the bumblebee-yellow body. I walk up and take it. He says, "How do you open it?"

I show him where to press and pop. I'm a bit taken aback by the size of his football hands. He laughs. "*Thriller*. That what you listen to?"

"Yessir."

"But you've got an iPhone."

I shrug. It is none of his business, my retro philosophy of purity, simplicity, and innocence that was the 1980s.

"Can you do that zombie dance?"

I roll my eyes. "There's so much more to Michael than little monsters. Give his lyrics a listen and you'll see the light."

His grin—a toothpaste smile designed to electrify teen girls—says I amuse him. "Oh, I know the word according to MJ," he says. "How it don't matter if you're black or white. But the Bard, now that's my boy. 'If you poison us, do we not die?'"

"'If you wrong us,'" I say, "'shall we not revenge?'"

I look over my shoulder. Tanay's face says she's not too fond of this exchange.

"Well, anyway, you guys go ahead," I say. "I need another minute."

"Come on, California, you know what you got to do," Tanay says. She taps her forehead. "My third eye says you're going to help us out now."

"Sorry, but I'm actually going back to California *tout de suite*."

They give each other a look. "All right, that's cool," Andrew says. He holds the door open, and Tanay walks through. As it closes, I hear her say, "She talks like a professor, but kind of crazy."

"Well, she'll fit in good around here," Andrew says.

They're gone. The last thing I pictured when I moved here was me taking up the cause of racial integration. *O, for my old school in San Francisco, where everyone's a whiter shade of some darker tone!* You don't know who the hell's gene pool crossed whose, where and when—and nobody really cares to ask. Here, there are too many allegiances, too many invisible high-voltage fences. And Tanay's third eye wants to know too much.

I survey my incendiary garb in the bathroom mirror. *Here's the 411, Deanna Faire: I do shower—often four times a day.* I remove the hoodie, and my hair lies flat against my scalp, a slimy sheath. It hates this Carolina swamp of humidity. *Why do you hate black so much, dearest Deanna? Would you like me better in Aryan white?* My face, a receding thing, heart-shaped, pale and slightly elvish, stares flatline back at the mirror. Mirror, mirror, me and Cindy in the mirror, reciting the three commandments of make-up.

1. What you make light stands out.
2. Correct a face so it becomes perfect: oval shape of ideal vertical/horizontal balance; almond eyes; and full balanced lips, not too thick or too wide.
3. Exaggerate features to fight the bright lights. But don't look like a ghost or a ghoul.

The other day she turned to me and said, "If only MJ had taken Stage Makeup 101."

And I said, "Yes, his visage is indeed an experiment gone awry. But who doesn't want to destroy their face?"

"I don't," she said. "Nor should you."

"I'm a freak," I said.

"Your freak, *c'est chic,*" Cindy said, and I smiled all the way to my insides.

A group of giggly, shiny-faced ninth grade girls bursts in on my reverie, thrilled they're so bad, bad, really really bad for skipping class. They ignore me like I'm a towel dispenser and chatter over Uggs and rings and bling-y things. Over sounds of one of them puking, I take one last look in the mirror and decide the All-Black Attack isn't a good look anymore. As The Great MJ would say: *Time for some glitter.* I have no idea how or what the new look will be, but I'll show these fools who's a superfreak before I stroll out of here forever.

Whatever I do, I'll keep the eyeliner. Normally, my pasty-white visage floats like a blank sliver of moon in a dark mop of hair; yet with black outlines, we have almond eyes full of age. I dare say I look kin to MJ's daughter Paris, which is a very good thing.

CHAPTER 4

SOMETHING TELLS ME SUNNY REVERE is lying when she says there was no one in our house at six o'clock this morning. I could have sworn I heard a voice at a lower register, then a Sunny giggle, and then the front door click shut.

I shower, then go back to bed, diving under the covers. I can't help but chew on the Deanna slur—*hippie ho, hippie ho*—stringy like a tough piece of celery you can't spit up. *What do I pay him for...* Oh dear saints and satans, what if Sunny's newest flame plays in Deanna's band? Only this time, it won't be the lead guitarist: no, Sunny has probably found something grassroots, authentic, and super-Southern—a banjo boy, Dobro dude, or mandolin man.

I have to go to school.

I tell a rumpled, slit-eyed Sunny I'll take the bus rather than ride her crazy train. Though she looks hurt and pouty, I do not care. I much prefer the B.O. of seventh graders to riding with a liar—a hippie ho who won't tell me who's latest through her revolving door.

On the bus, I waffle, wondering if Deanna could have crafted some massive lie just to torture me. I know her kind all too well: she's a Cheri Hamilton, the one responsible for several cycles of seventh-grade hell when Sunny and I did a stint in South Dakota. Cheri gets copyright for calling me Serial Killer (when I wasn't much for talking) and Grease is the Word (when I wasn't keen on washing my hair). Oh, the places she went: MySpace blew up in 2006, followed by a super-vicious situation on the new frontiers of Facebook in 2007. Let's just say it involved fake nude photos of yours truly and posts by every seventh-grade male on the subject of said party's body parts. But Deanna doesn't strike me as smart enough to spin intricate yarns. I fear she knows too much of something I don't. Hammering heart, sketchy breath—shift focus, shift now! I text Cindy while getting jounced around, shoulders slamming the window:

Where are you??? What if I told you I'll be there THIS WEEKEND?

Why won't she answer my texts? I know she was up all last night with dress, but still: why not text me from the wings, the car, the bathroom? It's been 5.3 days of nothing. My heart rattles in its cage. Something is up.

Off the bus and into the halls I'm still checking for some sign of Cindy life when some girl screams in my face, "Get *The Citizen*!" She thrusts a newspaper in my hands.

I prop myself against a wall and flip through this travesty. What do we have here but fashion rants against Uggs and a review of the Kardashians' latest reality trash? *The Advocate*—the paper Cindy and I wrote for back home—now that was a serious act of journalism. And it was online, Southern idiots; can you refrain from razing forests while you dispense drivel?

Lo and behold, page 2: My nemesis holds forth in her Deanna's Do's and Don'ts column, ranting and raving against freakazoid me.

Join the Team, People

If you dress weird and try to be a "character," you are disrupting the community. Now I'm all about diversity; who cares if you're purple, pink, or blue? But don't make your clothing a freak show.

*For example, don't freak people out with the black hoodie, jeans,
and eyeliner. Who wants to look like a terrorist? It's not funny
when you think about 9/11.*

Deep inside the brittle husk of me, something starts to
smoke. That's how we terrorists roll.

As I walk into AP Lit, people look up from *The Citizen*,
waiting to see what I'll do with my TMZ moment.

Deanna smirks when she breezes in, passing out *Citizens*
left and right. She sits down and tells one of her girls, "Looks
like Osama Bin Dancing didn't read the news."

Laughs like little knives all around. Blind and deaf Teasdale
passes out the AP practice exam. Tanay is nowhere to be seen.
Andrew zones in on the exam coming his way and Teasdale
calls, "Begin!"

Forty minutes to spew, but I can't write. Breathe. Count.
Count every brick in the wall. Breathe. Focus the hate on
Deanna's empire-waist blouse in front of you, a strangely big
and billowy blouse.

Wait a second. Why such an odd, formless choice for Diva
Dee who usually rocks the skintight? OMJ. What fertile ground
have we here? It's story time, folks. Let's start something,
shall we?

While Deanna activates a limited supply of brain cells, I
paraphrase MJ scripture with my blackest yet lightest felt tip
on the back of her chemise:

CAN YOU

FEED THAT

BABY?

She squirms only once. *Listen to MJ, bitch. Let the world
think you're a few months along.*

I settle back in my seat with a smile. I imagine Miss Dee's
debutante, sweet-tea entourage tapping her nervously in the

hall, minutes from now: "Um, Deanna, what's this about a baby?"

Welcome to Pariahville, sweetie; the weather's fine.

Someone clears a throat. I glance behind me. Andrew saw me do it. He lifts his eyebrows like, *It's on now.*

I choose branded harlots and write fast and brilliant. I will not let the Southern Abyss of Dumbassedness steal my GPA before I make my escape.

The bell rings. Deanna walks out of class clueless. I follow at a safe distance of 16 paces till she's swallowed by the hordes. No incident. Damn.

"Hey! Wendy!" someone calls behind me.

It's Andrew, looking too curious for his own good. Meanwhile, all girls in the vicinity look too curious about his body. "Why'd you do that?" he says.

Lemmings bash us from all sides; we're shoved together down the hallway. "I don't know; why do you engage in blood sport?"

"Usually the other team sees me coming." He's got a gleam in his startling dark brown eye, like he's got my number.

"Well, as a terrorist, I prefer guerilla warfare."

His grin says I amuse him. But I am impervious; we will develop no needless interdependencies in this backwards land. My ass will be leaving on a jet plane soon enough.

He says, "Like how you spoke out yesterday."

"Yeah, well, speak up, and someone calls the media." I wave *The Citizen.*

"She's mad because you don't scare."

"What I want to know is why she gives a damn what I think."

"You called her out," he says with a shrug. "Real talk."

"I wish it were that simple, good sir."

He jerks his chin to the side, saying, *Pull over,* so we find refuge from the onslaught near a locker. He pulls a sheaf of papers from his backpack while I rip *The Citizen* to shreds.

"Sign my petition?" he says. "To allow school prayer?"

I snap, "Yeah, this place needs all the help it can get." And I thought I'd met a sane one in the midst of this antebellum crazy—now he's a right-wing evangelical? Lovely.

He's waiting for me. The dude is serious.

"Okay, so is this for all faiths?" I ask. "Because that's the only way you'll get my John Hancock. I'm talking Wiccans, pagans, Satanists, Scientologists now. Liberty for all."

He doesn't bat an eyelash. "The Muslim and Mormon kids are into it, but the Jewish kids won't sign."

"Well, my guy needs worship, too." I glance around and see an opening in the stream of lemmings. "Later!" I dash from his holy halo.

"What guy?" he calls.

I yell, "He's bad, and I mean, really, really bad!" and get several withering stares for my volume. He looks confused a second, and then it hits him who I mean.

I've never met a dude like this one—a bona fide Bible thumper and class VP, happy to mix his church and state.

I glance at my phone. Cindy still has not texted me back. *Please, gods of music and ether and all things invisible: do not let my darkest of theories come true, that Good People don't exist, no matter how long a history you might have with them.*

The rest of the day, I see neither hide nor hair of Deanna Faire and her chemise. I am relieved, but I know I am stupid. I'll have to face her eventually, and the girl has way too many fans. Why do I do what I do? I don't know; they'll figure it out come arraignment time.

As school ends, I walk out of sophomore hall and see Andrew, tall and buff in his Steeple Mount High gear, hanging with his club of linemen headed for spring training. All of them slam each other like hunks of slaughterhouse meat. White dudes mingle with black. I stand corrected; in blood sport, let there be integration.

As I slink by, he yells "Hey!" and reaches to stop me.

I popcorn back like a cat. The linemen bust a gut laughing.

He says, "Watch yourself, girl; Deanna wants revenge." He gives a slight nod, like, *I'm not playing.*

I keep moving. I hear a lineman say, "Deanna better watch it or she'll get rabies from that freak." More lunkhead laughs behind me. I don't hear Andrew among them. I press on.

I tell myself I'm not scared because I have safe haven in the poor people's bus lot where me, rednecks, blacks, and Latinos without rides or licenses go. Meanwhile the Beauty Queen from a Movie Scene rules our pitiful campus from the student lot full of Beemers, MiniCoopers, and SUVs. But something has me just a little spooked, maybe because Andrew has that John-the-Baptist look, prophet knowing I'm headed straight for death.

CHAPTER 5

THE BUS LOT LOOKS POWER-TO-THE-PEOPLE safe, even though my bus is of course late. So whilst everyone else gets safely spirited away, I and the Misfit Toys crew must wait, exposed like zits on the bald, pocked face of the blacktop.

And right on cue comes my D-Day, Miss Faire, nose job in the air and sporting a fresh Swarovski crystal Indian blouse. How ethnic of her. She makes a beeline straight for me, flanked by her boy posse: famed sex machine and firestarter, Koyt Collins, and Graham, frat-boy twin, polo collars sky high. Tottering behind them on cheese-straw legs is Bethany, Most Likely to Faint from Lemon Water Fast, followed by chubster sergeant, Ziona, pushed down the chain after weigh-ins.

"Here's the future of America, folks," I yell, though my voice is thin. "Anorexic, pre-diabetic, and contagiously dumb!"

"Psycho!" Deanna screams. "You ruined my shirt!"

She and her minions descend. In my ears, Michael's breathy voice stays with me—*c'mon, girl, run!*—but Koyt knocks me down, flat on my ass, while Graham pins my arms. Koyt pries my Doc Martens off my feet and drop kicks them. The girls take my backpack and my Walkman; they take my hoodie. It's kind of a rape.

I tunnel back, vision fading, shooting straight backward into the gray, thoughts mumbling how strange is it to die in a cloud of Dolce & Gabbana, suffocated by Abercrombie & Fitch...

They bust open my backpack and scatter my small life everywhere. Deanna holds my iPhone aloft and smashes it to the ground. It matters not, as every inch of me's gone numb... till Koyt kicks me in the back. My skin explodes.

"Some *black* girl almost killed me in the hall!" Deanna hisses over me, breath hot in my eye. "She thought I was talking about baby mamas."

Another kick, vicious ache in my back. One of my ribs is screaming.

She yells, "And that top cost me seventy-five dollars!"

Behind Deanna I see Tanay and another girl advancing upon our little scene of horror—16, now 8, now 4 steps away. Tanay's companion is six foot and huge, very pregnant, with long flat hair spraying out in a fan around her shoulders. It's Teira Rae Benton, only it's said "Tee-err-uh Rah-ee." But nobody says that, either; they call her Mushi. The other day I witnessed her ripping out someone's weave in a cafeteria war.

Mushi yells, "Look at these white girls trippin'."

"Engaging in some violence," Tanay says, with relish, staring Deanna down. "Mmm, mmm, mmm: somebody might get suspended."

They're standing over me now. "What I want to know," Mushi says to Deanna, "is why you calling me out on your shirt."

Deanna shrinks back a foot, pointing my way. "*She* wrote it!"

Tanay shoots me a hand. I grab it, and it's solid and strong. She yanks me up. Something sparks in me. "That's right, I'm the scribe," I tell Deanna. "Message for you and your pals: starve yourself, starve the baby."

Tanay cracks up. Her eyes are dark brown today.

"She pregnant?" Mushi says. "Damn, that baby going to die."

Deanna screams, "I'm not pregnant!"

"Something wrong with being pregnant?" Mushi's eyes are slits. "That what you saying?"

We've drawn a crowd.

"Nobody's saying anything!" Deanna burns bright pink.

"You better shut that mouth," says Mushi. She takes a step forward; Deanna's whole crew recoils.

Deanna backs up, high speed. When she's a safe distance, she screams at me, "It's not over, bitch!"

"Yeah, skank. Watch yourself on Facebook," Koyt calls with a snarl, but he's already paces behind her. He's too dumb to be a hacker but rich enough to outsource.

"You still owe me seventy-five dollars!" Deanna shrieks.

"I'll whup that ass for a dollar!" Mushi yells.

Deanna whirls and stalks off to the tune of the crowd's laughter. "Boom!" Mushi yells. "You anamarexics need to eat you a sandwich!"

I'm breathing again, and the aches are receding. I see Tanay pick up my cracked iPhone. Now she's bringing me my backpack and shoes, and my Walkman, scratched and muddied.

Mushi watches me like I'm a strange and exotic animal, squatting in a cage. "What'd you say she is—zucchini?"

"Zuni," Tanay says. "That's Indian."

"She ain't Indian, she too white," Mushi says. "Why you drag me out here to save a cracker?"

"Well, you know me," Tanay says. "I love everybody, even black people."

Mushi snorts.

I kneel and put on my Martens, caked with mud. "I appreciate it," I say to my shoes. Adrenalin still pounds every corner of my head, and I'm full of disbelief someone just saved my ass. I don't suppose it would help to tell Mushi that my eyes do slant—ever so slightly—and I tan like a mug every summer.

"How'd you know to come here?" I say.

"Andrew told me," Tanay says. "I missed class because I was trying to stop a suspension—"

"Shi-i-i-t," Mushi drawls, "you just wanted to get out your exam. Ain't no charity thing. My ass still got seven days."

"Well, don't throw a chair at the wall next time," Tanay says.

"I didn't hit no one!" Mushi says. "Motherfuckers just looking to write me up, is what it is."

"Meanwhile, Deanna commits assault," I say. "Do they suspend for that here?"

Mushi says, "They ain't going to do shit."

"Her dad, he does plastic surgery on all the country club women around here," Tanay says. "And her mom owns half the ooh-la-la boutiques on Jefferson Street."

"The Faire cartel," I say.

Tanay is sizing me up. Why does everyone here look at me like they need to do a cavity search? "Come on, girl. I know you can do some drama because you bring the drama. Andrew says you don't scare."

"Says the dude stirring it up over school prayer," I say. "Will you please tell him I may look lost, but there's salvation right here?" I tap my forehead.

"Ha!" Tanay cackles. "Boy, you got his number. I guess he went John 3:16 on you?" She looks relieved as she hands me the rest of my worldly goods.

"He was unsuccessful in his mission," I tell her.

My bus rolls up in a cloud of suffocating exhaust.

"She worship the devil?" Mushi says.

Tanay chokes on a laugh. "Girl, you crazy."

I board the bus and find a seat near a rank ninth-grader. Tanay still watches me like she will figure me out somehow; Mushi, like I'm a meteor just landed, a steaming hunk of strange rock. If Sunny's ever said one true thing in her life, it's this: *Be careful what you owe people. Because they always want something.* She and Grandma are always battling it out over money, and every boyfriend Sunny's ever scored always has a catch. Now these two girls, who've just saved my life, it's like I've got a tab with them, and I don't know when it'll come due.

I dial Cindy on a fractured phone that still works, but it goes straight to voicemail.

CHAPTER 6

S UNNY IS DOING YOGA IN her room when I make it home, so thankfully I can dodge the rambling chitchat. The older I get, the friendlier Sunny Revere gets, striving after total BFF-dom, glad she need no longer worry about the state of my nutrition or hygiene. Not that she would notice the mud and bruises anyway.

Once inside my room, I start to shake. My pulse soars, my temples throb, my skin ignites. *Just some Deanna PTSD—you'll be all right—No, I won't!* My chest's tight as a drum; there's no air! Count! *Count!* Count knots in the pine of all doorframes—door to living room, door to closet, door to bathroom—1, 2, 3, 4, 5, 6, 7, 8, 9, 10, 11, 12, 13, 14, 15, 16. My heart's so fast I might die, I might die, I must leave all of this, right now, this life as a target—16, always it must be 16, the age I'll be this summer, which times 2 is 32, the age by which I will have won an Emmy or a Tony, and times 3 is 48, which is the age when I will be at least 16 years living in a far-flung region, Luxembourg or Madagascar or Nova Scotia...

I put my head between my knees; my breath is back in ragged bits. Focus on what you can count. I see 16 CDs in each of 7 stacks, as I own 7 of St. MJ's 11 solo albums. From the 1979 spark of dying disco brilliance, *Off the Wall*, through the 2001 *Invincible*, I possess exactly 16 copies of each for emergencies, study, and worship.

My eyes light on the best of the 7, the story of perfection: *Thriller*. My heart slows. 1982. I cradle the CD in my hands, Michael in all his sexy serenity of purest black and white. The best-selling album of all time and winner of a record-breaking 8 Grammys.

You'd wanna be startin' something should you say anything could ever beat it. No mere mortal can resist it, the very essence of our human nature. This is such an interesting revelation I become supremely calm.

I will pack 4 copies of each album for my journey. That, cash, and a couple changes of clothes. Cindy will know how to advise me. Ever since I went MJ, she is the only one who's ever understood. It all began that ugly March night when backstage I confessed my eternal love to Cyrus, the dude playing Orsino. Or, more like I asked him if he wanted to go for coffee.

I don't know what possessed me—stage adrenalin, thick makeup as my cover—making me think I could dare approach. Unforgettable, his face, a perfect blend of half-Persian and half-Irish, dark-as-hell eyes and eyebrows, hair combed back from his olive skin, thick and curly. So all that beauty looked me up and down. And said, "Never gonna happen."

My passion suddenly felt sick, perverse. He looked at me like I was a dog.

At Cindy's house after rehearsal, I told her what went down. "What?" she yelled. "Arrogant punk-ass bitch! Just like Orsino! I'll kick his—"

I cut her off: "I'm done."

"With what?"

"Love. I'll never marry, either."

"You just need to meet the right one." She turned on the radio. "If music be the food of love—"

"—play on," I said.

There on the oldies station was "Human Nature."

Melancholy, mourning, the why that lasts so very long. Michael's cry for understanding, ethereal and high. It rocked my very soul. And Cindy knew to let me have my moment, let the music swell, wash over me and say nothing stupid, like "I'm so sorry," because there is no sorry for what happens in life. It is what it is and you deal.

That night at home, I googled Michael Jackson. Images unfurled from every phase of his life, and 1981, 1982, 1983— that's where I landed, and that's where I stayed. I saw What the Man Once Was. Till that moment, he was just some white dude who put masks on his kids, androgynous crotch-grabber and clown face. Now I had to know who he was, before all this, at the height of his powers, before he began messing with his face. I asked, *What drives a man to the knife?*

Someone made little Michael feel tiny. Insignificant. Used. This mask was born of rejection. He made so much sense.

Right then, I texted Cindy: *Why doesn't Cy want me? Because I am a freak...*

My iPhone rang two seconds later.

"The same reason I fit so well in boys' clothes and other shapeless attire," I added.

Cindy said, "Get off your cross; somebody needs the wood."

"No, you will hear me out. I wasn't made for these times. I hate the Two Thousands, the Ohs, the Oughties, or whatever the hell we are. How bad is it I came into consciousness at a time when nothing matters? Fake celebrities on 'reality' shows; fake talents doing glorified karaoke on *Idol*; fake money in banks; fake friends on Facebook; a fake president for most of my waking life!"

"Wow, that was quite a rant," she said. "Now put a lid on all that crazy. Whatever's fake can't last. Like Cy. Fake-ass Narcissus, only loves his own face!"

"Noughts," I said. "That's it. We're in the Noughts. This is the Dark Age of Noughts."

Cindy said she couldn't agree more and that the only shred of hope left was hanging on Obama. I let that go, because what I was trying to say was so much more than politics.

The next day I went on a shopping spree and became the proud owner of myriad Michael masterpieces. From Best Buy, from Amoeba Records, and while trolling Amazon, I texted her: *It's on—watch the truth unfurl.*

After that, whenever we'd hear some airhead chick at school squeal at her fake BFFs, or watch one hang off Cy's super-fine physique while my skin burned red hot with envy, Cindy and I would look at each other and say, "Truth, motherfucker! Truth!"

People thought we were crazy. It was awesome being a Crazytown twosome.

But now Cindy is three thousand miles away and unreachable; make that 5.6 days she hasn't picked up. And it is still 2009, a bitterly dark year in the darkest pit of the Noughts. I am trapped here with only Michael's words to soothe me. To die. To sleep.

When Sunny busts in, sweating, half-naked in some unidentified male's boxers and a sodden *Twilight November 2008* T-shirt, I'm laid out flat on the floor in a half-doze, feeling hardwood work my shoulders like a brutal masseuse, CD on my solar plexus, listening to "Human Nature" on my stereo 16 times.

"Wendybird, don't you get sick of that album?"

I hit Stop on the remote; the song is ruined. I say, "Did you know at one time Michael Jackson owned 30 rats? He wasn't so keen on them when they started eating each other."

Sunny grimaces. "Gross! TMI!"

"And no, I do not get sick of this album."

"I can't believe I ever listened to it." She releases her damp flood of hair from its topknot; now her face looks ten feet long. "What about Lady Gaga? She's great about gay consciousness."

"Please." I close my eyes. "Pale imitation of Madonna."

Sunny takes some yoga breaths, whistling through her nose. "Sweetie, I'm headed to Nature Fare. I might have a friend over tonight."

"Is this gentleman caller the reason we left home in a panic?" My voice is cool, distant, adult: soon I will have no more need of her and her seventh-grade love affairs.

She flushes red to her roots. "Help me clean up. This house is a wreck."

I sit up. "That's not the only wreck, but never you mind."

"*Wendy!*" Her shocked face berates me with equine guilt. "We've gone through this a hundred times. California is over for me. You can't hide in this house forever. It's your fault if you don't try to meet people—this is your *life* we're talking about!"

"But *Mother,*" I nail her whiny voice, dead on, "if you don't get the hell out of here, this is my *sanity* we're talking about!"

More yoga breaths. "Find some empathy for others. It's not all about you." She frowns like I'm Fox News and stalks out.

"It's never about me!" I yell. I leap up and chase her out of the room. "Can I FOR ONCE get a vote before we run away?"

She has her hands over her ears and her eyes closed. "Listen to me!" I scream. I grab the nearest thing, a fearsome bowl Sunny made during her pottery phase, and hurl it at the floor. Gray-green-blue shards crack everywhere.

"You're a horrible human being!" Sunny is sobbing. "No one gives a damn how I feel!" The phone starts ringing, shrilling off its hook. Sunny's message kicks in: "This is Sunny and Wendy. Tell us what's on your mind. U.S. Out of Afghanistan! Adopt a cat today!" Beep!

"Wendy! Lydia!" Grandma snaps. "Stop screening and pick up."

"I can't deal with her right now!" Sunny shrieks. She grabs her Guatemalan fanny pack and storms out, swiping at tears.

I head for the phone. At least the dragon lady on the other end will listen to a fraction of what I have to say.

CHAPTER 7

As I pick up the phone, the front door bangs with Sunny's departure, shaking the house. "Hi, Grandma."

"Wendy, is that you?" The line crackles with static since she is in Bali. It didn't surprise me she wasn't stateside to greet us when we arrived a week ago; she and Sunny fight like cats, and fur flies to the point of baldness. But Grandma is forgiven all things because she's funding my trip to see The King this summer. My heart rate slows at the thought of Michael sparkling like a chandelier above me, 74.3 days from now in London, an eternity, but there will be Cindy and me screaming, swaying, jumping, rejoicing—

"Where's your iPhone?" Grandma says. She can do this because she pays for it.

"I didn't hear it. We were brawling."

"And how is the lady of the manor?" She sounds resentful she must ask. I picture the long, elegant line of Grandma pacing poolside in a silk kimono with fawning hotel staff hustling behind to bring her drinks.

"Same old, same old." I glance over at the mess I've made.

"Does she keep the place clean?"

I glance around. Every corner's furry with cobwebs or dust clumps bigger than armadillos. I hate our new digs, a passive solar house built in 1977, all brick and hardwood floors. There aren't enough skylights to make the solar thing work, so it's always too cold or too hot. The doors to my bedroom and bathroom don't lock, and I'm very afraid of what will happen when Sunny tries the wood stove. Grandma calls the place another addlepated liberal scheme even though she'll keep paying our rent. I decide a lie is in order. "Yes, when she's here."

"Who is she stalking now?"

"No idea." My stomach twists.

"Not that horrible MyFace dating. Parasites, each and every one. Lord knows how Lydia stands them."

"Indeed." Lydia is Mother's Christian name; Sunny, her adopted. Something to do with her astrological sign; Grandma still scoffs at the christening ceremony Mother had for herself back in the day. I'm pretty sure she also invented my name, Redbird Dancing, which is no doubt an insult to the Zunis.

"Where are you keeping that debit card?" Grandma says.

"On my person."

"Good. You never know what she'll drag in next. Brilliant idea, that travel wallet. What did I tell you? Haven't been mugged yet," she says.

Grandma's never been places where mugging is even possible.

"Why are you loitering around that house?" she snaps. "Don't you have some after-school activity you could do? You say you want to be an actress—join the drama club. Don't be a misanthrope."

"I've given up theater."

"Nonsense; that's your talent."

"These kids are trying to get me to do a scene, but—"

"Do it! You need more than grades to get into college."

"It's a bit part, just for class." The devil rises within, so I add: "And I'd be the only white. *A Raisin in the Sun.*"

Her silence throbs like a threat. Finally: "Don't know it."

"It's about racism and housing desegregation in the 1950s."

"Everything was better then."

I mutter, "Yeah, if you were white."

"What's that?"

"There was never a Golden Age, Grandma. If you study history—"

She cuts me off. "Bullpuckey."

"—if you study history, everything's always sucked. It's just a matter of degree and who happens to be oppressing whom."

She says like I've never spoken, "Nowadays there's too much hoo-ha about people's feelings." Uh-oh, here we go. "No one speaks his mind because everyone's afraid of race-based lawsuits. I'll say it, if no one else will: races don't mix. Not because one's better than the other. People just don't like mixing."

I count to 4, a quarter of 16, so I don't blurt, *Easy for a rich old white lady to say.* Seeing MJ this summer overseas is worth the muzzling.

"Remember where you come from, Wendy. Don't let anyone tell you you're less because you're white." I love how Grandma ignores I might be mixed. She's not a big fan of my may-be-Native-American genes, I guess because they own casinos that take her money.

"Grandma, you've lived in the South too long."

"You haven't lived here long enough," she snaps. "We're going to Mass when I get back."

"How's Bali?" I say quickly. I do not relish another religious field trip.

"Having a splendid time."

"When are you coming back?"

"I'm steeling myself to see your mother again. Just remember: You're better off being near me, where I can supervise her."

Inside a switch trips; some supervision! I feel a singe in my back, in the vicinity kicked by Koyt. People act like they care, but no one gives a damn how my day really went.

"I have to go," I say.

"I wired you money," she says.

"Thank you." I almost say, "I'll make good use of it this weekend," and stop myself just in time.

She snaps, "Unpack *all* the bags, Lupita, not just the jewelry!"

I hear Lupita say, "*Ay!¡ Disculpa, tuve que ir al cuarto de baño. Esta comida me hace sentir tan mal!*"

"That is entirely too much information," Grandma says. "I told you not to have that papaya."

"Grandma," I say, "you are a misanthrope."

She chuckles and we hang up.

I must keep on her good side because I'll sure as hell need support when she gets the news I've left for the Left Coast. But now, I need Cindy most of all.

I skirt around shards of Sunny Revere's masterwork to get to my room. It was a shitty thing to smash it, but so is uprooting me. I find my iPhone. Then I leave the house, scattering tumbleweeds of orange-black hair left by our most recent foster calico moved on to permanence.

I emerge into the sunlight and run down the cracked driveway, hitting speed dial for Cindy. She will, must, has to pick up this time.

CHAPTER 8

WHEN CINDY'S PHONE GOES STRAIGHT to voicemail, I stalk down the street and unleash with a rant.

"Well, hello, Long-Lost 'Friend' Screening Me! Where are you, pray tell?" I'm breathing heavy with a fast stride and rush of words. I want to hit something, someone. I pass our hipster neighbors' house, folk musicians stumbling with bedhead onto their cluttered porches, rubbing crust out of their eyes. "Fine, whatever, thanks for the radio silence!" Now I'm passing the Coexist Café where the Soy What latté is today's special, next to Nature Fare where Sunny meanders this very moment, hunting fair trade coffee and a man we can't afford. I'm sweating through my clothes. Cindy can't do this to me. Not freaking now. "Oh, and FYI, I just had the shit kicked out of me at school, but never mind. This is it, Cindy. Don't let me d—"

Her call cuts through just as Star Man, a local loon sporting an afro of gray fuzz with stray dreads, almost runs me over on his pogo stick.

"Hi," I say, trying to sound calm. Now I wish I hadn't left such a psycho voicemail—

"Girl! What's up!" She sounds normal, she sounds like perfection, she's Cindy.

"How'd it go last night?" I say, my voice bright.

"We sucked. Emily sucks the most, but we'll survive."

Emily is my understudy. I'm ridiculous for panicking. Cindy is the essence of calm, the rock in the midst of my swirling neuroses. "Sorry, I should be there."

"Not your fault."

"No, I should've stayed. No more cowardice. You'll see my ass this weekend."

"You're coming to the show?"

"I'm leaving this hellhole, for good."

A pause. "You mean, come live here?"

"That's right!"

Another pause. "Where are you going to stay?"

"Well, I thought—" My heart drops. "I thought, I mean, if it would be okay—maybe I could stay with you till I get settled." More silence. "I'm thinking about emancipation."

I don't know what I expect—cheers, applause, parades— but what I get is quiet. "Girl," she says finally. "That's a big-ass step."

"Hell yeah it is!" My voice rings out, loud like a little kid. I don't know what I thought—I guess because Cindy's mom is cool, organized, stable—that they could keep me at least a couple weeks while I work things out.

"Are you sure?"

It hits me hard what I'm asking—and whether I'm worth the asking. My chest gets tight. Stupid fantasies; stupid me.

"I mean," Cindy says in the silence, "aren't you going to take your APs, you know, finish school?"

I feel my heart grow cold as moon rock, I am shooting backward, backward, and light years away from her, into my own private outer space.

"Never mind," I say. "Forget it."

"Wendy, come on now, don't be like that—"

"Never mind I hate rednecks, debs, and all things Southern. Never mind Sunny has a new secret man and there's a half-ass understudy ruining the play I should be in, tonight!"

My voice is shrill across the three thousand miles.

"I'm sorry," Cindy's voice is small. My rock sounds like a pebble.

"No, I am," I snap. I'm an add-on to her life, a needy parasite hovering on her edges.

She says, "You think...you'll join a play there?"

Jesus. No real talk for almost a week—and all she can freaking ask is, *Will I join a play?*

"Acting is over."

"You're too good. Wen, come on now. You'll get through this."

"I've got to go," I say.

"I'll call you tomorrow."

"Uh-huh. Whatever."

Silence. It's ugly, I feel ugly, but if we're being honest here, we both know what's up. We're not twins anymore, till death do us part. Why should I expect Cindy's nuclear family—that hot fusion of loyalty and normalcy—to welcome me? It would be too good to be true to live in a house that smells like fresh laundry or buttery biscuits, and mingle with people who get up and show up at expected times.

"I hate that you moved," she's saying. "I really miss you, girl. You can visit anytime, you know that, but like, live here? I don't know if Mama's down with that. I mean—"

"Break a leg tonight, why don't you."

I hang up.

CHAPTER 9

M Y HAND AROUND THE PHONE is wet with sweat. I will not cry. I will not scream.

A crowd of obese tourists, 4 people wide, jostles me awake: I've walked myself into downtown Steeple Mount, aka Mainstreamia, where Deanna Faire lookalikes roam Jefferson Street past trans-fat food joints and stores stuffed with cheap Steeple Mount U sports memorabilia. So it surprises me I'm standing in front of a tiny red door, decorated with tiny doll heads, missing eyes—16 of them. The number restores my breath. Above the door, a tilted sign: IN VINTAGE VERITAS.

In the front window, a dusty red leather jacket. OMJ. It looks a little small, but a tight fit would be all the better. And check out the burn mark on the left arm. The Pepsi stigmata, a sign of Michael's sacrifice for the masses when he caught fire that fateful day.

To hell with everyone. I'm going rogue with MJ. At least I can trust him to do what he says—the man who never stops says, *This is it*, and means it.

I step inside the dusty coolness of In Vintage Veritas and find a world of MJ-approved, '80s items. Heaven. I am transported by polka-dot blouses, big boxy jackets with padded shoulders, and all other kinds of classic. They make up for the dark-red bruises I see blooming on my lower back in the changing-room mirror. I suit up in a pair of tight black pants, cropped at the ankle; a white T-shirt; and the glorious red leather cloak of a King. Beauty; truth. All I need is white socks and black loafers.

To everyone in my life, let me say, *Sayonara*. I will survive these 74.3 days with a righteous rage and a righteous look, and I will sell Cindy's ticket to a worthy stranger outside the O2 Arena. She never really liked MJ as much as I do; it's nothing to her but frivolous amusement, a tag-along free trip to Merrye Olde England. She never even memorized a single lyric, while I know every one from three quintessential albums. She wasn't the one who stayed online two days straight to get us tickets, beating out 1.3 million people. This is it, baby. See ya.

And the next time I see Deanna, let me face her in the rich-car lot, a crowd circling us. Brilliant in shiny red jacket, slim black pants, and pure-white socks, I stare down my nemesis. She bares her teeth.

Someone ropes our hands together. Switchblades pop, spark, and slash.

The crowd parts like the Red Sea; Tanay appears. She puts hands on our shoulders, shakes her head, and shows us the way: snap, row, slide…

Tomorrow Steeple Mount High will see my real face. Let 'em all turn to stone.

I'm careful and know how to bargain, so I score not only these fineries but also a rust-orange Members Only jacket; black leggings with only a few nubs; a sea-green, sleeveless ruffled shirt; barely scuffed black ballet flats; a long droopy sweater with a green and white argyle pattern; and a pair of stone-washed peg-leg jeans. All for seventy-four bucks! My debit card goes through, since Grandma shows her love in green.

I head back on the bus to Millboro and get out at the Coexist Café. I order a Soy What latté. We must celebrate.

How it's going to be is calm, collected, strong-ass Wendy. Wendy who no one rattles, who no one breaks through.

I sit at a table by the window, sipping my drink, plugged in to Michael and Paul, "The Girl is Mine." My phone pings with a Facebook friend request. Some random older dude named Shaye Tann wants to be friends. I click into Facebook, where I see my account's been hacked.

Lovely. There are now fake nude photos of me with a fire crotch posted. Deanna can't even get the hair right. Or maybe that's the point. Why wouldn't Osama Bin Dancing rock the red beneath the hoodie? Come on, couldn't I be a hermaphrodite, too? It would have been *way* more original to post my double dose of sex organs.

I deactivate the account. This is the best policy, as I have no "friends." One learns the hard way when one stupidly maintains MySpace two weeks too long in seventh grade.

I gather my bags to leave, just as Sunny and her new suitor stroll in, arm and arm.

CHAPTER 10

T HE NEW DUDE HAS EYES like Cy. Dark brown with the
longest lashes I've ever seen, and dark eyebrows, too.
He's got blond hair to his shoulders. He could be thirty
or forty-something—hard to tell, since he's wearing tight
hipster jeans, boots, and a crimson cowboy shirt with silver
embroidery. There's a roll of posters under his arm.

At the sight of me, Sunny glows like a red light of shame.
"Oh, sweetie!" she chirps. "Didn't know you'd be *here!*"

The dude extends his hand to me. "Shaye Tann. Nice to
meet you."

We shake, and his hand is strong and warm. No
condescending simper on his face like, *You pimply hormone
beast, please don't bite.* Just those eyes taking all of me in.

"You just friended me," I blurt. How did he know I'm her
daughter? This can't be a yesterday romance.

"That's right." He smiles. Sunny beams and beams.
"Somebody looks like she just stepped out of 1982. What's in
the Walkman?"

I shrug. He holds out a hand, and Sunny nods, like, *Do it,*
so I let him have it and hold one of the headphones to his ear.
A smile breaks across his face like a beam of light, shot from
the sky. He hands it back.

Sunny butts in, "That's right; I raised a retro girl. Though
in her millennial world, Michael Jackson is The King."

"The King?" Shaye says. "True that. But if you're really, truly retro, Elvis is the King, right?"

I shrug.

"Let's sit down," he says, waving at the table I was leaving. "What's your poison, ladies?"

A retro phrase that for some reason makes my skin crawl. "I'm not thirsty."

"Ever had Italian soda?"

I shake my head.

"Trust me. You'll love it."

He leaves and Sunny and I sit down. She leans forward, eyes bright. "Hot, huh?" She giggles.

"His nose is too big."

"You mean hawk-like. I love that look. Yum!"

I shudder. "How'd you meet this one, Mother?"

"Oh, the usual, online." Her eyes dodge mine.

"God, you move fast. I don't even know where my classes are."

"Come on, Wendybird. He's in the music industry. Think of the free tickets!" She's glowing like a nuclear reactor. For all her crazy, her smile is rock star and straight, white arches of perfection. Perhaps that's what sinks each new man.

She's telling me all about his Harley and what a great driver he is when he comes back with an Amity Latté Swirl for her and a Sopranos Chianti-something for me. He's got a Sapporo beer for himself. "You've seen *The Sopranos*?" he says, like of course I have.

"No." I look at the bottle. "Is this wine? Because I'm underage."

"It's virgin, don't worry," he says, and laughs. Sunny giggles, eyelashes fluttering like a seventh-grade girl's.

It's all-natural grape soda. Not bad, actually.

"So, remember when Elvis died?" Sunny leans into him

like she's known this stranger all her life. "Wendy, your grandparents and I were driving somewhere—what was I, nine?—and the radio starts playing Elvis songs over and over, to the point where your grandpop says, 'Sons of bitches, I don't want to hear this trash!' Then the DJ says, 'My friends, The King is dead.'"

I can't help it. "When was that?"

"August 16, 1977," Sunny and Shaye say together—perfectly timed. They laugh. He's looking at her like he's just seen the light. And right before me I see Sunny bloom like the big, overblown sunflower that she is. Shit, here we go again. True love made to last—what, three weeks?

"The King?" I sneer. "Michael Jackson has won eight Grammys, three of them for vocal performances in pop, rock, and rhythm and blues. Top that."

"Hard to," Shaye says, like I might be smart. "Elvis only won three for gospel tunes. Though he did record over seven hundred originals. He had about five number-one R & B singles and seven number-one singles in a time when singles were the way pop music was done. And you have to keep in mind he started before the Grammys were even in business."

"So you're a music expert." I glare at him. But I will admit: he's the first adult I've met with anything valid to say about music, ever.

"Actually, I'm a manager and publicist." He's not spooked in the least by my tone. His eyes say he gets me, perhaps even can read my frustration. "I work with A & R at companies, which means I rep new artists and sign them to a label."

Well, well, well.

"I don't suppose you rep one Deanna Faire."

He looks surprised. "Yeah, just signed her this year. You like country?"

And there you have it, folks. This would be The Man.

"Uh-oh," he says to my silence. "You two aren't BFFs?"

I could spew all my virgin grape stomach acid across this table. "There's a B who needs to eff off."

He chuckles like I've got some wit. "Could this win you over?" He picks up his roll of posters and slides the rubber band off, unrolling the stack. There before me is a nine-by-sixteen glossy of Deanna Faire, glowing in a lime-green dress and matching fringed boots as she's draped seductively across a blue velour sofa. Her face is soft and thoughtful, like the angel Gabriel just whispered heavenly secrets in her ear, while a mandolin dangles carelessly from her French-manicured hand. Above her sheath of smooth blond hair, curlicued letters unfurl: MY GRASS IS BLUE, the same color as the sofa.

"God, she's gorgeous," Sunny says wistfully, like she wishes Deanna were hers.

"She's a sociopath," I snap. "I've got bruises on my back from a beatdown!"

"What—she hit you?" Shaye stares at me.

Sunny says to him with an embarrassed giggle, "It explains things, doesn't it?"

"It sure as hell does," I say. I want to stand, but my liquid legs won't move.

He folds his hands, well manicured, cleaner than anything Sunny's ever held before. He looks me straight in the eye. "Deanna's pretty possessive. She doesn't like it when I turn my phone off, and I've been doing that more than usual." He glances at Sunny, and she blushes pink. "She's hot on this particular label, and when I told her I wouldn't pitch to them, she got mad. That was the day we ran into her at the Starbucks, right?" Sunny nods. "She's over it now; or at least, I thought she was."

"Oh, she's a little diva," Sunny reassures him. She Who Remains Latched to His Arm, giving him squeezes and big soulful eyes, avoids my gaze. "I told her to chill out and that you're new to the school and how you two ought to be friends." She gives me a look like, Isn't this brilliant?

"Let me get this straight," I say slowly. "Deanna knew you were dating before I did? And you told her my name?"

Shaye doesn't flinch at my laser glare, but he's rattled. "It's only been a few weeks." He glances at Sunny, looking for help.

"A few *weeks*?"

Shaye says, "We were kind of active on Facebook." He looks genuinely sorry.

So Sunny hid her posts to Shaye from me, but not the rest of the world—Deanna, not only witness but stalker. Never mind Jerome and Shaye at the same time—and me none the wiser. Sunny looks caught in a vise of her own devising.

I stand. "Thanks a lot. I mean, really, Mother: Thank you. Deanna Faire has traced my ass to yours, and every day at that damn school, she hunts me down!"

"Wendy!" Sunny squeals. "Is it really that bad?"

"Yes!" Acid at the corner of my eyes, but don't cry, don't cry, even though I can see she doesn't believe me.

"I mean, all we did was flirt in those posts," Sunny says. "I wouldn't even call it dating." She nudges Shaye. "What can you do online?"

I shove my things under my arm, slam the chair into the table, and stalk off.

"Wendybird, don't be that way, come back!"

Dude number three for the year 2009. I'm outside the Coexist, I'm storming past an overgrown yard full of metal sculptures, skeletal figures with arms thrust skyward, armadillos in mangers emerging from the weeds, and patrons swatting ticks and mosquitoes while sweating out their lattés. Once again, here we go, I can't do a damn thing. I hear myself gasping, trying to find breath, but this humid air suffocates my lungs.

I want my little knotty pine room, right now—its tight ten-by-ten parameters, the soothing sight of my MJ collection, and the peace when the headphones descend. That's the only known quantity in this life full of x. One never knows what the goddamn status is.

CHAPTER 11

ODAY, THE DAY AFTER CINDY'S Betrayal, The Day After Sunny's Surprise, and The Day After I Found MJ Attire, I rock the new look. Crisp white shirt, circulation-cutting black pants, regulation short white socks, somewhat scuffed black loafers (raided from Sunny's closet while she sleeps, as always, like the dead), and of course, *la pièce de resistance*, the red leather jacket. I consider placing red flames on my crotch, too, but that's carrying color coordination a little too far.

How it's going to be from now on is this: No one will ever mess with me again.

My chariot of choice is the Steeple Mount EZ Rider. It smells a little musty and an old lady stares while I whisper-count multiples of 16 toward calmer, but nevermore shall there be school bus hell. Note the safety factor: Deanna's posse never stoops to ride with the unwashed masses.

My iPhone chirps with a text. Cindy: *You got beat up???*

So she finally heard my voicemail rant.

Too late, sister. Way too fucking late.

I turn my phone off and stare out the window, my heart erratic, hateful, and sad.

I arrive at school nervous as a cat. I dodge the fools of these halls, this zoo of swarming, too-close bodies, not sure where my swagger went. Yet I find myself making eye contact all of a sudden, because I am seen with interest, not shoot to kill. What is this? Do I actually get approving looks? Some hipster girl with fuchsia punk hair stops me and asks me where I got my jacket. She asks if it's vintage and I nod. She's not joking. Am I succumbing to the admiration of the dull, sheep-like masses?

I pass more lemmings in all my glory, light-footed, music cranked in my Walkman. "The Way You Make Me Feel" is making me feel just a bit giddy. "*Whee-hee!*" I sing out, way off key.

Now people turn away, eyes rolling. Much better. Snickers and hoots trail me to class.

"Wendy!" A hiss behind me.

It's Deanna Faire, strangely unaccompanied. Alone in black shiny military jacket with poufed shoulders, shiny black leggings, and sky-high heels. Sexed-Up Sergeant who looks, strangely, up for a chat.

She beckons for me to follow, and we enter an empty classroom. She closes the door, and we have a stare-off.

"Look," she says. Her eyes are bright blue, like the Xanax fog is gone. "I—this is kind of getting out of hand. I think we should just make a truce, you know?" She smiles, bites her lip, and mumbles. "I'm sorry about the fight. Really."

There's something practiced about the language, like she's reading from a script. Is she afraid I'll report her ass?

"I effed up. With Facebook. I'll like put an apology out, okay?" The eyes plead; the lips purse. They wait.

Who twisted her arm? Teasdale?

"Not even great Neptune's ocean will wash the blood clean from your hand," I say.

"Okay, whatever," she says, looking fierce. "Shakespeare— I'm not a total dumbass. I'm just saying, I'm not blaming *you*— you can't help what your mom does. I mean, I should know." She rolls her eyes. "I told him he just needs to focus and now we're cool."

So that's it. Careers are at stake. What do you bet Shaye Tann pulled her aside and said, "Don't be a Mean Girl—it's bad for your image." That's how he got her on board.

"Jesus," she says, and sighs. "I'm trying here. Can't you say *something*?"

I let the silence lap around us, deliciously cool. Count 1, 2, 3, 4 beats.

"Don't ever come near me again," I say. "I don't want to see your face."

That face falls. "God, you're a nasty bitch!"

She shoves past me—black skids across red—and flings the door open. She spins and says with a sneer, "I don't care what he says. I'll do whatever I want. Like anyone cares what happens to *Wendy Redbird Dancing*." Her look says, *I will ruin you.*

She's gone, and I'm alone with the roar of the hall in my ears, loud as the blood beating my head.

I don't care: I'm bad, I'm sick, I'm strong.

I march to class and discover Andrew has taken over my desk, a Venti Starbucks plunked there like he owns my real estate.

"That's my seat," I say.

He kicks back in my chair. "You want to sit behind Deanna, looking like you do?"

He flashes me a grin and waves his hand at his old desk, inviting me to take up residence. "I'm just saying."

"I don't need you to be fashion police," I say, but go sit there anyway.

"Tanay says you'll change your mind," he says. "We still need someone."

"Where is she?"

He rolls his eyes. "She says she can't pass the AP, so I bet she's hiding out."

"But today's just practice."

"You can't talk sense to a girl running scared."

The bell rings and Deanna slides in, eyes searing me all the way to her seat. My jacket might well combust. I give her a big-ass grin. She snorts and looks away.

Tanay comes in right behind, her eyes wide and frantic.

"I'm here, right?" she snaps at Andrew, who chuckles to himself and shrugs.

Teasdale chatters at us nonstop while she passes out papers—"I know y'all can pull fours and fives on this!" Deanna mutters to her minions about my ensemble, while Tanay stares at the AP prompt like it might bite. Teasdale sings out, "Begin!"

Prompt: *In some literature, adolescence is portrayed as a time of innocence; in other works, as a time of terror...*

I got this—*Catcher in the Rye* is full of terror—so is *To Kill a Mockingbird*—that's it—

"Hey, Fire Crotch!" Deanna hisses, just loud enough for our back corner. "Oh, Fire Crotch...."

People are cracking up. So her hackwork got some serious local traffic before I deleted my account.

"Please," I say loudly. "Don't project your STDs on me."

"Oh-oh-oh!" some dude yells, and the back corner erupts. Tanay is laughing, and Andrew's trying hard not to, shaking. Deanna is now Fire Face.

"Whore," she spits, glancing at Teasdale, whose hearing has just now activated. "Just like your mom!"

"Wendy, Deanna—this is an exam!" Teasdale calls.

"How hot is that?" I say to Andrew, pointing at his Starbucks.

"It's cold," he says. "Why, you want it?"

I stand and grab it off his desk. "Then there will be no lawsuit," I say, and pour it on Deanna's head.

A lovely cascade of latté drools down that sheath of salon blond; then it trickles down the anamarexic shoulders puffed up with satiny sheen. I shake the last drops out on the crown of her hateful head.

The class explodes.

She rises, gasping and wringing her hands. Then she lunges at me.

I believe it's Andrew who pulls her off me; all I hear are shrieks. My white shirt is soiled with latté; my jacket has earned some new wounds.

Ms. Washington arrives to escort me out of class. Tanay pleads to come with, but Ms. Washington, after a slight pause, shakes her head with a curt no.

After Sunny Revere is called yet not reached, I do some time in the hallway chair outside Ms. Washington's. I don't yet know my verdict while she chats with the principal. Tanay finds me there; she grins and shakes her head.

"Damn, girl: you're going to destroy her entire wardrobe!" She sits next to me and sighs. "What's this fire crotch, mama's a whore mess—did I miss something?"

"She hacked my Facebook and posted fire crotch pictures."

"Oh, hell no." Tanay's lips set in a grim line. Then a look like she's older than me, like she knows better, as she says to herself, "Here I thought I had me another Mushi situation."

"Which would be, what?"

Tanay leans forward, staring at her toes that are today glitter blue. "Mushi's got that borderline personality thing. Can't help herself, but she won't take her meds, neither."

"But nobody messes with her," I say. "What I wouldn't give to win a war, just one time."

"But if you can't shut your damn mouth…" Tanay sighs, shaking her head at me. "She just told some teacher she was going to 'whup that white ass.' Ms. Washington wouldn't cut me a break there." She gives me a hard look. "Sometimes, you've got to bite it back. You feel me?"

"So you're what, the savior for lost causes?" I say sharply. "Don't waste your time here."

She gives me a look. Then she gets up and walks into Ms. Washington's office.

Five minutes later, I am called in, and I am not suspended; instead I receive ten days of detention. "Praise Jesus," Tanay says, when I come back out.

"Fine by me. It's not like I have anywhere to go," I say with a shrug.

Tanay stands over me like I'm one stupid child. "You're lucky I saw that beatdown and there's a million witnesses."

I know I'm being an asshole. I stand up and pretend to consider my abused jacket. "Yeah, detention is way better."

"Girl, your ungrateful ass needs an escort."

I rub at a latté stain. "Right, I'm dead meat."

"Hey, anybody in there?" She snaps her fingers at me, and I look at her. "Because you're acting kind of crazy."

The way she's looking at me, I don't know why, but tears leap to my eyes. "Let's just say I'm over everyone."

She nods, like I need not explain further. The bell rings. "What class you got next?"

"AP History."

Tanay pulls out her phone in a pink rhinestone case and texts someone. A minute later, Andrew strolls up.

"Walk California to history," she tells him. "You know where all the la-dee-da classes are." Then she glares at Andrew. "I'll never get fours and fives like his ass does, all the damn time."

"Come on, girl, you got this," he says. "We have not yet begun to fight."

"John Paul Jones," I say.

Andrew points at me. "Studied that last night," he says.

"We'll see if I pass one," I say. "Every class here is in a different place than where we were back home."

"Shoot, your moms pulled you out of school right before the APs?" Andrew shakes his head. "Sorry, no disrespect."

"Tell me about it," I say. "But I will accept nothing less than a four or five." He's nodding, and I feel the old competitive drive kick in, the way Cindy always got me going. We used to try to beat each other's scores, and most of the time, we came out dead even, to the A- or A+.

I catch Tanay casting glances between us, none too pleased with this exchange. It's clear AP English is her only advanced class, never mind Andrew is her territory. I will not trespass there.

"So when's practice?" Andrew asks. "This project is worth twenty-five percent of the semester, y'all."

"Tomorrow at lunch," Tanay says. "Wendy, you good?"

They're both looking at me. One will soon escort me to class; the other just got me out of a suspension. This equals one serious IOU.

"Yeah. I guess it's better than hiding in the bathroom, my usual lunchtime haunt."

Tanay and Andrew exchange glances. Andrew says, "I don't know about y'all, but I ain't going to be late."

He glances at Tanay as we leave. The last look always tells you where a guy's heart lies. There's never been a dude who's done that with me.

"Be good, California!" Tanay calls as I follow Andrew. "Stay in school till we do our play!"

By 3:00 p.m. I've had a Dee-free day without further incident, thanks to Andrew and Tanay taking turns to get me to class. But he's got weightlifting and she's got something to do with Mushi after school, and my detention doesn't start till next week. So I high-tail it solo, top speed, to the front of the school and EZ Rider bus stop where the public eye should protect me. Not even Deanna's crew is stupid enough to try a gang bang at the city stop right near the school marquee.

I'm not there a minute when I see Deanna Faire's baby-blue MiniCooper, full to busting with minions, do a leisurely drive-by, traffic backing up down the avenue behind her. My heart stops: she's slowing down for me.

"Hey, Osama!" she screams. "Wait till you hear from my lawyer!"

"Hey, bitch!" Bethany shrieks out the passenger side, only a few feet from my weak, scuttling ass. "We've got a present for yoooou!"

I see Koyt in the back seat with a huge spray can, scrambling to get out. Will they paint me black? Thank MJ, the EZ Rider bus hurtles toward us, the driver's face broadcasting death as he leans on the horn. The Mini-Cooper doesn't budge. At the last second, he swerves around Deanna and ends up several feet past the stop.

I skirt the waiting crowd and scramble aboard. The driver is cussing a blue streak. My heart might just leap out of my chest and bounce down these steps.

I find a seat at the back and crouch down, peering out the window. Bethany's flipping me off and so is Deanna. They're waving at Koyt to get back in. The bus grinds and roars to life. Deanna's car is now riding our tail.

The death bus rolls on. This time, I am 100 percent alone.

CHAPTER 12

A HEART-SLAMMING 15 MINUTES LATER, COUNTING way past pi to heavenly infinities, I spill out onto Jefferson Street. I start a mad dash past restaurants, sports shops, abandoned storefronts where homeless camp and cheer me on. Nonstop honking right behind me, bile in my throat—praise MJ, they're stuck at a light—but now Koyt's getting out at the corner, sprinting my way, picking up speed!

I dodge prospective SMU frosh ignoring parents asking if they want a SMU T-shirt; I knock arms with a panhandler who hollers, "Illegal download!" I seek nooks, crannies, burrows, till I find a dark little store—Album Alley.

I dart in. Inside the shotgun store stands a hunched dude behind a counter, his face Neanderthal and scowling, gray pompadour hair brushed away from his temples. Everywhere stacked ceiling to floor, nothing but LPs sheathed in plastic and leaning towers of CDs covered in dust. I stare at him, panting.

He glares back. "Desperate for music?"

Through the window I see Koyt lumber by with Graham on his heels, right past the store.

"Would you look at that: Wendy Redbird Dancing." A voice behind me. I turn. At the back of the dank shotgun store stands Shaye Tann.

I've never been so glad to see someone in my life. He's got on a tight black T that says Martin Guitars. His hair is mussed, like he might have been in a fight or just rolled out of bed, but it makes him look super young. "You okay?" he says, walking toward me.

I gulp a breath. I could hit the floor and go fetal, clutching the manic heart in my chest. "Your client—she wants to kill me."

"What's that?" He walks slowly, smiling, his hands tapping the rows of CDs and albums flanking him, like a blind man might do with a cane.

"She and her thugs are"—I breathe—"looking for me."

He grins. "Seriously? Well, you're safe. I got your back."

I watch him walk to the window and peer out. I close my mouth and try yoga breaths so I don't sound so desperate. My heart hammers in my ears.

He turns and smiles at me. "All clear." He comes back, and inches away, I smell something sweet like bread. His eyes have a slight glaze but he's speaking clearly. Grandma slurs after her four glasses at dinner, and it only takes one for Sunny to get stupid. I think he's had a beer or two.

"It must be fate you're here," he says. "Look what I found." He points at a basket of cassettes on the counter near the hunched proprietor, who scowls at Shaye like he's Satan. Shaye starts rifling through. "Perfect for your Walkman." He pulls out Phil Collins, Cyndi Lauper, Howard Jones, and Rick Springfield, and places them in my hands. I count to the perfect 4, breathe deep, count again.

"Thanks." I glance through the window again, but not a Deanna minion to be seen, not a murderous MiniCooper to be sighted.

"Hey," he says, and touches my arm. "You okay, really?"

"They had spray paint," I say.

He raises his eyebrows. "Jesus, were they going to tar and feather you?" He rubs my arm before he pulls his hand away.

"That's what I thought! I mean, I know I said she has STDs, but she hacked my Facebook with porn pictures—so I threw a latté on her—"

"Bunch of delinquents, y'all are," Shaye says with a grin. He's really hard to hate. Then his face shifts, scanning mine, like he's worried there's no smile. "I guess she needs more than a talking-to, then."

Behind us the curmudgeonly Neanderthal snorts, like all the phlegm of the world is in his throat and soul.

"I'll be fine," I say with a shrug. I can't show him so much baby. "Don't worry about it—"

"No. Something's got to be done." His dark eyes look Dad Knows Best. He shakes his head. "I let her get away with too much, and she expects miracles 24/7. I deserve a life, and you need to feel safe. We have to get you two on the peace train."

"You don't need to, it's okay—"

"Sshhh." Shaye grabs my arm. "You hear that?"

A dirge-like, echoing song moans from dusty speakers teetering above. Some guy swears he's become comfortably numb.

"You know this, right?" Shaye says, looking at me like I of course would know. He closes his eyes. "1979." He opens his eyes. "Does it pass inspection?"

"I can do 1979," I say. "*Off the Wall* released that year."

"Nice." He lets go of my arm and gives me that look like I'm beyond brilliance. "My go-to song, freshman year in high school," he says. I do the math. So that would make him forty-four—a few years older than my dear mother, Sunny Revere. "I was zoned out on pot, total delinquent, hating everyone. No one got me, you know?" I nod. His eyes are so dark, penetrating. "But you hang in, okay? You'll find people who get you." That crooked grin has so much confidence, I get a little thrill.

He leans against the counter, considering me. The Cur rolls his eyes and steps back in disgust. "So what's in your Walkman right now?"

"*Thriller.*"

"Let me make a confession here. 'The Girl is Mine'? What's that bit about, I love you forever—?"

"Endlessly."

"Yeah, that's it. MJ really hits it there. I'm a sucker for that kind of mess."

I can't tell him how much that song moves me, too—how I've listened to it a thousand times, hoping one day I and Cyrus might live the dream.

"You think I'm cheesy." He's grinning.

"Not at all," I say, a little too loud. "I mean, songs today, there's no true romance. All we have is Gaga's bad kind. Or like, the Black Eyed Peas plastic kind."

"You go, girl." He looks impressed. "It is a shallow age. But you got to admit, Gaga can bring it. I'd rep her." He glances at his watch. "Listen, I've got to bounce." He tosses a few dollars on The Cur's counter, then turns so only I can see and mouths, "Asshole."

I want to laugh but keep a straight face.

He pats my shoulder and then squeezes, like, *It'll be all right.* "Listen, I'll hang around front on my bike, keep an eye out. That girl doesn't have the patience to search every store. She's got work to do if she wants to go anywhere, and I'll tell her that myself."

"It's cool," I say with a shrug, like getting chased is child's play.

"No, it's not," Shaye says. "I owe you. Your mom and I—we didn't mean—we had no idea—"

Talk of Sunny's romance turns my stomach. "It's okay," I say, holding up my hands. "You two just enjoy your geezer love."

"Oh, oh, oh!" He swats me. "I'll have you know I'm wa-a-a-a-y young at heart."

He grins and leaves with a wave. Let's just say, he is too hot for Sunny.

I hear the growl of the Harley as it revs up, and then the roar as he pulls into the street. The Cur hunches forward over his counter, watching him ride away. "Some lookout," he growls.

I do not want to know what makes this man mad. But I do need to get home somehow; walking and busing it are not the way. I wish Shaye had offered me a ride on his bike.

I take a breath and say to The Cur, "Is it okay if I hang out?"

"Why not? Seems to be Charity Day."

I have no idea what that's about; didn't Shaye just pay him? The man's a weird bird.

I dial Sunny at the animal shelter, her haunt since we came.

While I wait for the shelter staff to find her, I say, "What was that 'I am numb' song you were just playing?"

The Cur's caterpillar eyebrows shoot skyward. "You don't know? Jesus." He shakes his head. "And I thought, *Play what the people want,* the few overplayed ones I could actually stand. It's Pink Floyd, 'Comfortably Numb.'"

Now there's a phrase I can get with. Like MJ in his hyperbaric oxygen chamber. Michael would understand why I have to wave a freak flag, then dive deep, go under. Yank the teeming invaders off your scent.

I go stand at the window to wait for her. In the dusty display, mysterious albums sag and lean, the singers' faces trapped in black-and-white stills—Sonny Rollins, Chuck Berry, Everly Brothers, The Platters—or in hectic, colorized prints—Ziggy Stardust, The Animals, Aretha Franklin, Dusty Springfield. Tourists wander by but no thugs.

A few minutes later, the Mirage Colt pulls up. As I step outside, Sunny Revere rolls down the window and calls, "Wendy, what in the world—why couldn't you take the bus?"

With Sunny it's best to sift out troubling information, as she's flummoxed by most facts. Facts require decisions, and Sunny's best at dithering. Except when it comes to animals.

Then things become black and white. We've been foster parents to a million cats, and no surprise, there's a heart-rending squeak from the back seat.

"God, Mother, not again." I get in and lean my head back, closing my eyes. No wonder she's willing to come: baby on board.

"This one will be a snap to place," she says. "Two years old, really sweet. Irresistible!"

Squeak, squeak, squeak from the cloth carrier behind me. I've learned not to look because the cats never stay. Based on recent patterns, it's probably another calico. Sunny Revere has a thing for patchwork coats of indeterminate breed.

She pulls into traffic without looking and there's a strident honk behind us. I jump, but it's just another SUV riding our tail till she turns off and saves humanity the trouble of swerving around our puttering red carcass. *Squeak, squeak, squeak.*

She says, "What'd you get? And how'd you get the money?" She eyes my loot like it could be converted to essential oils or yoga DVDs.

"They were free. I ran into Shaye at the record store."

"No way."

"Yes way."

She's strangely silent. I bet the woman is jealous.

Then she says: "What did he ask of you?"

My stomach clenches on a sudden memory—me, ten years old, the day her skeezy dude Nelson made his dramatic exit. She yelled something like this question, sobbing, and I sobbed back, not getting why we both were crying and snot-faced. Sometimes, I wake in the middle of the night with that memory, so nauseated, I might hurl all over my bed. It makes no sense.

I snap, "Mother, what the hell?"

She stares through the windshield biting her lip.

I say, "What, like, would I shine his shoes? Or tell him what a fantastic parent you are?"

She turns pink. "You're nasty. Horrible."

Sunny Revere is an insecure freak. She will lose Shaye Tann in the next twenty-four hours. You can bank on that.

Then she says, "I don't know what I'm talking about," with tiny conviction, and leans forward over the steering wheel. The way she's peering through the windshield, she might just be blind.

We drive home in silence, save for *squeak, squeak, squeak.*

CHAPTER 13

WHEN I JOIN TANAY AND Andrew for practice in Teasdale's room the next day at lunch, I tell them what went down on Jefferson Street with Deanna.

"Oh, hell no," Tanay says. "Not on my watch."

She grabs my hand and drags me out of the room.

"Hold up!" Andrew yells behind us. "Where y'all going?"

"Wait your turn," Tanay says. "We'll be back."

We stalk empty hallways, thanks to a zero tolerance policy that herds the masses into cafeteria, classrooms, or off campus. "What if they catch us?" I say.

"They won't." Tanay points. "See that?" There before us, at the end of the English wing, is one of Deanna's glossy propaganda pieces, only this time with

CD RELEASE PARTY
7/04/09
THE SHADE

blasted across the bottom.

We look at each other. Then we rip the thing off the wall into a zillion shreds.

Then we scour every inch of the academic wings and destroy 15 more.

"This is vandalism, you know," I say, as I stuff the remains into a trash receptacle.

"It's the Lord's judgment," Tanay says. "God told my ass to do this in a dream."

"I love the Lord's will," I say. "Nevermore shall I be a heathen."

We slap hands. My smack's a little off.

We come back to Teasdale's room looking innocent. "You look real good today," Tanay says as we come in the door. I've come to school garbed in my peg-leg jeans, blue ruffled blouse, and a '50s ponytail, which apparently '80s girls wore back in the day. This is a milder look for sure, topped off with a less flashy jacket of Members Only, one that hopefully won't have to serve as flak jacket. She adds, "You're skinny as hell, girl, like a bird beneath those costumes!"

I want to tell her thank you for this and for a lot of things, but I don't know how.

Andrew says, "What you two been up to?" He's looking at Tanay.

"I got secrets," she says, and bats her eyelashes. She looks really cute herself in a short red miniskirt, red feather earrings, and an olive hoodie made of some soft material, the edges frayed on purpose.

"Oh, I know that," he says. I feel like I need to leave this private room, so I turn away and pretend to be very interested in my copy of *A Raisin in the Sun*.

"Wendy!" Andrew says. "What's she up to? I know you can't tell a lie."

"I plead the Fifth," I say.

"Aw, sh–" Andrew cuts himself off, grinning. "Girl, I know you, and you been bad."

She shoves him in the chest. "Get serious now. I want that A."

Andrew throws up his hands. "And y'all acting like I'm the one holding us up!"

I'm skimming my part. I remember this play from eighth grade. Mr. Lindner's a nervous, racist white man who doesn't want the black Younger family to integrate a white neighborhood. I am to be shouted out of the Younger house by Andrew in his role of Walter Younger. Tanay is playing Ruth Younger, Walter's wife. It's good there's not much personality to my role—a bland, glad-handing guy—because ever since I was ripped from California, I'm not feeling too inspired to get crazy on stage.

"Wendy, come through the door like it's the door to our house," Tanay says. "Andrew, get your ass over here." She points to a spot next to her, in front of Teasdale's SMART Board.

I go to the doorway just as Teasdale comes in, munching on a long carrot and reeking of garlic.

"Oh, wonderful, just in time!" she sings out. "I totally want to see this." She takes a seat like she's our director.

I enter the pretend doorway and face Andrew and Tanay. "Uh—how do you do, miss. I am looking for a Mrs. Lena Younger?"

Teasdale shakes her head. "No, Wendy, *nervousness.* You are the only white person in this black neighborhood, and you're not used to being a minority." It's like she's talking through a condescending megaphone.

I take a deep breath. I've never acted in a show where I stood out like a sore white thumb. "Uhhhh. How...do you do... miss. I...am...looking for a Mrs. Lena Younger?"

"No, no, Wendy, that's not it. Why don't you try pausing before the 'Lena Younger.' Blacks are all the same to you, so names don't really stick."

Cringe. But Tanay watches me with sympathy.

I do it yet again, pausing at the right time, but I sound and look like cardboard. Frankly, I'm a little freaked with everyone hot-lamping me. Teasdale nitpicks every word, Tanay's looking disappointed, and it goes this way till the end where Mr. Lindner tries to scare the Youngers with a warning that hints whites will bomb their new house should the Youngers integrate his white neighborhood.

I'm just about to panic when it hits me: Sunny and Mr. Lindner would sound exactly the same—white, whiny, and guilt-tripping. I shift my voice to Sunny Revere in a head-shaking, told-you-so trance:

"Well—I don't understand why you people are reacting this way. What do you think you are going to *gain* by moving into a neighborhood where you just aren't *wanted* and where some elements—well—people can get awful worked up when they feel that their *whole way of life* and everything they've ever worked for is *threatened*."

A pause. Everyone watches me, startled. Andrew spits, "Get out." His eyes bore holes in me exactly the way black Walter would look at white Lindner invading his home.

"Bravo!" shrieks Teasdale. "Wendy, that's it! That voice, that whole demeanor."

"Yeah, girl," Tanay says, coming over and slugging my shoulder. "That was good."

I want to laugh because how mortified would my progressive mother be to know I channeled her to play a racist. But I feel good; I didn't let Tanay down.

I rifle through the pages and tap a scene. "You guys skipped something. When I come in, you're supposed to be dancing!"

"What?" Andrew acts confused. Tanay looks mad, but not too mad, and I'm delighted, because they clearly know what they missed, and plus the hot lamp's off me.

I say, "There's a bluesy, sexy record Walter puts on. You're romancing your wife."

"My wife?" Andrew says, like that's the craziest thing he's ever heard, but grinning, he grabs Tanay's hands. He drags her around the floor in a waltzy, ridiculous way.

"No, no, no, bodies close," Teasdale says.

If Tanay could blush...she looks like every nerve's at full attention as Andrew yanks her closer. He does not mind this in the least. They do a stiff-legged twirl around the front of the room.

"Okay, we'll have to work on that," I say.

"Hell with you, Wendy," Tanay says.

The first bell rings, and Teasdale gets up to go to her desk. We hear rustling down the hall and slamming of lockers as the hordes begin their advance.

Mushi's large frame appears in the door. "Tan*ay*!" she yells. "Where you been?" She looks between me and Tanay like, *What you doing talking to Sideshow Whitey?*

Tanay's face is a wall as she says, "Girl, your ass could've been in this."

"Shit," Mushi says, "I ain't doing no damn play." But she looks a little too pissed as she says it.

"When you coming back?" Andrew says.

Mushi says, "Week from Monday. Mugs think they showing me something."

Teasdale glances up from her desk, looking nervous. Andrew shakes his head slightly and says, "I'm gone, y'all." He leaves.

"Yeah, go on with your bad self!" Mushi yells after him. "You the big man on this campus." Then she turns to Tanay. "And now you all bougie." She looks darts at me, then back at Tanay. "Hanging with these emo bitches. I guess you think you something." She stalks off.

In the hallway we hear her holler, "Used to be homies, but we ain't shit no more!"

Tanay stifles a sigh with an embarrassed glance my way. My heart's trying to chop its way out of my chest, but I shrug like it's no big deal. "Hey, she didn't call me Osama. I consider that a plus."

Tanay cracks up. We go down the hall, jostled by thick and distinct streams of white sheep, black sheep, brown sheep, yellow sheep. We're our own little Oreo stripe. She has to shout. "Hey, you think you could help me out with this exam?"

The AP English exam is in six days. I see a glimmer of hope on her face—hope mixed with massive fear of that looming score of two. "Sure—yeah—I mean, I guess."

"Want to come over for dinner tonight?"

For a second, I'm petrified. I hear myself say, "I can't. I mean, I would love to, but..."

I can tell she sees through me. She shrugs. "Sure, whatever."

"I mean, Andrew—he's the one getting fours and fives on the practice ones—maybe you should ask him."

"I don't have time for his mess." Tanay's face gets hard.

"But I guess you could, I don't know, sit with me in detention, I mean, if you want—if they let you—"

"All right, then. I'll meet you there." She scans the hallway. "I don't see the diva or her damn posse. You okay?"

"I'm okay."

I scan her face for judgment and repulsion, but her look is chill as she leaves me. Somehow she forgives my freak, and I have no idea why.

CHAPTER 14

WHEN I GET HOME, SHAYE is sitting on our doorstep, smoking a cigarette. His Harley is parked in our driveway. The Mitsubishi Mirage is nowhere to be seen.

"Where's my MIA mother?" I say.

He shrugs. "Uh-oh, something's up," he says. "What's wrong?"

"I'm fine," I say. At least, I think I am. Tanay acted totally cool, but I still feel weird—like I ran from a gift of cash, or shoved away an ice cream sundae.

"Sit down." He pats the step next to him.

I sit on the edge, a little in front of him, while he takes a drag on his cigarette. The smell is sharp and pungent but somehow comforting.

"They hunting you down?" he says.

I shake my head.

"Good. That's what I want to hear. You making any friends?"

"I guess." *Except when I screw it up,* I want to say. It's like I can't help myself.

"You guess? Doesn't sound too promising."

"There's a—there are people who seem decent. I don't know—I can't explain it." My heart flutters as I feel his gaze. I blurt, "But no one's worth the time."

"Tell me about it." He sighs. "Welcome to my world. That's the music industry. Everyone's fickle, and everyone's a whore." He says the last word so casual, with such little emphasis, that it doesn't sound anything but true. And like I'm old enough to get it.

"And you don't want to get burned," I say. "Have someone take advantage, you know?"

"True that." He inhales, deep, then releases smoke through his nose. In the fading afternoon light, it looks regal, leonine. A shaft of sunlight cuts through the trees and strikes his hair into fire.

He's saying, "But you get up every day and you take that risk, right?" He peers at me. "I mean, you come from trail-blazing stock. Seriously. Look at your mom."

I laugh, harshly. "Yeah, look at her." But it rattles me a little to think he respects Sunny picking up stakes. Could there be something brave to it?

He's waiting like I need to explain, so I add, "Thanks to Sunny Revere, I no longer have a best friend. How can she expect me to start over again and again?"

A pause while he stubs out his cigarette. "Wendy, I've got one piece of advice for you. Wherever you go, wherever you are, let people in. Because you get one shot at this life." He looks at me. "You know that saying, how it's better to love and lose than never love at all?"

I shake my head, but my heart pounds. What he's saying echoes deep. I still miss Cindy like the devil. She can't save my ass, but that was never her job. She was a damn good friend.

Before I know it, I'm telling him about her and MJ and how we had this thing about letting the truth unfurl. How I miss her more than anything and I don't know if Tanay can really come through, if anyone can, which is why I didn't go over to her house.

He listens like he really gets it.

When I'm done, he slaps his hands on his knees and says, "You know what you need?"

"What?"

"You need to lighten up. You think too much." He pulls keys out of his pocket and dangles them in front of my eyes. "Come on," he says. "Let's take a ride."

He's already walking down the flagstones, now down the driveway, and though I'm standing up, I don't know what to do. I haven't been on a regular bike in ages; motorcycles seem like a quantum leap of adventure.

"Come on, girl," he calls. He's sitting on his bike, unhooking his helmet. "Let's put Dancing back in your name."

I follow and get on behind him, awkwardly. He twists around, handing me his helmet, grinning. It's heavy and smells musty like cigarettes but sweet sweat, too.

"Grab ahold," he says. "Don't be shy."

I put my arms around his waist—basically hugging him—and the engine roars with monstrous life. My heart shoots into my throat. I can feel his ribs, a tight waist, and then I'm wondering if I'm clutching too hard but I do not want to die.

"Lean with me!" he hollers over his shoulder. "When I go around corners!"

"Okay!"

"You ever get soundtracks in your head?"

"Yeah!"

"Cool! So what's our song?"

"Uh, 'Beat It'!"

"Yeah, baby!"

With a deafening snarl, we're off like a bullet through this heat. Suddenly, for the first time since I've landed in this forsaken place, there's a breeze. The cluttered porches of hipster houses look quaint at this speed, homey, come to life with beer sippers and bongo players and toddling babies. And there's so much green: the lush blur of oak and birch and the occasional magnolia, dark and shiny with heavy leaves; and loud and hard, the chatter of cicadas whirring in my ears. I'm clinging to him but somehow I'm weightless, while I feel him solid as stone, shooting us through space without fear.

We pass the downtown bustle on the green outside Nature Fare, where hippies stroll, laugh, let their dogs and kids run wild, and listen to a sitar player. Shaye calls, "Now!" whenever there's a corner, and I lean with him, hoping I'm getting it right.

We pause, growling, at a light at the edge of Millboro, before it bleeds into downtown Steeple Mount. Shaye calls, "Me, it's 'Photograph'!"

"What?"

"Def Leppard! Ultimate soundtrack!"

We take off again, and I hug tighter as my heart hits my throat. I will have to look that one up.

We shoot down Jefferson Street, and it's awesome because Mainstreamia can't handle the truth of this muffler. We're like an earthquake past the chain restaurants and the tacky sports shops; loitering teens look up, sneering like they could be cousins of Deanna Faire. Especially the one who is Deanna Faire. In a pack of blond lookalikes and a gaggle of frat boys, she stares, mouth hanging open as we pass.

"That was your client!" I yell.

"Oh, shit!" Shaye laughs as we burn through a yellow light.

"Ooh, you're in trouble!" I yell at the next light. "Fraternizing with the enemy!"

"Enemies?" he says. "It stops, today."

A small thrill races across my skin. I let my chin touch his back as I readjust and hug tighter. I think he just said I'm safe.

Then he yells, "Let's go make peace."

"No!" I hear myself yell. But he's turning left at the next light, he's headed back the other way on Jefferson, going towards Deanna, and he doesn't seem to hear me.

CHAPTER 15

W E PULL UP OUTSIDE OF Sparky's, teen scene and college hang right smack in the middle of Jefferson, known for its red meat and milkshakes. Deanna's crew hanging outside includes some of her minions but mostly what look like older dudes with backward ball caps and Steeple Mount U sweatshirts. Shaye cuts the engine; I stumble off. My head roars with wind, like I've just pressed a million seashells to my ears. Deanna watches us disembark with a snarl on her face.

Shaye beckons to her and goes into Sparky's. I pull off the helmet and follow him.

The two of us stand in the lobby, looking back to see if Deanna will come.

"Table for two?" chirps the perky hostess.

"Three," Shaye says.

Deanna strolls in, her face slightly pink and her ice-blue eyes roving, as if someone might see us together and that would be very, very bad.

We follow the hostess to a booth. Shaye points us where we are to sit: across from each other. He sees I still have the helmet and cracks up. "I'll take that."

Dee glowers at me, like I don't deserve such attention.

He pulls a chair from another table and sits on the end, like a negotiator.

He says, "I heard there was a chase yesterday—"

I interrupt, "With gallons of paint!"

Deanna's face goes stone cold, like a murderer on the stand.

"Dee," he says, "is this true?"

I don't like him calling her Dee. She shrugs and won't look at us, staring instead at the table carved with graffiti of penises and lost loves. "She's destroyed two outfits."

"Hey, how ya'll doing?" chirps a perkier waitress, shoving menus at all of us and talking only to Shaye. "Want to hear about the Sparky Special?"

"No, thanks," Shaye says. "We need a couple minutes."

Perky Girl's face falls like she's been dumped. She skitters away.

"Now we could exchange cash—" Shaye says, "—and pay for the destruction of property and whatever. But there's fault both sides—it's getting violent—so let's stop all this seventh-grade shit."

"I tried to be nice like you told me!" Deanna screeches. "And she was a total bitch about it."

"Like you really meant it," I say with what I hope is heavy sarcasm, but my voice sounds little-girl under Shaye's gaze, younger than seventh grade.

"I'm not saying y'all have to like each other," Shaye says. "Dee, your career's at stake. A mean Taylor Swift is the worst PR move. This one—" he points at me "—could start a blog or upload a video to get every parent in America foaming at the mouth. Then there won't be any tweens buying your records." I can see the panic on Dee's face. He looks at me. "And you. You're too smart for this. You get into trouble, don't the colleges find out?"

I suddenly picture Grandma tanning my hide, then skinning me, then making said hide into a couture purse.

Deanna and I glance at each other. He's making too much sense.

He grabs Deanna's hand. "I won't spend any less time promoting you. I got your back."

Her face melts. She's got him in a tractor beam, willing him her way. Like she wants him, body and soul.

Then he grabs mine. "And I've got yours, too. I love your mom, and I want things to work."

His hand is warm, really firm—but he loves Sunny Revere. I hate the needles pricking deep inside, needles I don't know why, maybe because she doesn't deserve it, this kind of love.

"Truce?" Shaye is saying. He puts our hands together.

Our fingers fumble against one another, and then Deanna and I shake, limply. We don't look at each other.

"Say it," he orders. "Say, 'Yes, Shaye, it's a truce.'"

"Yes Shaye it's a truce," we mumble.

"Good." Shaye leans back, smiling.

Deanna stands up, not looking at either of us. "I have to go."

Shaye considers her, looking slightly irritated. He waves her off. "See you tonight."

She stalks out. "What's tonight?" I say, trying not to sound too curious.

"We have a meet with Redblood Records. She's chewing her nails to blood and fasting like crazy, but the deal's in the bag. She'll be the star she's always dreamed of."

I take small pleasure in the thought of Deanna Faire getting ulcers despite her meteoric rise. "I don't trust her," I say.

"Listen." Shaye takes my hand, clutches it a second. I can't look at him. "She's a publicity hound. She won't mess with her rep. She heard me loud and clear. It's over."

I glance up at him, and those dark eyes tell me it's so.

He lets go, and leans back. I miss his hand already. "So," he says. "I'm buying. What's your pleasure?"

Perky Girl is back and hovering. "Tell us about that special," Shaye says with a grin, and the girl melts and chatters away.

After the long litany, she looks disappointed when we say we want ice cream sundaes.

When we get home and I clamber off the bike, I stand, then stumble again. I wish so badly I had more coordination. I hand Shaye the helmet, hoping I don't look like I'm ten. His hair is wild around his face. He swats it away, and the OCD in me sees tangles I want to fix.

"How old are you?" he says. "Sixteen?"

"Almost. July 24," I say. "Why?"

"Because you sound a lot older. All your fancy words, like 'fraternizing.'"

"Yeah, well, what can I say? I'm a nerd." Again, can't look him in the eye—he notices so much.

"Nerd's good," he says. "But you know how to dress. Not all nerds know that." He gestures at my clothes as I perch on the curb. I wonder if I'm turning bright red. I see the Mirage is back now, and I realize I'm disappointed. Shaye leaves me wanting just a few moments more.

"Who's that?" Shaye says. I turn and see a burgundy Mercedes trundle into the driveway, almost ramming the bumper of the Mirage. Behind the wheel is Grandma, sitting ramrod straight and dripping with pearls.

CHAPTER 16

GRANDMA ROLLS DOWN HER WINDOW when I approach. "Are we still doing this London junket?" she snaps.

"Yeah," I say. Grandma's already told me she plans to stay at The Ritz and shop Harrods the whole time; though she considers MJ "loony tunes," it's still worth a chance to shop her heart out. I say, "I thought you were in Bali another week."

"The heat was atrocious. And then I had Lupita whining every day about missing her kids," Grandma says. She gives Shaye a withering glance in the rearview mirror. "I suppose that's him."

I nod.

"Well, get in and away from the Hell's Angel. I'm taking you to dinner, et cetera."

I get in as the front door bangs. A sleepy Sunny Revere steps out of the Passive Solar, just woken from yet another mammoth nap. She flutters her fingers at Shaye, and I look away. She's wearing a tank top without a bra and frayed jean shorts sewn with old Girl Scout patches. Her face falls when she sees me getting into the car with Grandma.

"It'll do no good, Virginia," Sunny calls. "She's spiritual but she's not *religious*." She looks at Shaye, like he might add something supportive.

Grandma yells out my window, "*Spiritual* doesn't mean balls. Do a deed today, Lydia, do a deed."

Grandma has trouble picking up today's slang. When she does, her phrases sound more sexual than she ever intends. I glance at Shaye. He winks at me and grins like, *Good luck.* I want to die. Sunny's arms are folded, she's giving us a look of disgust, and I say to Grandma, "Are you two related?"

Grandma lights a Virginia Slim. Her laugh rasps like sandpaper. "Lydia's views are quite convenient. A rock can be full of 'spirituality' as long as there are no commandments on it."

I learned long ago not to take sides in this war of attrition. Frankly, poised between the spiritual but not religious and the religious but not spiritual, I'll take atheism, thank you.

"What's this one called?" Grandma says as she pulls the Mercedes out of our neighborhood and away from my dear mother body-slamming Shaye.

"He's not so bad," I say. "Shaye Tann."

"What is he, number eight this year?" I see the slow fade and bleed of lipstick into the lines around her lips as she inhales.

"Number three."

We have several moments of silence for this, till I realize she's pointed the Mercedes to St. Anthony's Catholic Church. "This isn't dinner," I say, but before I can protest, we're walking up to the dark stone Gothic chapel. It flanks the big modern white church where she normally drags me, the Sunday or Saturday services overflowing with harried fathers toting bawling toddlers and jiggling women shushing seven-year-olds showing no sign of the age of reason. Today we're relegated to the late-afternoon service at the chapel where rich old ladies like Grandma get special delivery from Father Bill before their early-bird happy hours.

Grandma marches us into the cool, dark little building, lit at the end like someone's funeral, and plunks us in the first pew. I watch an altar boy and girl light remaining candles and try not to trip on their albs. Grandma snorts because she hates girls doing things around the Body of Christ. This one wears pink Skechers; Grandma gives her the evil eye.

There's no music or fanfare for the eight of us in attendance; only Father Bill processing down the aisle with his two altar servers in tow. Father Bill sports white hair; a red, veiny nose; and a round potbelly and skinny legs like he nips his bottle now and then.

I've learned the hard way over the years to fake a face that's intent with listening, because Grandma doesn't do excuses. In her world, I'm going to a very good public school, her alma mater, and am finally wrested from the snake pit she considers San Francisco. In her fiction, I'm on my way to becoming an actress on Broadway, despite its hijacking by the gays, or a journalist for *The New York Times*, despite its raging liberalism. The fact I'm a hell of a lot more focused than Sunny is a huge thing with Grandma, so she will cultivate me like a crop till her dying day.

I wake up during the penitential rite where Grandma rattles verses off like an old pro. For a second I wish I believed the same as this cultish, chanting brood, spilling words that wrap life into neat little balls.

I have sinned through my own fault,
in my thoughts and in my words,
in what I have done,
and in what I have failed to do...

Grandma explained this chant once as having something to do with "sins of omission." I do believe when the Church thought that one up, it had to be thinking of Sunny Revere.

Father Bill says, "And may almighty God have mercy on us, forgive us our sins, and bring us to everlasting life."

Our tiny group rumbles, "Amen."

I take a deep, slow breath. I keep thinking of Shaye and that ride, his joining my hand with Deanna's, how he's telling me to take a risk on Tanay, how everything looks different from the back of a motorcycle. Dare I say things are looking up? Here where I'm prisoner to Grandma's rituals, where her Chanel scent surrounds me with its military might, I feel something like safe. It's not like Sunny will ever darken a church's door, demanding we renegotiate how the service goes, and it's not like Grandma will ever change. I want to touch her, lean close into her silk jacket like a little girl and sniff the same scent forever.

Father Bill's voice is gravelly as he monotones his homily verbatim:

"Gratitude. Count those blessings. Even in your darkest hour, Christ's light shines through. What candles can you still see shining in the dark? Bow your heads. Let us count as many as we can."

I duck my head so Grandma won't elbow me. I'd count anyway since I'm damn good at it. Next to me, Grandma sighs. I wonder what she enumerates. Maybe as she searches for bright things to count, she remembers the irony that her child, Sunny, casts only shadows.

After Father Bill tells us all to go in peace, Grandma takes me to Chubsuckers for dinner. It's another one of our rituals ever since I came to visit as a kid—upscale fish dinner at the place hung with nets and anchors and full of Steeple Mount's upper crust. I'm feeling hungry, ready to eat hearty, till I see the place is packed and what time it is. Tonight will be dangerous because dinner will go past 8:00 p.m. I've learned the hard way to never call or see Grandma after 8:00 p.m. or before 10:00 a.m., as she is not the nicest of persons during that stretch.

We're not seated till 7:00. By that time Grandma has had

one and then another Tom Collins with extra lemon at the bar. Hoo boy.

Thankfully the waitress gets us our appetizers fast, so we glut on raw oysters and hush puppies. Grandma orders a bottle of Pinot Grigio. I don't get a sip, even if I am almost sixteen.

"So tell me, what is this play thing?" Grandma pours herself a very full glass.

"It's just some scenes we're doing."

"Do you like them?"

"The scenes?"

Grandma takes her first big gulp and flutters her hand at me. "The people—them!"

"By 'them,' do you mean 'the blacks'?"

"Who else would I mean?"

I hide my sigh. "I like Tanay. She's cool. So's Andrew."

"Tanay," Grandma says it with a sigh and takes her first big gulp. "At least it's not LaQuisha or Shanaynay."

I let that hang a good thirty seconds while I do a dramatic head swivel. There's not a black face among the whiteys dining on calamari here at Chubsuckers. I say slowly, "Some people like to invent names. Your daughter is one of them."

"Your name should have been Emily," says Grandma. "But none of us had a say in the doings of your mother. This boy—who's supervising all of you?"

"There's plenty of supervision, Grandma." I stuff a hush puppy in my mouth so I don't tell her she's racist for thinking the black boy wants a piece of this white girl. "Maybe you should come see us. Get to know some black people."

"I'm taking you to see that loony tunes, aren't I?" Grandma barks. She tips her glass for last, nonexistent drops. "Hell's bells, where's our food?" She glares at our waitress sweating beneath a huge tray as she rushes toward a table of ten, then frowns at me like this is all my fault. She snaps, "So what does this shaggy-head boyfriend do?"

"He manages musicians."

"Hmpf. Watch yourself. Musicians are heels."

"And what is a heel?"

"A contemptibly dishonorable individual." Grandma nibbles on a hush puppy, then drops it with disgust on her plate.

"He sets up record deals. He doesn't play." I hate to think that he's doing a deal for Deanna, this very moment.

"But will he play, as they say, your mother? No doubt." Grandma smirks at her own sour wit.

"He'll soon figure out he's wasting his time."

Grandma's overplucked eyebrows soar sky high. "Dear God—so she's got another waiting in the wings?"

"Lately she's been so lovestruck, she may have met her match." The waitress places swordfish before me but now I can't eat. I can't help but have noticed Sunny's stopped glancing over her shoulder at other men.

"He's a little too pretty," Grandma muses, attacking her pecan-encrusted halibut. "Clothes horse. You can tell he checks all his mirrors. Could be a Rock Hudson. I never got over that." She sighs. "Your mother will wake up one morning and discover he's a fruit."

"He is NOT gay."

Grandma gives me a sharp look but says nothing, as the third glass has been filled.

I count all my images stored of Shaye, 4 strong impressions I recycle on the regular: strong nose, dark eyes, the masculine way he walks, the way he looks at me. No, he can't be gay. I start my swordfish as it looks good again.

We finish our meal without another word, which is fine by me. I think of Shaye and his stark contrast to all other suitors and their sins throughout the years. Sunny's dudes have always pretended to talk to me but only because they want to know where she keeps the pot. When circa age seven I learned to say, "in the kitchen by the stove," they'd get bored and go away. That was the easiest to deal with. The worst was the drinking and the drugging and the disappearing that always left Sunny a puddle of tears.

As we leave, I remind Grandma of my upcoming July birthday and current permit so she'll let me drive, never mind I don't want her behind the wheel after four glasses of wine and two stiff drinks. Driving her Mercedes feels like steering a tank but I pretend everything's cool, entertaining her with Sunny tales till she interrupts, "So have you joined any activities?"

"Grandma, I've only been here a week."

"You should write for the paper."

"It's a rag. It's stupid."

"Your excuses are stupid."

"I'll get into college. Please don't worry about it!"

"If you're lucky, you'll get into Piedmont Tech. Just like your mother—a complete waste of potential."

This is how Grandma's tipsiness goes—sharp banter with a sudden swerve to morose nastiness. It's exactly 10:09 p.m.

Then she snaps, "Well, you'll be rid of me soon. I'm headed to St. Thomas next week. If you're lucky, I'll kick the bucket soon after."

"Grandma, don't say that."

We drive the rest of the way in silence.

As I pull into our driveway and cut the engine, I wonder how I'll stop her from driving home. Grandma hates her daughter, so I can't invite her in. If I drive her home, I'll break the law driving myself back. She has no idea how she tortures me.

She interrupts my thoughts. "I've got something for you." She stretches her arm over the back seat with a groan and retrieves a book. It's a thin blue paperback, worn and cracked, titled *Our Friends The Saints*. Pale martyrs grace the cover, eyes cast heavenward and hands clutching roses and chalices. I flip it open. Copyright, 1956. On the first page is printed, "Saint Agatha—the Pure Virgin." It's a golden-haired woman draped in purple robes, carrying a palm frond, backed by Roman pillars. She has a wrench in her hand, no doubt the instrument of her torture. I imagine nipples twisted off, so I close the book.

"Thanks." What do you say to a book like this?

"This was mine," Grandma says, like something's caught in her throat. "I used to read it every night. And pray I'd get out of that house."

I stare at the pale-as-death martyrs. Grandma's never said a word about her childhood. All of a sudden I remember a photo Sunny pulled from a box when I was younger, a black-and-white photo she said Grandma tried to toss. It's of a young and skinny Virginia with primly-waved bob and legs tucked under pleated skirt, looking straight up at an unknown photographer who's shot her up close and uncomfortable. She looks fifteen or sixteen. Grandma's mouth is twisted like she's biting back words. I recognize that look. It's on my face most days in the mirror. I wonder what my great-grandparents were like.

"Don't let Lydia see this." Grandma snaps. "She'll burn it and make you do moon chants."

I take a deep breath and say, "Grandma, you shouldn't be—"

"I know." She puts up a hand. "I'll snooze, dry out, yada yada yada. Just don't tell *her*."

I say, "I'm checking in 15, 30, 45, and 60. If this car is gone—"

"Call the cops." She waves me off.

I get out. We never say goodbye or kiss goodnight. It always surprised me when Cindy used to tackle her grandmother and smack a kiss on her cheek. I figure Grandma's cheek would be very powdery and dry; you'd get a mouthful of couture makeup.

As I come inside, I find Sunny in front of the TV dancing up a storm to Madonna, "Don't Go for Second Best," limbs flailing, hair flying, sweating streams of horse sweat.

"Wendy!" she gasps, waving like she hasn't seen me in forever.

I dodge past her. In my room I get my laptop and my history text. With these and the *Saints* book, I set up shop in a chair near the front window. I peek out. Grandma's Mercedes still slumbers there. A burst of happiness deep inside. Grandma's doing what she said she'd do.

I flip through the *Saints* book again. Now I see martyrs not so scary—St. Rita, St. Rose, St. Clare—more angelic without any heavy artillery. Then I search Google for quotes about loving and losing. I find what Shaye was saying: "'Tis better to have loved and lost/Than never to have loved at all."

Alfred Lord Tennyson, a great Victorian poet, took seventeen years to write a poem in honor of a friend who died suddenly. I read it all, all one-hundred-and-thirty-three cantos. It's like Shaye knew about the death of me and Cindy. I glance at my phone—the record deal must be done, and at this hour, I bet he's not coming over, but I kind of wish he were, so I could say something like, *Thanks.*

I move aside the curtain every few minutes to check on Grandma. I'll keep doing this long as she needs me.

CHAPTER 17

THE NEXT DAY AT SCHOOL, I find the lyrics to Def Leppard's "Photograph." I download the song, insert headphones, and find the darkest corner of the Media Center to contemplate what this might tell me about Shaye Tann. Then I play the Youtube video, over and over—full of tight pants, dead starlets, screaming guitars, and yearning.

The wild and free woman full of mystery—she who makes a man feel like a child—that is not, never has been, never will be me. Deanna Faire, on the other hand—she who was just signed to a major country record label and hangs with college dudes on Jefferson—like it or not, she has sophistication. Glam as Marilyn, a wanted woman. Dudes don't care how twisted you are inside. Outside is all that matters.

A million questions fill my head. *Shaye, why this song? Did someone break your heart? Who's wilder and freer than you? Do you prefer blondes?*

During the next class change, I see the celebutante, aka Diva Dee, flanked by minions, but she only glances at me. I am dead to her, and her reputation shall remain intact. That's good, right? Seventh-grade drama, over. Yay. Shaye doesn't have to play mediator anymore.

Then why do I feel so sad?

My phone chirps. I pull it from my pocket. It's Shaye. *Hey WRD take a risk today*

My heart goes wild, staccato crazy. How odd is it that just when I was thinking of him—what witty thing to say back? I'm paralyzed—

But he's written more.

How's that funky strong fight

O, sweet relief! I know this land.

I text back, *You know I'm gonna stay alive*

He texts, *Right on. See u soon.*

OK bye, I text back, and I catch myself smiling. How nice it is, not having to explain. And I like how he calls me WRD.

Ever since I woke this morning, I've kept the image of us on repeat: speeding down Jefferson Street, the motorcycle roaring like fire, turning Deanna's face to fire. Us shooting through space at 132 beats per minute, just like a certain song, bells tolling *Danger, danger, Deanna—no longer can you beat me, kick me, tell me it's Faire.* Someone's got my back, bitch! I don't care what label you just signed: 132 beats per minute is now the reigning speed of my life. Divided by 16, it's 8.25 minutes—more than auspicious!

She has no power anymore. Shaye's thinking of me, right now. I am safe.

At lunch practice before Andrew comes to meet us, I tell Tanay I can come over to her house, anytime.

"No, you can't," she says, and my heart stops.

She grins. "I'm just playing. You got detention, girl, remember? But don't worry, I can wait on your delinquent self."

"Okay," I say. My racing heart slows down.

"But let me check with Mushi; sometimes she comes over and I don't know if I can handle both your dramas at the same time."

I blurt, "Well, don't let this be a charity event."

"That's what I'm saying." Tanay grins and slugs me in the shoulder.

Andrew walks into the classroom, which is good, because I'm nervous beyond words at what just happened. As we rehearse, I keep thinking of the Top Ten Reasons Why It Would Be a Mistake for Tanay to Take Me In, and then I think, *Jesus, she's not "taking me in," it's just homework and hanging out.* What did Shaye say? *Stop thinking so much. You need to lighten up.*

I wake up to Andrew and Tanay arguing about Mushi. Tanay thinks if the scene between Mama and her rebellious daughter Beneatha gets added in, Teasdale will surely give us an A.

Andrew shakes his head. "I'm just saying, that girl wears you out."

"But she's good!"

"She'll have, what, one day to practice when she gets back?" Andrew's face is hard.

"She don't need one practice. She's that good!"

"Good for trouble—" Andrew catches himself. "The three scenes we got are fine."

"Easy for you with your A," Tanay seethes. "Wendy, come on, speak up!"

"I think I'm staying out of it."

Tanay waves the book in my face. "Look at this scene. This boy's all about Jesus, but he won't let me do the one scene about religion!"

I skim it. It's the one where Mama slaps Beneatha for hating on God. I'm with Beneatha; I've never known God to come through with a miracle. Ever.

"Girl, you've got to let it go." Andrew puts his hand on Tanay's arm, and it's like she calms at his touch. Then suddenly I notice his long red and white polo has a dark stain at the bottom, the edges are frayed, and his Jordans have a gray sheen and a little give, like they could be an eBay snag. Funny, he's so good-looking, I missed these other details.

Tanay says, "Wendy, let's do your part now. Because I'm done with his ass."

Andrew sighs and flips pages.

They decide to do the Ruth and Walter scene where they fight over eggs and money, and then we run the one with me. I get my racist white woman voice even more nasal with just enough Sunny lilt in it—a work of art, truly—and I get Tanay and Andrew cracking up.

When we finish, Tanay gives a quick glance at Andrew and says, "You know what, California? Tonight would be a good night to come over."

"What about Mushi?" I say.

"I forgot she's suspended." Another glance at him, but he's grabbing his books, not listening. Does she want to invite him, too?

"My granmama will make you a meal to remember," she says to me. "And preach you the gospel." Still no reaction from Andrew. "You can stay for dinner, right?"

She looks hopeful, at me this time, despite all the energy shot Andrew's way.

Against alerts screaming from every nerve ending, I say, "Sure."

CHAPTER 18

AFTER DETENTION I MEET TANAY at the drop-off circle. "Bet you don't miss that bus," she says as we wait for her mom.

Behind us, someone hollers, "Hey! Hey! Tanay!"

We turn, and it's Andrew striding up in Steeple Mount athletic gear, his neck and arms shiny with sweat, with Mushi trailing many feet behind. "Give us a ride?"

"Get off me, boy," Tanay says, fighting a smile. No doubt the glint off his sculpted arms is making her heart race; I have to look away myself. "Forget your sorry ass."

"Come on, girl, let me in your world." Andrew's grinning.

"My world don't like your kind." She glances at Mushi, who's still taking her sweet time to get to us. "What the hell? They catch her trespassing—"

"Where else she got to go?" Andrew says, low. "She just showed up at the weight room, said she wanted to hang."

"Who dropped her off?" Tanay sounds just like a mom.

Andrew shrugs. "Like I can keep up with all her connections." Then louder: "That's right, the Lord told me you going to be my wife." He orates like an old-time preacher, then bear hugs her.

Tanay tries to squirm and slap her way out of Andrew's grip. Mushi has arrived by now and snorts like these two are too stupid. A ring winks on Andrew's left hand. I need to ask Tanay what that's about.

He releases her and looks at Mushi. "That's right, I'm a G for Jesus."

He and Mushi slap hands, cackling. Then Mushi shoots a glance at me. She says to Andrew, "What, now you down with the swirl?"

Andrew stifles a laugh. I have no idea what they're talking about; must be a white-girl slam. Tanay looks pissed.

A new silver Acura hatchback with tinted windows pulls up next to us. Tanay taps the passenger side window. A woman lowers it. "Mama. This is Wendy Redbird Dancing. Can she come over for dinner?"

Ms. DeVries looks me up and down. She has elegant, Nefertiti features and dark caramel hair in a low chignon. She's wearing a yellow sundress with a knotted black scarf and a black silk jacket, very classy. Except for her eyes, she doesn't look a thing like Tanay.

She says, "Fine, get in." She is not pleased.

Andrew and Mushi step toward the car. The eyes of Ms. DeVries widen with the wrath of God. "What is this?"

"They need a ride," Tanay says.

"Mmm, mmm." Ms. DeVries grips the wheel and stares through the windshield. "Get in. Don't bring any food in here."

"Yes, ma'am," Mushi and Andrew say.

In the back seat, I have to sit half on Tanay's lap and with my thigh crammed against Andrew. Mushi shoves her seven-month self into the front seat, grunting. The car smells minty fresh—not like cats, sage, or garlic—while Coldplay blasts that song about ruling the world. Ms. DeVries turns it down. Tanay smells sweet, like Jolly Rancher mixed with coconut oil. I hope I'm not crushing her.

At the light, Ms. DeVries snaps, "Where to?"

"We're right downtown, off Jefferson," Andrew says. The look she gives him in the rearview mirror could melt steel.

Andrew looks at his hands. Beneath me I hear Tanay stifle a sigh.

"Right downtown" is fifteen minutes through Steeple Mount till the main drag of Jefferson forks. The right fork would take us into Millboro, but we take the left, which within seconds becomes a ghetto: shotgun houses tagged with loopy, unreadable graffiti and fronted by either scabby, rusted cars or gleaming Nissan Altimas and Mercedes. One house is black with mold creeping up the sides, its windows like gouged-out eyes. Toddlers stumble outside another house, unsupervised; a little ways farther, some heavy-lidded dudes, hunched inside hoodies, stare our car down, down, down as we pass. Needless to say, I'm the whitest thing for miles.

"That's me," Andrew says as we come up on a light blue house with a fresh coat of paint and a dirt yard. Next door, the house literally crumbles, ringed with police tape.

"Me, too," Mushi says. "Walk'll do my ass good."

No one says a word as Mushi groans her way out and Andrew exits after. The dudes down the road eye us like fresh kill. They whistle and shout for Ms. DeVries.

"Thank you very much," Andrew says to Ms. DeVries, who gives a curt nod. "Bye, y'all," Andrew says to Tanay and me. He heads up the cracked walk and disappears inside.

Mushi heads down the street toward the questionable dudes, her progress unhurried, untroubled, like a steamer that will plow right through anyone.

"Sorry, Mama, I know this place is jacked up," Tanay mutters as we pull out.

"What did I tell you," Ms. DeVries says low, like her teeth are gritted. "She can come to us, but that is it."

I'm trying to picture Andrew studying for APs in this neighborhood. Or Mushi raising a kid here.

When we're back on Jefferson, Tanay says, "Wendy did real

good today, I mean, well." She's all chatty like she took speed, and her voice has shifted in color from black to café au lait. "She's the one I told you is playing Mrs. Lindner—from the neighborhood that tells us not to move."

"Where do you live?" Ms. DeVries has her eye on me in the rearview mirror.

"I live off Oak in Millboro."

Ms. DeVries pulls out a cigarette—the same kind Tanay carries—and cracks the window. Tanay lights it for her. I feel the strain ease with each puff. Coldplay still sings the same song: something about swords, shields, and missionaries in foreign fields.

"You're part of that green living community?" Ms. DeVries says.

"No, Mama, her mom's just a hippie." Tanay glances over her shoulder and rolls her eyes at me. She adds, "Wendy's real smart and she's helping me get ready for the AP."

"This girl better pass this class. Nothing less than a three," Ms. DeVries says.

"I got this, Mama."

"I'm not playing. Your grades are an embarrassment. You keep this up, and you won't find a safety school to save your life."

I make myself very small in the back seat and reconsider the wisdom of this field trip. Not another word is said the rest of the way.

Tanay's house is on a wooded street just outside Millboro, a ranch with dark red siding and fronted by hot-pink azaleas, a mowed lawn, and trimmed shrubbery. Everywhere, a guard of thick woods, the presence of deep foliage, giving me the feel of acreage and great privacy, neighbors nowhere near. By the doorbell is a little purple plaque reading, *God Bless This Home.*

I follow them up the flagstone path. Inside, everything is clean, gleaming, and attractive: pale wood floors, shiny white and black furniture, an art deco poster over a white sofa of a skinny black woman with a silver feather sprouting from her head. The great room flows into a dining room, which leads to a spacious kitchen where an elderly lady, not much over five foot but looking fierce, holds court over a big pot on the stove. The air smells rich with pepper and bacon.

Tanay goes and wraps her arms around her. The woman turns to check me out with unsmiling brown eyes. Her hair is a silver-gray bob, smooth and stylish. Her skin is dark as Tanay's and her nose as broad. I don't know where Ms. DeVries fits in all this because she has a skinny nose, high cheekbones, and caramel skin.

Tanay sees my face and laughs. "Mama's a redbone," she says. "This is Ms. Sadie, my Granmama, my daddy's mama."

"Hi," I say, and my voice cracks.

"She don't like hambone?" her grandmother says, glaring at me. "I can't fix for no vegetarian."

Tanay says, louder: "Granmama, this is Wendy. She eats meat." Tanay looks at me and mouths, "You eat meat?" I nod.

"She makes the best collards and ribs." Tanay sighs with pleasure. "What do you want to drink?" She opens a gleaming silver fridge, space-age compared to ours.

"Anything," I say. Tanay pours us Diet Cokes. Ms. Sadie watches me the whole time, and I pretend I don't notice.

"She know the Scriptures?" Ms. Sadie asks, loud.

Tanay chokes on her drink. "Granmama, I don't know." She gives me a look like, *Sorry.*

The kitchen opens into the living room with its pristine white furniture and a wall of photos, a family Hall of Fame. I follow Tanay as she gives me the tour of portraits going back several generations—the ancient sepia-tone pictures, then black-and-whites, and then color, the most recent of a Marine who looks like Tanay, and then lots of Tanay and her mom. On the far right side, several pictures of what I assume is Tanay as a baby and Ms. DeVries as a teen or twenty-something with a very black man with an '80s mustache—I'm guessing Tanay's dad.

"That's Daddy," Tanay says. "He died when I was four."

"I'm sorry."

She shrugs. "I really don't remember him. That's Eugene." She points to the Marine. "My big bro-bro. He just got deployed to Afghanistan. Third tour."

I blurt, "I wish I had a sibling."

"Nah, you don't. A brother, he'll jack you up." Tanay smiles, and I can tell she's crazy about him.

"What's redbone?" I say.

Tanay laughs. "High yellow. Light-skinned."

I consider the huge parade of photos, with tons of shots of cousins, aunts, and uncles at picnics, games, and church gatherings. I wonder what it would be like to have a whole pack of people who knew your history and who'd notice if you went missing.

"Does she mind I'm here?" I mutter, because I can't get Ms. Sadie's eyes off me. She's even peering around the corner from the kitchen.

"Don't worry, she's blind," Tanay says cheerfully.

"Wow," I say stupidly. "She gets around good." Here I thought I was being skewered by laser eyes.

"Yeah, don't ever try to run from her. Granmama can do the hundred-yard dash."

"So you all live together?"

"Yeah." Tanay looks surprised I'm asking.

"There's no way; it'd be World War III in our house."

"Well, most days, Mama tries to kill me," Tanay says grimly. "But Granmama? She'll put you under the ground. See, she and Ms. Washington, they're tight at church. That means I can't play nobody. Everybody's watching."

"Wow. Wonder what that's like? I could be MIA a week and Sunny wouldn't notice."

Tanay cackles. "Please. You do not want my situation. Come on, let's go study so I can get smart."

I follow her down the hall thinking how full-time supervision is solid like stone, dense and deep. The kind of rock that might cut you some days, but still feel amazing beneath your hands.

CHAPTER 19

ANAY'S YELLOW ROOM SHIMMERS WITH orange and pineapple hues. There's a zebra throw across a queen-sized bed and big posters of Jennifer Hudson, Mary J. Blige, Lauryn Hill, Missy Elliott, and Beyoncé. Tanay jerks her head at the corner, where I see a pink glitter backpack and a bunch of bags from Hot Topic, The Gap, and other stores. They appear to be stuffed full of worldly goods. "That's Mushi's. She stays with us sometimes. Mama called the social worker but they're so backed up, they can't investigate." She sighs. "Nobody wants to touch crackheads."

"What was it she said about you being bougie?"

Tanay's lips get tight. "She was calling me white."

"Because you hang with me?"

"Because I do my schoolwork and act too damn happy. I haven't been in a fight in ages. Now in middle school, yeah, the two of us were all up in it. I almost didn't graduate and Mama about killed me. Moosh can't get over it; she thinks I'm betraying her or something." Tanay sits down on her bed. She kicks off her shoes and today she's got red toenails. She gives me a fierce look. "She can sit there and blame me and you and every white person in the building, but at the end of the day, what you do with your life is on you."

"Yeah," I say. "You only get one shot." That makes me wonder if Shaye has texted me since I got here. I could check, but I feel nervous—nervous to see he hasn't texted, and nervous Tanay will think I don't care about her.

Tanay points at her desk where there's a computer and all our AP English books. "All right, let's do this."

After we make notes together on every book, listing themes and key passages, Tanay tests me on terms I didn't learn back home. Then she asks me to go over a paper her mom is making her write on *Of Mice and Men*, since Teasdale will take extra credit. It's a draft already bloodied by Teasdale's pen, writing that sounds no more like Tanay than I sound black: i.e., plagiarized from some cheap-ass source straight off the web.

I flip to what's stapled behind: a rough draft with only a short paragraph, in Tanay's big loopy pink handwriting.

Crooks is a side and not the meat. What I mean is he is reduced, reused, and recycled. Look at Curley's wife how she treats him. She calls him the epithet of nigger. Then he explains about Lennie how he is very lonely. Throughout history black people have been treated like a side and not the entry to the main meal. We are tired of being sides.

"Don't look at that," Tanay says, ripping it off. "That sucks."

"Why do you say that? The food metaphor rocks—sides, entrée. Put that thesis here." I tap the plagiarized pages.

Tanay shrugs. "I don't know, I lost my nerve. You going to do this thing for me or not?"

"You mean write it?"

"Yeah."

"No, I can't do that."

"Oh, oh, so that's how it's going to be." Tanay looks half-amused, half-mad. "You're bad as my mom."

I flip through her book to the scene between Crooks and Lennie. "Get three quotes that prove Crooks is a side. You already have one." I tap a quote, but I can't read it out loud. "Put this whole thing in there."

Tanay looks, and reads it aloud: "Well, you keep your place then, Nigger. I could get you strung up on a tree so easy it ain't even funny."

She makes a wry face but says, "Yeah, that'll do."

We move to her computer. Tanay's screen saver is a picture of the Obama family. I teach her what I learned in eighth-grade advanced English: "Sandwich the evidence. The introduction is the top piece of bread. The meat's the evidence; and don't forget the condiments, or commentary, where you explain why this is such a kick-ass quote—ketchup, lettuce, pickles."

Tanay gets it in five seconds. "Slap some jalapenos on that mug."

I wonder how she missed all this before tenth grade, and how without this, how much misery AP must be.

When we're done, Tanay jumps up with relief. She goes to her dresser and presses Play on her iPod. The speakers boom with Rihanna who pleads for the music not to stop, electric pulsing chatter, more Noughts fluff, till I hear Michael. "Whoa, wait!" I yell. "That *mama se* in the background? That's from one of the best songs ever. 'Wanna Be Startin' Something.'"

"I know. Here comes more, especially at the end," Tanay says.

We listen to Rihanna's robotic chant over Michael sampling, and I'm wondering for just a nanosecond whether Tanay would ever in her wildest dreams consider going with me to London to see *This is It.*

"This is good," she says, "but 'Man in the Mirror' is his best."

"Oh no no no." I proceed to explain how excellence culminates in *Thriller.* "'Man in the Mirror' is a nice piece of sentiment—I'm not against it—but if you want to change the molecules in a room, you need to listen to 'Human Nature.'"

Then she says, "You think he messed with those kids?"

I take a deep breath. Clearly, she's not a travel partner for London. "No way. He was just pretending he was the dad he never had."

Tanay doesn't look convinced. "But didn't he bring them into his bedroom and shit?"

"He doesn't get that celebrities can't tuck kids in, give them cookies and milk—he's just a big kid!"

"I don't know. Something doesn't seem right."

"He's a freak, yes, but not that kind!"

Tanay holds up a hand. "No offense, just wondering."

And here I thought the song could be a sign. I guess it's still just me and Grandma. I note the Rihanna song is on repeat. "You like this song," I say. "A lot."

Her eyes dart away and I know there's a story behind the obsession. She says, "You see how my mom was in the car, about Andrew?"

I nod. "Does she not like him?"

"No, it's not that. It's just…Mama worked hard to get where she's at, so did Granmama and my granddaddy. So they try to keep a million miles between them and the ghetto."

"So, what if he, I don't know, asks you out? Will your mom let you go?"

"He can't date till his junior year because of his church or something."

"That's weird as hell."

"You mean holy. Boy is serious." Then she gives me a look. "You ain't into him, are you?"

"What? I mean, he's hot—but no. Not me." Like I could be any form of competition.

"I'm just a jealous fool." Tanay shakes her head. "That's because you can't trust a bitch around here." She hugs her knees. "Mushi likes to mess with him, but she's crazy. Plus, the boy doesn't know what he wants. Had me thinking the other day he was going to ask me out. Told me how good I listen, how stressed he is with all he's trying to do, sports and school...boy was this close to my face." She pinches an inch of air. "Then he backs off and acts like we never had that conversation."

"He was all over you today," I observe.

"Yeah, he's got these phases," Tanay says. "Like, this song? Eighth-grade dance, him and me. This was our song. We had two weeks where we were together every day." She smiles to herself, and I can see she is stuck on him the way I used to be on Cy. There's no stopping the thoughts about the person; they invade every waking moment. This fact she shares is like a small jewel, and I hoard it to myself. It's like Shaye said— payoff for blazing a trail, for taking a risk.

"Why does he wear that ring?" I say.

"Oh, that." Tanay rolls her eyes. "Purity ring." When I look blank, she adds, "Means he's saving himself."

"And here I thought he was trying to save me. He doesn't appear to be gay."

"No way! He ain't a fag!" Tanay picks at chipping red polish on her thumb. "I'll be honest; sometimes I'm sure as shit we got something going—that he's just about ready to commit." She glances up, her eyes wide, almost begging me to dispute what she's saying—but I can't. "Then I freak out, you know? I know I'm just one of a million girls he talks to every day. Makes me so damn nervous, I don't know what to do."

I don't know what one says in these situations. All I can wonder is what would it be like to have anyone interested enough to ask me out. It feels like something that happens to other people in foreign lands, not in my ZIP code.

"You like anybody?" she says.

"Not a soul."

"Come on! You don't have somebody, nobody, back in California?"

"Unrequited, yes."

"Ooooh....What's he like?"

"Cyrus? I don't know." She is so damn curious!

"Cyrus, huh? Tell me! Come on now!"

I want to tell her that I'm so done with them, but boys like Cy are strange, exotic creatures—and not to be trusted. "Do you ever get the feeling you'll always be alone?" I say instead. "I mean, are there just some people who can't find their tribe?"

"You act like you want to be left alone, but I know you don't really," Tanay says like that's dismissed. "You've never dated anyone?"

"Ouch. How'd you guess?"

She gives me a look. "Come on now. Dancing, you're cute as hell—I'd say you could be a real good-looking woman—but you got a stop sign all over your face."

Her look is so frank, so curious, I almost crack open beneath it. Why am I the kind of girl who counts things incessantly, who in the shower scrubs hard as she can what I guess you could call a body? In straight, fast lines, resting nowhere, 16 for each limb? Then a quick swipe in nooks and crannies. I rarely shampoo. I remember Shaye looking my outfit up and down, saying I'm a nerd who knows how to dress. I wonder if he thinks I'm cute as hell.

"I don't know," I say slowly. "Maybe because the sand's always shifting? I don't know where the wind'll blow us next? I mean, why get attached? I don't know."

Tanay's quiet a moment. "House built on sand, huh?"

"Yeah, another metaphor," I joke, but she doesn't smile.

She says, "Granmama's making me memorize this Scripture. *And the rain descended, and the floods came, and the winds blew, and beat upon that house; and it fell: and great was the fall of it.*'"

"Sorry, don't get it."

"Maybe someday you'll get your own place and it will be built on rock."

"Oh," I say. "You're goddamn right I will."

We slap hands, and this time I don't miss.

"Girls, dinner!" Ms. DeVries calls.

Nobody talks for most of the meal, but the food's amazing. The collards are hot, spicy, and smooth. The ribs are fall-off-the-bone sweet. I try to eat slow and tidily, even if Ms. Sadie can't see every smudge on my face. I count leopard spots in the tablecloth. I've never eaten off an animal print.

"So you two are doing this project together?" Ms. DeVries says finally, looking at Tanay. "Is it A material?"

"Of course," Tanay says too fast.

Uncomfortable silence. Finally I say, "This is much better than takeout."

Tanay snorts. "Of course it is."

"I mean, that's all we eat at my house. Unaffordable organic food in eco-friendly boxes."

"Are you serious?"

"My mom'll get a wild hair and cook sometimes, but it has to be like, Winter Solstice or something."

That gets everyone smiling.

"Mama, want to hear something funny?" Tanay's voice is higher, a little too loud. "Andrew tried to preach it to Wendy, her first week here."

Ms. DeVries shakes her head and smiles. "Why am I not surprised?"

Tanay looks pleased, like she just pulled a good PR move for Andrew.

"She ain't saved?" Ms. Sadie says.

"Uh-oh, this conversation's over," Tanay says, standing up. "Granmama, it was real good." She grabs my arm and drags me back to her room. I say a choked thank you over my shoulder.

Tanay begs to drive me home with her mom supervising, but I learn that Tanay's driving privileges are currently revoked due to her D in AP. Tanay's still chipper, though, as Ms. DeVries takes us through downtown Millboro, maybe because she sees a dude engaged in mock sword play—antique blade and bad-ass self—doing *Karate Kid* moves in the park. She begins to comment on him, the braless, the tattooed, and other circus freaks.

"Tanay!" Ms. DeVries says. "You are not the day of judgment."

"But these people need a mirror, Mama!"

"Shut it."

"Tanay has a harsh yet truthful tongue," I say.

"Thank you," Ms. DeVries says to me, perhaps before my full statement registers, then to Tanay: "Truthful, I don't know. Salty as a ham hock, this one."

"She said I speak the truth," Tanay crows.

"Only One does that, and it is not you."

I hear the capital letter loud and clear. This mama-daughter speak fascinates me, since for Sunny Revere, there are many truths, depending on who she's talking to.

We pull into our little neighborhood. "I love these millworker bungalows," Ms. DeVries said. "So quaint."

"Not bad for a hippie commune," Tanay jokes. But she's watching me funny, like she doesn't feel quite right about letting me go.

We bump into my cracked driveway. There's light burning for once in the windows behind our beaded curtains, and Sunny's actually tidied up the front yard and raked the moldy leaves away from the house. The dead violets in cracked plastic planters are gone, and it looks like she watered all the browning ferns; they're now draining just outside our front door. I don't see Shaye's Harley or his helmet, which is too bad, since I have a lot to tell him.

"I really appreciate it," I say.

"No problem," Ms. DeVries says.

"So are we doing another rehearsal tomorrow?" I say as I get out.

"Damn straight!"

"Tanay!" Ms. DeVries says. "Cuss again, that iPod's gone!"

"Mama, I'm trying to get you that A!"

They pull away, snipping at each other, but laughing, and I stay standing near the door, watching. Part of me wishes they were taking me back with them, that I could have a piece of that calm they keep under their roof.

CHAPTER 20

SINCE BEING OVER AT TANAY'S, I'm irked whenever I step inside the Passive Solar and sniff must and mold. All of Sunny Revere's shortcomings seem bundled up in the unclean state of this home. I even think about calling Grandma in St. Thomas and pleading for a service to come scour this place top to bottom.

It doesn't help Sunny's been MIA on random nights, either—a schedule beyond tracking. I don't know where Shaye lives, I would very much like to know, and I imagine she is there.

I could be wrong, but I think Shaye senses what's missing, too, because when I come home after detention Friday night, he's already making dinner, standing over our greasy stove with a wok in full play. The house smells like lime and soy. For the first time ever, I couldn't be happier that Sunny's given her latest love a copy of our key.

"Hungry?" he says with a grin. He's wearing a tight blue gingham shirt, jeans so worn they look streaked with rust, and some massively cool black ostrich cowboy boots. I have to say, he's the best thing Sunny Revere's dragged in yet.

"What are you making?"

He fakes a Brit accent: "My special stir fry. It's quite saucy." He winks. I feel myself smile, a little.

"But I'm way behind schedule. Getting your mom off to

her health care forum was tough; she took a nap and once she's down for the count—"

"Yeah, she sleeps like the dead."

He grins. "Watch this for me, will you?" He hands me the wooden spoon that's working onion, garlic, and ginger in the wok. He grabs a bowl and starts whisking coconut milk, lime juice, fish sauce, soy, and chili paste.

"It's so cool to come home to smells," I blabber, poking at the food in the wok. "I mean, I didn't even know this stove could work."

"Your mom's a liberated woman."

"Right-o, free at last, thank God she's free at last. Am I burning this?"

He comes and peers over my shoulder. He smells like mint and something heady, exotic—maybe it's the Sapporo beer on the counter. "No, you're doing great." He swats my arm, like, *Don't be so paranoid.*

"You like shrimp?" he says. "Or are you veggie?"

"Oh, I'll eat anything," I say. "It pays to scavenge."

He laughs. "Your mom likes fish, I know that much. But forget chicken and beef."

"And dairy, unless it's goat, and no gluten," I recite, and "nothing processed, nothing refined, nothing from a box." I pull a face. "As a child, I dreamed of Doritos and Girl Scout cookies."

"Aw, man, she didn't let you be a Girl Scout?" Shaye grabs a handful of carrots, mushrooms, and cauliflower, and tosses them into the wok. It spits up oil, tiny stings on my hand. "Those cookies are like crack, man." He gives me a look, and maybe it's just the heat of the wok blasting my face, but it seems like he sees me like an equal, an adult. "I bet you would've been a good girl and gotten all the badges. Real cute in that uniform, too."

"Ha!" I study the vegetables like they're of great scientific curiosity. "Yeah, I'm an overachiever."

While he chops and I stir, I tell him about the APs and how it sucks trying to figure out what they covered here that I didn't in California. Then he asks me what my risk was. I tell him all about Tanay and Andrew and the scene that's working out so far. About Tanay's house and her intense, gorgeous mom and her fierce and scriptural Granmama. About how Tanay didn't get the background I got in school and how she's smart, just not book smart yet, and I wonder about that. He listens while I stir, occasionally coming over and tossing in more veggies, and finally pouring sauce over everything. "Good for you," he says. "Better to have loved, right? Don't you feel alive?"

I realize that yes, I do. I nod.

"And it's good you're connecting, getting out there—your mom's been worried."

I snort.

"And how about Deanna?" he says, leaning against the sink. "Is she listening to her A & R man?"

I look away. His eyes are very dark tonight and incite strange thrills. I say, "Ever since the peace treaty, yeah."

He folds his arms and smiles with satisfaction. His shirt, open several buttons, isn't skeezy like Sunny's prior guys. Things are smooth, fit, tan—not pallid or flabby. "Yeah, well, she and I had a little talk after that. I told her if she didn't chill, I'm walking."

"Whoa, really?" I sound stupid, about ten. My heart is hammering with happy.

"Really."

He'd lose a client—a big client like Deanna—over me? I want to say thanks, I really do, but I can't, I feel so strange under that gaze, or maybe it's the fact I can't think of a time someone even changed their schedule because of me. Thank

MJ the door bangs, and Sunny blows in, hair flying, but face ecstatic about the health care justice fliers she has in hand.

"Oh my God!" she says with a rush of breath. "We are making a difference!"

Her hair is chocolate brown today, streaked with gold, and it looks damn good. She's lost years with the color upgrade. And there's shimmery eye makeup applied, and a whiff of scent—something lavender and musky—a whole new deal for one Sunny Revere. My mother is pretty, for the first time in ages, and I am stunned.

Shaye Tann has changed her. And he's looking at her with this possessive, lusting glance that I hate but can't stop seeing.

We sit down to the first set table in a long while, after clearing it of cat hair. Through Shaye's dinner, Sunny fills our ears with grassroots talk. "This Health Justice Now group is so committed," she says, leaning across the table, peering at us like we're her next converts. "We're going by every trailer in the state to make sure people know the lies being spread about this reform. You know The Right is trying to get low-income people voting against their own interests!"

Throughout the speech, which lasts about ten minutes, Shaye keeps glancing at me, smiling.

"Speaking of poverty, ten minutes from here is a major ghetto," I say. "I saw it when we dropped this dude off the other day."

"Really?" Sunny looks as if she's seeing me for the first time. "We should go there, too!"

"Where were you?" Shaye says with a frown.

"It's the left fork off Jefferson—a total hellhole." I warm under his concerned gaze. "Andrew lives there; he's like super smart, super athlete, and class VP."

"Uh-oh, do I smell a crush?" Shaye teases. "What, is this dude hot? Is he buff?"

I flush red to my roots. "He's Tanay's territory. I'm not messing with that."

"Sweetie," Sunny says to Shaye, grabbing his hand, "this meal was amazing."

She tries to hold his gaze extra seconds, but he's looking at me. "And what do you think, WRD?"

"You're a kick-ass chef," I say.

He grins. More thrills dancing down my gut. I don't know, I've never had a dad before. And he seems to give a damn like one might.

Sunny interrupts with a shrill, "Baby, let's dance off these calories!"

She bounces out of her chair like a little girl, races over to the stereo, and starts blasting Elvis's "Wooden Heart." She runs back and drags Shaye out of his seat into the living room, trying to make him dance. I want to look away. He tries to keep the beat, gamely, as they almost stumble into the wood stove. It all looks so stupid and forced, never mind Sunny's horse head bobbing in time to the music. Finally she gives up her little bizarre tango, then hugs him, hard.

"Did I ever tell you about my Elvis obsession?" she says, looking up into his face like they're the only two in the room. "When he died, I was only seven, so I didn't know who he was. I made my mother tell me all about him because everyone seemed so upset. Then I got so obsessed, I played her Elvis records 24/7. I used to set up the album cover on my dresser and watch his face for *hours*. I kept thinking his eyes followed me wherever I went!"

"Is that true?" I cut in. I've never heard word one of this. Let Grandma blow this myth to smithereens.

"Well, Wendybird, you of all people should understand. Shaye, weren't you just saying how cute her little obsession is?"

"Little obsession?" I snap. "Uh, I'm not five."

"Ladies, ladies," Shaye says with a grin. "How's about some more wine, baby?"

Sunny likes that plan and races off to pour her and Shaye another glass.

Then she makes a fake attempt to convince me to stick around—"I'll let you sip some, sweetie!"—but I beg off with the excuse of exams. Because she's already ogling Shaye, having yanked him to the couch, her flesh pressing his like a two-should-become-one sandwich. *Ucch.*

Behind me I hear Shaye say, "I told Wendy I talked to Deanna. Sucks to know I'm representing a Mean Girl."

Sunny giggles. "Mean Girl, ha ha ha. You're so hip to what kids are into!"

I hear him say something low, and then Sunny murmurs something a little too lusty and growly, and then their voices dim and I'm afraid to think what might be occurring.

I close the door to my room, then kick off my shoes so they slam the wall. Ballet shoes don't make much of an impact. I turn up Michael and block out whatever teenage hormonal behavior is going down under our roof.

Tanay is right: I will one day leave this house. To do so, I must make Grandma proud enough to pay for a decent college. I must make quick work of AP Bio, AP Lit, and AP History. Therefore I let myself be suffocated by genomes and phylums, Puritans and Poe, and racists and Reconstruction.

When I look up, it's because I hear a bedroom door slam somewhere. It's midnight and that means more sexual shenanigans. Though I'm still betting on Shaye's departure within the week, as Sunny Revere stoops to compete with her own daughter and behave like a first-class fool.

He said he'd lose a client over me. That is something. Maybe he and I will stay friends, no matter what. He is solid, not one of those countless hollow Sunny men I've had the pleasure of surviving. Maybe that's why he can put up with her crazy, reach through my various force fields. Maybe—and again, all bets are off—he will stay. Maybe with him, things for once could settle down.

CHAPTER 21

MY ALARM CLOCK WOULD STOP working the day of the English AP, making me too late to catch the bus. And Sunny, whom I have to wake from the dead, who hates rising before noon, keeps me waiting so long I'm paranoid I'll miss the exam. At 7:45, I'm sweating outside her bedroom door, tempted to drive myself and break the damn law. Then I scream at her all the way to school. "I will not get a two! You want to trap me here forever!"

"You're out of your mind, Wendy," Sunny yells back. "Calm down. I'm taking you for a hormone test."

She is glad to drop my screaming self off at school, where I race to Teasdale's room.

I land with one minute to spare. The proctor glares at me.

Deanna sneers my way, with just a squirt of venom. She's been de-fanged, plus she knows her blond, oversized head rattles empty. All she has to her name is a thousand posters plastering our hallowed halls, broadcasting that career-making CD release party. Hate to think of Shaye sitting close to her in a booth, engaging her in conversation about tracks, takes, and sound engineering—it seems such a waste of his wisdom. I wonder if he hates her burnt vanilla smell, too—if he despises like me that taut, undernourished skin. There's no way he could be transported by her ridiculously fake and Auto-Tuned beauty—there isn't a square inch of that surface that hasn't been retouched. Though I will admit to conditioning my hair lately, taming it behind my ears or in a ponytail, and sometimes stealing some of Sunny's shimmery eyeshadow. Just a little.

Tanay is late but the proctor still waves her in, frowning. She sits down and stares at her desk.

"You've got this," I whisper.

"No I do not," she says. Her hands tremble. "Help me Jesus, I'm going to throw up."

"Dig deep, girl," Andrew says.

"Begin," says the proctor.

Afterward, none of us are sure how we did. We walk to the drop-off circle since we're off the rest of the day, talking about each prompt. Or at least Andrew and I do. He thinks he's pulled a four or five, and I know after talking to him, I begin to feel I'm somewhere in that vicinity, too. Meanwhile Tanay looks like she wants to cry.

Andrew grabs her right there in front of the school and hugs her for a long, long time. I look away, pretending I have a car coming for me.

She doesn't invite me to her house. I count light poles and SMU shirts from the EZ Rider on the way home. I tell myself I'm too wiped to socialize anyway.

I find the Passive Solar blessedly empty. I land in my bed. Shaye and Sunny aren't canoodling, Sunny's not rhapsodizing about health care justice, and the latest foster cat has been placed, so I can go under without disturbance.

I wake with a start when I hear a tap on the door. My heart's like a jackhammer.

Shaye peers around the door. "Sorry—did I wake you?"

I sit up quickly, "No, no, it's just I startle like it's 9/11." I rub my eyes, not sure if I'm making sense.

Shaye grins. With him my lines never seem to fall flat. "Come on, I woke you up."

"Just dozing," I say. "Where's Sunny?"

"She called and said she'll be here in a few hours." He's got a bunch of CDs. "I brought the '80s girl some more music." He says this almost shyly, like he's afraid to cross my threshold.

"That's cool." I try not to look too like a stop sign or whatever Tanay says I am.

"So, what we got here is Whitesnake, INXS, The Bangles, Bonnie Tyler, bunch of classic." He steps into the room. "Though you probably know all these."

"Actually, I don't," I say. I wave at my CD stacks. "I have what some consider very limited tastes."

"May I?" he says.

I nod and he goes over to my dresser. "Very nice. Not an album missing."

"I'm a purist if nothing else."

He grins and lays his CDs on top of the *Thriller* stack.

"Easy now," I say. "Nobody touches that but me." He's moved the perfectly-aligned stack a half inch left.

He holds his hands up. "I'll let you fix it," he says, mock serious. "Don't trust myself in this—sanctuary."

"That it is," I say, trying to stay calm. As soon as he leaves, I'll leap up and straighten and restack—

"We ought to shop downtown on Jefferson sometime," he says. "The dude at Album Alley's an asshole, but if you want real music, that's the last great place for it. You in?"

"Sure." I shrug. When I wake from naps, the world feels shady and full of gray. I can't shake a feeling of doom, much less believe some guy would be this nice.

"You okay?" he says. His face furrows with concern.

"I'm great."

"No, you're not."

What to say? That it's not a matter of if but when the ax will drop with all good things? *Dude, I know you'll soon sicken of Sunny Revere, see through her makeovers, and find yourself obligated to take the teen on a field trip, and you really don't want that hassle...*

Instead I say, "I just had an exam. I studied my—" I want to say ass, but the way he's looking at me so intently, I want to sound older, and it feels weird to mention body parts. "I know I passed, but...anything less than a five is unacceptable."

"You're hard core."

"No, I have to get the hell out of here." I glare. "I am not living with Sunny Revere the rest of my life. Life begins in London."

He's quiet, contemplating me for a second. Then he points to the bed. "May I?"

I nod, and he sits at the far corner, on the edge. "*This Is It*, right? As only the King of Pop can do." He leans forward, staring at the floor. "Music is everything, isn't it."

I nod again. I feel a lump in my throat—another symptom of waking from a deep nap, laced with fear that I've missed something, that I should have been more alert.

"Deanna called me in a panic this morning." He chuckles. "Wanted to know her future in this business, since she thinks she failed that exam."

Why do we always have to talk about that B? "So what? It won't slow her down one bit."

He says with a grin, "You're right about that. She's a blonde who can sing."

"Thank you." I slap the bed. "Bubblegum talent, gone with the next chew. Bubble brain, head too big for that body, bimbo-bitch-racist—shall I go on?"

Shaye drawls, "Damn. You are one cynical girl." He's giving me that look like I'm older than he thought.

"Dude, seriously, though, how can you rep her?" I reach for my iPhone—still cracked, courtesy of his client—and call up her website. I read for him the astounding lyrics:

"I'm a bootstrap kind of gal
Do things my own way
Don't have to tell me how
I'm not afraid to pay!
Don't want no handouts now
Don't want free meals or help
This gal goes alone
And I never kiss and tell!"

"What is she," I say, "Britney Spears gone Tea Party?"

"You got to give her props—that's an original."

"Does my mother know you rep a right-winger? And what's this 'kiss and tell' crap—"

"Listen." He grabs my foot to stop my next onslaught. "Sunny called and said you two fought like cats this morning. She was all torn up." He lets go.

"She's always torn up! Please!" My voice sounds shrill.

"Maybe if you stay calm, she'll stay calm."

"Um, is this going to be your role?" I snap. "U.N. ambassador? Because I no longer negotiate."

He laughs. "Chillax," he says. It hits me I'm leaning forward, seething. "Look at you. You're shaking." His eyes rove across me. "I bet your blood pressure's out the roof."

"I don't keep track of it." A lie, since I count my pulse on the regular.

"Come here." He beckons to me. Those dark eyes are hard to refuse. I scoot forward a couple inches, not sure what he's about. "Turn around." I do, slowly. Then I feel his hands knead my shoulders, and though it's strange—I never get or give back rubs—the pressure is amazing.

"I don't know why she called you, I mean, it was a typical fight," I chatter, because the quiet unnerves me. "Why drag you in?"

"Ssssh," he says. "You're not relaxing. There are some serious knots in here." He works between my shoulder blades. "You're too young to carry all this tension."

"Yeah, well—"

"Release your shoulders." He presses them down, and I realize I had them up near my ears. "This hurt?"

I shake my head no. His hands are very strong. Warm, firm, knowing what they're about. He stays on my shirt, thumbs pressing deep, and I feel something crack between my shoulder blades. It's nice—really nice—and strange—to be touched. Sunny Revere, she's not hands-on, not unless she needs something.

He squeezes my shoulders, like maybe a dad would, then lets go. I want his hands back, immediately.

"Thanks," I say, scooting back against the wall. I can't look him in the eye.

He stands up and glances at my CD player. "You want some tunes to get you back to sleep?"

He's always thinking of what I might need. Yet thus far, no IOUs. No corrupt, hidden adult agenda.

I say, like it's no big deal, "Yeah, hit me up with 'You Are Not Alone.' *HIStory* album. On repeat, please."

"You got it." He goes to my CD player.

I watch him search for the CD, and maybe it's because the very mention of sleep drugs me, and I want more precious oblivion, that I don't mind him touching the CDs now. Or maybe it's I trust him more than I do my own mother. I watch him take the time to straighten everything, stack it tight with perfect four corners, and I feel my lids droop a second. If only I weren't wired like such a freak, able to sleep only a couple hours at a time…But Shaye doesn't seem to care about the OCD. He treats me like I'm normal, just like Tanay. They've looked past the hoodie, the unkempt hair, and the Jackson jacket, too. I wonder why.

I sink down on my elbow, trying to keep my lids open. Now he's put the CD in my player. I hear him say softly, almost to himself, "There was a time when you had to stop when you heard a song."

"You mean like the radio. No repeat."

"Exactly." He glances over his shoulder at me like I'm brilliant.

"What'd they do back in the '80s without repeat?" I think I just slurred my words, then blink hard.

He laughs. "I have no idea how we ever survived."

The song starts. We're not alone now. I think he says, "You get it." He's looking at me like I'm fine china, not to be believed. "But you always get it."

My eyes close as he leaves, the door clicks, and I think how strange it is, all this peace. It hardly takes a minute for me to slip away, into thoughts of MJ writhing near sunset Greek columns, silk black shirt flying open to ribs pushing through smooth flesh. All the while, the man-woman lips sing a safe, mannequin song.

CHAPTER 22

THE NEXT DAY AFTER THE AP History exam, Sunny finds me in my room, looking like she's been chastised. Her hair swings in fuzzy little-girl braids around a face that looks older, weaker—like she's fighting her age with this silly hair.

"Wendybird," she says. She moves my laptop so she can sit right next to me on my bed.

"I need that."

"Come on, talk to me a minute."

I sigh and slam my AP bio text.

"Listen." She stares at her hands. "I'm sorry I was late getting you to school yesterday."

I chew the inside of my lip. Here we go.

"I know that exam was important to you."

"Do you, now?"

She sighs. I count three seconds this time, odd because she's an odd number, never balanced or in time. I think how my Bio teacher was saying last week that a sigh from Jesus or Julius Caesar still circles the globe—that the air molecules from their lungs have been recycled for centuries. If that's so, then Sunny Revere's legendary sighs will ensure a billion folks don't suffocate from here to eternity.

"About the Mean Girl," she says. "If you need me to do anything—and I mean anything—I'm there for you, okay?"

"Thank you, Mother. What a kind offer." I stare, unblinking, while she searches my eyes for irony. Sunny Revere, like anti-bullying Facebook posts and parent workshops, can never do a damn thing. Just another hoarse shout from the crowd while the cage fighters spill blood for the cameras. Suddenly I feel ancient, but strong: it's like I can taste living on my own one day, and it won't be scary.

"Shaye said you didn't seem mad anymore, so I'll take this as forgiveness," she says.

"Shaye's quite the diplomat."

Her face gets soft and goofy. "He's so much fun. Tonight we're going to Midnight on the Green."

"You kids have yourselves a swell time."

She nods with a vacant look, pats my leg, and leaves. You can tell she's already thinking about the hipster festivities; how she's going to make a million new girlfriends while parading Shaye around. That's always the way; Sunny has a knack for meeting new people who manage to mooch off our food, crash on our couch, and paint murals on our walls. Funny how none of them call when we need money or when we split for another state.

I return to my Bio notes. I read somewhere that the Bio textbook was a hell of a lot slimmer in MJ's day. A cell had what, a nucleus? How simple it all was. If only I could answer only those questions available in 1982.

If Shaye were here, he'd laugh to hear me say that.

Focus! Alleles, phenotypes, and Punnett Squares dance on my twenty-first century head. I could seriously fail. My stomach really turns when I'm asked, *True or false: most hybrid offspring that survive the zygote stage die before reaching reproductive age.* This question feels personal, as if the AP exam knows some people, like me, aren't even mules—more like mutants with low viability. If I have to write an essay about heredity, should

I describe the twisted tree I sprout from? I wonder how much Shaye knows of Sunny's dysfunctional romantic past and my imaginary father.

My iPhone chirps. It's Tanay.

COSTUMES. We got to step it UP.

All caps says she's through pouting about her supposed two on the AP. After I survive Bio, I'll see if she wants to hang out. I've even flirted with the idea of her coming over here, but so much might humiliate me here, I don't know.

If she wants costumes, then we have to do it right: go 1959, all the way. How can I look like I'm a '50s girl?

Grandma.

I text back, *ON IT.*

I leave Grandma a message, having no idea what time it is in St. Thomas, hoping she'll grant me access to her mansion's walk-in closets in her gated community.

I must fall asleep, because all I know is I wake with the Bio text pressing my side to numbness like an anvil. I check my phone; it's after ten, and Grandma called while I dozed. Her message says Lupita has already left one of Grandma's Chanel suits by the front door.

Now that's service as only Grandma and her minions can deliver. I race there and find a garment bag draped over one of Sunny's half-finished mosaic tables, one that's made it through three moves, a mess of faux gemstones and mirror chips. The night roars with cicadas, making the neighborhood seem alive with thick heat and invisible insects. The motorcycle and car are still in the driveway; Sunny and Shaye must still be here, buried in her room.

When I try on Grandma's suit, I know I've won the lottery. Tanay will be thrilled.

It's a late-1950s Chanel of soft brown wool tweed: a cardigan jacket trimmed with gold buttons and a wide collar and fat cuffs. I try on the straight skirt that skims slightly below my knees. There's a soft pink silk blouse, matching the lining of the jacket, with the whiff of mothballs. But it's all good as yesteryear. Oh, and a pillbox hat. In the mirror I see hints of Grandma in my trim figure, svelte and sassy. Maybe she stalked the halls of old Steeple Mount High once upon a time when everyone looked like Deanna Faire, though I guess it would have been poodle skirts and whatnot. I walk into the bathroom and preen and strut.

A knock on my door as I pirouette for myself in the bathroom mirror. I come back into my room and kick off the heels. I can't recall the last time sometime knocked. "Who i-i-i-i-s it," I croon for Sunny's benefit. No doubt she's trying to impress Shaye with how she really respects my boundaries.

"Wendy, okay for me to come in?" Shaye.

"Yeah," I say. Why does my heart pound so crazy?

"Wow," he says when he walks in. "Look at the retro girl now."

"This is the garb of a racist."

"Put on the heels," he says. I slip my feet into Grandma's pumps.

"Walk a little," he says.

I stand and clack forward a few feet, but I know I look stupid, like a baby giraffe trying to walk. Those eyes will see what a little awkward fool I am.

I look up and he's shaking his head, saying, "Mmm," like Elvis, the randy lion.

"So what's up?" I say quickly. "How's the diva?"

He smiles. "Now that the deal's done with Redblood, we've booked her CD release party. It'll be the biggest thing in town come July. Pretty cool, huh?"

I shrug and turn to pick up the hangers. I pull off the jacket. I want his business to do well—but he still hangs with a diva ho.

"Hey," he says softly, "You're coming out with us tonight, right?"

"To what?" I know, but I relish hearing a drawn-out invite, knowing he is including me where Sunny will not.

"Didn't Sunny tell you?" He shakes his head, amused. "It's a pre-solstice celebration at midnight tonight, out on the green at Nature Fare. Beer and torches and gluten-free goodness."

"Uh, beer's not gluten-free." He reaches out to swat me, and I dodge him, grinning. "Yeah, she told me, but I doubt I'm invited. Plus I have exams." The Nature Fare green, a dusty patch of dying grass, is where Millboro folk bring their kids to run wild. Some dude is always playing bongos and mosquitoes are a guarantee.

"Well, I guess I'll catch you later then?" he says. He looks disappointed. He turns to leave.

He does care about the crazy crew beneath the roof of this Passive Solar; he does! We may not be blond or about to release CDs, but we must be worth something—

"Hey," I call as he's going out the door. "Thanks for— taking care of things with Deanna. It like—it's made a huge difference."

For a moment he looks surprised, like he has no idea what I'm talking about. Then his face shifts with recognition. That crooked smile.

"No problem," he says. "You know I'm there for you."

At 1:30 a.m. when I can't sleep, I go to Facebook. I reactivate my account. I must know what they're up to.

Sunny and Shaye are tagged in a photo on the green, their faces lit yellow by torches. She laughs big with her horsey mouth, surrounded by women who look like her twins in boho chic. She flips the camera off with a long, bony finger.

Beneath the status update, I wish I could type, "My role model."

I run my lines and go to sleep.

I dream of a white-hot heaven where St. MJ and I raise fragrant, spindly hands to bless all the lepers, one of whom is Deanna Faire. She, like Dorian Gray, glows like a thing of beauty till I get up close and see all the sores weeping from her face. I tell MJ she should be ousted from the heavenly realms.

He doesn't agree or disagree. I want to laugh but I can't. Something tells me Deanna is my mirror image, and it would be me laughing at my own diseased skin.

CHAPTER 23

I WAKE TO SOMEONE TOUCHING MY feet. Rubbing them.

I jump up, snatching my feet away. It's dark as hell. There's someone sitting at the end of my bed.

"Wendy?" It's Shaye, and his voice is soft. "Sorry. You don't like foot massages?" His hands move away.

I take a breath. "Um…what time is it?"

"Three."

I rub my eyes. I can barely see him. He seems hunched over in the gloom, at the end of my bed. My heart flutters. This is more than strange. I have no idea what he wants; all my senses are fuzzy.

"How was it?" I finally say.

"Oh, baby, it was debauchery—this one goes to eleven," he says, with a Brit accent and a giggle. His tongue sounds thick.

"Where's Sunny?"

"Passed out." He cracks up, his voice higher than usual. Great. I feel my stomach twist; Sunny has always had a thing for alcoholics, always ready to two-step them into sobriety. But because she can never keep from waving a wine bottle in front of them, they always go down in a puddle of weakness. I clutch my knees, hoping I am wrong. Please don't let Shaye have this Achilles heel, when so much else is right…

It's very quiet. I say, "Are you okay?"

He sighs, a long one. "Just can't sleep." I smell the beer like a dense fog pressing down. "Don't want to. I mean, why sleep when the dreams are from hell, you know?"

"I know." I wrap my arms around my knees. "I never can, more than a couple hours."

"Yeah," he says. "I always see your light on."

I don't know what to say to this.

"You see us on Facebook?" he says.

"Yeah." I shrug. "She inspires me, what can I say."

"You got to let go of the hate, girl!" He grabs my foot again, squeezes it. "Come on now." He starts rubbing again. His hot hand on my skin sends thrills of fear but also strange yearning.

"I can't; if you were her daughter, you'd get it," I say, a little too loud. His fingers are finding every toe, stroking each one. He's giggling uncontrollably, saying something about "Foot in the Door" and "Foot Up Your Ass" beer they tried tonight. Then he stops rubbing and says. "Hey. I really like those photos you have in your album. On Facebook."

"Which ones?"

"The ones when you were little." He means the ones with the bowl cut, circa age ten. Back then I grin stupidly at the camera, without a front tooth, like I own the world. Was he looking tonight—or does he mean from before, when he friended me?

"Thanks."

He sighs deep. "The innocence," he says, like it's a piece of candy on his tongue, something to suck on and make last forever. "Jesus, I could weep forever, you know?"

He's totally drunk.

"You need to go to bed," I hear myself say. A forgotten memory comes into focus: something with Sunny's hateful, horrible Nelson dude back in San Francisco. I was ten and he got drunk all the time. But now I remember specifics, like ghostly forms pressing through cobwebs: I led him one night to the living room couch and commanded him to "Stay!"

Shaye's not rubbing my foot anymore, but he's got such a strong hold, I don't know how I'll pull away. "Nah, nah," he says. "It's too damn cold in there. I mean, old. Ha!" He chuckles. Then his voice drops, serious. "You know, you're lucky she doesn't lay a hand on you."

Okay, another drunk *non sequitur*, but we'll go with it. "Yeah, she takes pride in never spanking. Unlike Grandma, who beat my ass one time when I was five and I ran into the street. She and Sunny got into a public brawl over the incident."

"Not what I meant, girl, not what I meant." His hand releases a little, but it's still there, now it's a caress, and my rogue foot wants all of it. "Ease that pain, girl, come on." He starts humming, off key, something that sounds familiar, high-pitched, staccato. His fingers go back to massaging my toes, then they're stroking, and something shoots straight up my leg to my softest, deepest part, and I tingle everywhere. He's still humming, light. I feel my body tense, not wanting to move an inch, because something's rising in me.

Suddenly the song cuts off, and his voice changes. He drops my foot. "I am drunk as hell," he announces. "I am one stupid asshole. Forgive me." In the dimness I see him sit up, press his elbows on his knees, and toss his head like he's trying to wake. Then he stands up fast, shaking the bed.

He walks slowly to the door and catches himself against the frame. "Sorry, Bird Girl, funny young thing," he says. "Going to see the King this summer, aren't you? That'll kick ass."

"Uh, yeah...yeah, it will."

"Wish I was going with. Now you listen to me." Then his voice shifts to cold, military. "Get to sleep."

"Okay," I say. I shrink beneath the covers, slipping that straying foot beneath the sheets.

I lie there, trembling with surges, coursing so fast from head to toe. I burn with something I haven't felt in ages, maybe except for a few times backstage when I stood inches from Cyrus, waiting for a cue. Quick, don't go where your mind wants to go—stay with Cy, tall and lean Cy, hell, even naked, naked, naked, try to think about his male equipment even, but dammit, it won't stick—Cy turns to stone, smooth and untouchable. Instead I see the scene I want: Shaye kicking in the door and devouring me with hungry eyes, coming and laying flat against me, a gentle press, igniting me to flames. We are there forever, him giving me feelings I can't escape, burning with irresistible urges making me rise to him and give him whatever he wants, as long as he wants.

I can't help it; my hands descend. *He's on me, he's on me, he's on me.* I shudder.

I twist in my sheets. Dirty girl.

I curl into a ball. I feel darker than a pit. I don't know what's come over me, but nausea rises hard in my throat. Something is very wrong: with me, my thoughts, my body.

He said he was sorry—that he was drunk. It's just temporary insanity—he's not thinking bad. I'm the one touching myself like a Deanna whore. I know she wants him too. I saw the lust at Sparky's, the melting his way, pulled like a magnet...

Can this guy be as good as he seems? Should I feel so drawn, his image a constant presence in my mind? His arms are sculpted, and his hair is mussed just enough to let the darker roots show, the perfect contrast of blond and brown. Jesus, I'm certifiable for my obsessions. I don't know when to say when. The point is, he's cute. He would be a very cute stepdad. And that is all. The most decent one I've ever seen.

So let me pretend to be normal. I am not sure this freak can do this, but we must sure as hell try.

CHAPTER 24

THE NEXT DAY, I COME into Teasdale's room at lunch for practice and find Mushi draped all over Andrew, whispering something in his ear.

Tanay is nowhere to be seen.

Mushi gives me a flat-eyed look, like I'm part of the door. Andrew, on the other hand, looks caught.

"I guess you got to do your Oscar thang," she drawls over a big yawn. She squeezes his shoulder. "Well, I'll leave you be, boo."

She gives him a look of ownership and sails out, one hot mama ready to pop.

I bury my face in *Raisin*.

"Wendy," I hear Andrew say.

"What?" I say, not looking at him.

"That—don't think—"

"Don't break Tanay's heart," I tell the pages of *Raisin*.

"Nah, nah!" Andrew leans forward. "That's not—that's not what that was about."

I give him what I hope is a look of death. "Was that a case of what-would-Jesus-do or a case of what-would-a-player-do?"

"It's not like that!" Andrew sighs and grips the desk. "Back in middle school, Mushi and I had a thing, but we—we've not been together in years!"

"Except till now."

He falls back in his seat, sighing with exasperation. He peers at me. "Are you going to say something to Tanay? It's not what you think."

He doesn't look like he's lying, but then again, Sunny Revere always looks truthful, too. "Why does she keep sneaking back on campus," I say, "other than to see you?"

"You think I can stop her?" Andrew looks more than frustrated. "I'm just trying to do my thing, get through school, get my scholarship." For a moment his face contorts, a brush of pain, like he could cry, but he gets control of it. His shirt looks pressed, clean—but the jeans, they look crusted with dirt, like they could stand alone.

"Look," I say. "I know you and Tanay—I don't know. Just be real with her if you're with someone else."

"I have never lied to her." Andrew looks me in the eye. "I don't make promises I can't keep."

"Fine," I say, shutting my book. "Please just don't reek of promises you might make, okay?"

"What's that?"

"Don't act like—we don't want—I don't know, I just wouldn't want someone to lead me on!"

"Lead you on about what?" We turn. It's Tanay behind us, looking mad.

My mouth dries up. I think I may look guilty. Andrew, he looks worse than me.

Tanay's eyes flit between us. "What is the problem?"

"Nothing," Andrew says with a shrug. "We're just waiting on you."

"Waiting and conversating," Tanay says sharply. "Fine. Keep me in the dark." She slams herself into a seat and opens her book.

My heart is in my throat. I don't know what to say, but I'm afraid to mention Mushi and afraid I meddled. I feel my gut ache, the way I always feel when Sunny and one of her suitors start kicking up dust. Tanay and I were due for trouble, I guess; relationships always fall apart by the third week, from what I've seen.

I hate she looks at me like I could steal Andrew—or like I could have a man's hands on me at night.

After a minute, Andrew says, weakly, "We only got a few days before we do this thing. So, we should practice, right…"

"I don't know," Tanay snaps. "Y'all want to practice, for real?"

"I do," I say.

"Well, get on up, then," Tanay orders. "Go do your thing." I can almost hear on the end of her statement, "white girl."

I go stand at the door and wait for them to set up like they're in the Younger living room. My eyes rove the room: there isn't enough space in this shrinking room for the three of us, and sure as hell not enough bricks or tiles to count.

Tanay slams the desktop. "Hell, I don't know why I even try. Look at us! We don't got furniture; we don't got costumes! We won't even pass!"

"I have a Chanel suit, 1959," I say. "The year the play was made. I promise you, I will look like a rich racist."

An odd moment of silence while Tanay and Andrew glance at each other. Then they crack up.

"All right, Mrs. Lindner, let's kick your ass out our house," Tanay says, and stands up.

I take a breath because she's smiling; I let the doorframe hold me up. 48 tiles I can see from here, gray from eons of student scuff marks: Tanay and I are still friends.

Andrew looks at me with gratitude, but I cast my eyes away.

I hear my phone chirp. I know it's Shaye—what I've waited for with every skin cell since I woke. I want to grab it but wait till I'm walking down the hall after lunch.

I'm sorry... he's texted. *I mean it...sorrier than u will ever know.*

I lean against a locker. *It's ok. No problem...we're cool.*

My heart warms, and my mind lands, then dances away from the feel of his hands on my feet. I should be writing him sorry, for reading too much into a simple touch.

Good, he texts. *Good good good good*

Then, a minute later: *You're a good girl. It makes me a better man*

I head to AP Bio smiling. He has a good heart. And I can't help but feel happy that he cares so much—and that he owns what he does. As we review adaptation and Punnett Squares, I hate to think Tanay is being played, by a boy. Andrew is not a man. How to tell her—what can I tell her without saying too much about Shaye but telling her to wait for something better?

I decide to stay out of it. But I must keep her in my life.

When Mr. Pennings isn't looking, I text her beneath my desk.

Prison ends today. Thanks for getting me a short sentence

She texts back *LOLOL*

After school Tanay meets me outside the classroom just as Deanna and her minions stroll by—like Deanna has kept tabs on my release date.

"What're y'all doing?" Deanna says with fake nice.

"*A Raisin in the Sun,*" I say, warily.

"Oh, right, a play P. Diddy was in," Deanna says slowly, every syllable dripping mockery, like. "Well, I'm sure ya'll will get an A."

Her girls giggle.

I snap, "Do tell, Scarlett: what's your brilliant plan?"

"Original songs I wrote, which I've linked to every novel we read this year," Deanna says, like she's light years older. "Teasdale guarantees an A if you create something *new.*"

"That's not on the assignment sheet!" I say.

"Wendy, Wendy, Wendy—haven't you learned to read between the sheets—I mean, the lines?" Deanna says.

Then she gives me a look like, *I know what you did last night.*

They stalk away, Bethany and Ziona trailing her and chittering like greedy, gleeful squirrels.

I feel sick to my stomach. Shaye wouldn't—no. He wouldn't dare tell her what happened between us. There's no way. But what—what the hell was that comment?

Tanay grabs my shoulder in a panic. "What the fuck? Is that true, what she said?"

"No, no!" I yelp, my best Oscar face pasted on. But something like lead presses my chest because all I can think of is Deanna and Shaye, Shaye and Deanna, pressed closed together in a tight sound booth. "Teasdale said we're supposed to do something original *with the literature—connect the dots,* remember? Original songs, my ass. If you're a horny old Republican, maybe. Everyone will be like, *What the hell?* when she starts singing."

Tanay does not look convinced.

I tell her as we walk to the drop-off circle how I'll make the speech after we act, explaining to Teasdale that Karl Lindner, my character, is a modern-day Simon Legree with violence hovering in the background—that I can connect *Uncle Tom's Cabin* dots to *A Raisin in the Sun* dots no problem.

"It's not enough," Tanay moans. "The bitch said 'every novel.' We've got to up our game!"

"Well, *Huck Finn's* another easy one," I say. "I'll connect us to every damn book. I got this."

"Come over for dinner and we'll do it together."

"Uh, no thanks," I say. "I'm kind of stressed. I mean, I'm pretty sure AP English was a four or five, and History, a four, but I need Bio to be a four, for sure. You know, to be competitive anywhere."

It's out of my mouth before I realize how that might make her feel.

"Right, mmm-hmm," she says, looking away. "You super students, can't think of nothing else but climbing that ladder." Her lips press tight and I know she's thinking of the scene earlier between me and Andrew—like I've come between them, again.

"Sorry." My voice is weak; I keep seeing her fade away from me—everything is so tenuous, shifting. "I could hang out some other time…if you want." My heart beats fast just to say this.

She shrugs. "Whenever. I got nothing but time." She starts to walk away, then stops and turns. "Don't pay me any mind. I'm just sick of things, I guess. It ain't you."

"Okay," I say.

Her heavy look and the weight of all things follow me home. Counting the pass of light poles and pedestrians doesn't soothe; I need to see Shaye to know what's rooted. What doesn't move. I admit to myself as the EZ Rider nears Millboro that part of my saying no to Tanay was to get home as soon as possible, just so I might catch a glimpse of him.

Neither he nor Sunny Revere can be located when I get home. But Shaye has left me a note on my pillow. It reads,

For your play you need Motown—Supremes, Jackson 5. Period music. And a record player. I'm on it.

His signature is big, strong, and sharp. It reminds me of his nose, his arms, his hands.

Some of the weight lifts, and I smile. Funny how the potential stepdad gives so much more of a damn than the biological mother, who can't even remember I've got this project, much less any major exams. If he'd confessed to Dee that he talks to me late at night in my room, strokes my feet, he wouldn't be acting like this. On my side. Thinking of me, this way.

I hole myself up in my room with an old container of hummus and stray organic carrots, reciting bio facts aloud till my head spins. I keep looking up every time I hear the house creak, thinking it's Shaye come back, but there is no one, all the adults are gone, and it's just me and my tedious path towards a 4 in a subject I hate.

When he wakes me later that night, I'm not surprised. I crane my neck to see my alarm: 2:00 a.m.

"Hey, girl," he says softly. He's on the far edge of my bed, like he won't stay long.

"Hey," I say.

"Study hard tonight?"

"Super hard." I rub my eyes. I don't move, maybe because he's so near my feet I wonder if there might be another caress.

"Man, you're motivated," he says with a sigh. "Where do you get that from?"

I snort. "Ha, not from you-know-who."

"Your Zuni dad, I guess?" It sounds like he's smiling. "Where's your dream catcher, Bella?"

"Uh, that's a cliché of indigenous peoples and I doubt the Zuni—if I am indeed that—would indulge such white-people fantasies." He chuckles, so I rant on. "What I really want to know is, is my dad really out there, living in a pueblo, or is he running a casino? Is he a deeply devout, summer-solstice pilgrim as I've read these Zunis are, or, is he a drinker, smoker, midnight toker, holed up in some ghetto, severely addicted to online poker?"

He's cracking up. "Nice, nice. Guess you wouldn't smoke a peace pipe with him." He scoots back on my bed, still an inch from my feet, and props his back against the wall. He tosses one leg over another; I see leather of cowboy boots glint in the gloom. "Ever smoked pot?"

I don't know why, but the question makes me freeze. A

whiff of déjà vu, something spooky, so I chatter, "Nope, total nerd. But if my dad the pipe smoker is dead, then and only then does he get a major pass."

Shaye tilts his head back, and I can see more profile now in the gloom, that craggy, strong, and hungry look that seems so loveable right now. "If he's an asshole—and clearly he is, I mean, he left you—you're lucky you don't have to deal. My dad was a doormat. And my mom? Cold as ice. Mental, really. At least yours *feels* things."

I feel a pang. I picture Shaye a little boy, running up to a dad who averts his eyes while his mom yanks him back and smacks him, hard.

"You're a Leo, right?" he's saying. "And Sunny's a Gemini."

"Which means what—we hate each other?"

"You're fire. She's air."

"Airhead, yes."

"Geminis are hard to pin down but they spice things up."

"Geminis never stick to anything."

"Geminis love adventure."

"You can't trust them."

"No, it means you can't sink your claws in her. That drives you crazy. And you—you always need to know where things stand."

I feel a little thrill in the bottom of my gut. He gets me. Totally.

"Know how you feel," he says. "Believe me." He must mean his mom—and I've learned that when people tell you a story, they only tell you the parts they want you to hear. He says, "Just—try to give her a break, okay? Her heart's in the right place. She's trying to settle down."

I nod, heart fluttering, unsure. Sunny Revere, settle? Here, till my senior year, so I could graduate with Tanay? To hear it from him makes me think it could be possible. But it also means he's lobbying for her. She's first in his head. Twisted I am, to hate that he loves her enough to sit here and plead her case.

"All right?" he says.

"Yeah," I say. My voice is little girl.

"All right then." He smacks the bed with his hand, like he's going to get up, and it tremors. But he doesn't move. "Listen. I'm really sorry I woke you. I hope I didn't freak you out."

"No, no," I say. I'm willing him with my every nerve to hang out, just a little more—not go just yet—

The silence shimmers with the unsaid. I can't breathe. Then he says, "I just—I had to see you."

A wave of warmth washes over me. No one in my life has ever said that to me, Wallpaper Girl, who sometimes becomes Freak Girl, and then always becomes Underground Girl. I have no idea what to say except, "Okay."

"Good night," he says softly. His voice is full of warmth. "Or I guess, good morning."

I feel myself smile. He leaves.

I lie there, thinking about all he's said, how he's sharing his deepest parts, parts I bet Deanna Faire doesn't know. At least I have that. He's in this private space with me, needing me and my attention, and totally there for me, willing to stick it out with my crazy mother.

Who wouldn't have feelings for him?

I curl into a ball, hugging myself. I'm a lonely nerd who has never been touched, who touches herself. I will have to staple oven mitts to my hands, no, baseball gloves, just something to keep me from going south and feeling things only freaks feel.

I am weak, but at least I know these feelings, all feelings, will one day pass. They must all go underground, the way viruses like HIV do.

CHAPTER 25

O N THE WAY TO SCHOOL the next morning, I admit to myself that my persistent thoughts of Shaye equal a full-blown crush. For a second, I see Deanna Faire in a slightly forgiving light. And when I enter the school and see her and that skeleton crew pretending to prop up the main wall of the school hall, see the nervous energy flitting through those bony limbs, I know the lacquered face and smooth flat hair are sculpted daily to draw not just him but everyone, The Public, and she, like me, is just another little girl who wants attention.

I finally have decent potential for a stepdad. Why be a freak and complicate it?

It's good I haven't seen Sunny in two days. I've heard the door bang at night, her voice low and urgent with Shaye in her room, but it's better this way; if I looked her in the eye, she might see my strange lust and pry it out of me.

After the Bio exam is over, I know I've passed, but probably with a three, not a definite four, and the instability of that fact makes me not just panic and count ceaselessly—but want to talk to Shaye, bad. In fact, I live to see him again; I'm sorry, I do.

So when he comes into the room later, around 3:00 a.m., I am so grateful, I'm full of a story to tell him about genomes and cellular respiration, of genetic leanings and inescapable breaths, of hope that I will get to a highly-competitive college and a decent theater program and somehow there figure out what country I will live in, near Good People.

Before he sits down, I say in a rush, "What if I never find a way to leave?"

He sits close to me, near my waist, not the foot of the bed. He's quiet a moment. Then: "I thought you wanted to stay put somewhere."

"I do. But I need to get into a really good college and leave—this."

He takes my hand. The grasp is so strong, so warm. "Wendy. I don't want you to leave. Ever."

His hand caresses mine. My heart overflows. He can't help himself. I can't help myself. I don't know what to do.

The sheets rustle and the bed creaks as he slides next to me and lies down. He's facing me, his hand still holding mine, and I stare up at the ceiling, my whole body trembling.

His face—his nose, his breath, is on my cheek. The smell of his skin is strong, like ripe leaves in fall, like a whiff of bread or something fermenting...his hand tilts my face toward him, and I feel lips, soft, searching lips, taking mine, mine lift up to his, I don't know what to do with mine, but he does. The kiss lasts a long time, it's just lips, and then it's tongue, there are thrills all over me, and the whole time my body rises, rises, rises with it. I'm burning south of the border.

He pulls away with a sigh. His hand leaves my cheek, slides down my neck, like it might go farther. Then it stops. His breath catches and he rolls away, facing the wall.

"I'm sorry. I'm so sorry." His face is in his hands.

My heart pounds so hard it hurts. I sit up with a gasp for air. "No—it's—I—"

Beneath his hands, I hear him mumble, "It's just—you're so beautiful."

Nothing but the sound of my breathing. I can't believe

that's true—but he is here, in my bed, making blood surge to every surface—

He sits up in a rush and leans on his knees like he hurts. Then his head whips around. "Wendy," he says, his voice pleading. "Please—can you not—please don't say anything."

I nod, speechless.

"You won't?"

"I won't," I say.

He grabs my arm and squeezes it. "I'm sorry, I can't help it—you do this to me." I see a glint of his smile in the dimness and want those lips right back where they were. "You're ... delicious. These legs..." He runs his hands down them, and I twitch, even though they're beneath covers. "Look at you. I mean, look at you."

I have never really looked. I don't know what he means. I just know his hands need to stay, keep doing what they are doing.

"I have to go." He crawls off the bed and walks to the door. From there he says, "Good night, princess."

"Good night," I whisper.

I'm rolling, descending into waves of endless, overwhelming sensation—I think this might be love—my body roaring his name and wanting back his hands—that face, those lips, that tongue. I want to go with him wherever he takes me, I want to go to that forever town where I am completely his, till the end of time...

Minutes later, I have to give myself feelings, now that I know what it is to be kissed.

When it's over, I feel a rush of hot and creeping shame. He is with Sunny now and she doesn't know and though I always hate and fear the secrets she's kept from me, now that I have one, a burning one, horrible—I have driven him to this and I don't know what to do with my betraying body.

Except want him back, and want more.

CHAPTER 26

I WAKE AT 6:00 A.M. WITH the strangeness of last night on me like a shroud.

He kissed me—right? I shudder with the horrible magic of it. Every skin cell vibrates as if his hands just left me. *It happened—and it felt so good. But it's so very weird, right?* I dress with this question pounding in my head.

—But then again, he said all those nice things.

I tell myself this as I pad softly through our kitchen— clean for once—and find an apple to take with me to school. Our cupboards, never ever stocked, have been full since Shaye appeared. Normally, the best I can do for breakfast is expired almond milk and stale rice crackers in one of those indestructible hippie pouches requiring surgery. Today I might take a banana—or a granola bar. So much choice. This arm that reaches, the hand that holds these things, everything about my body feels different. Like there could be hidden beauty there, unseen till now—womanly attractiveness, in me, almost sixteen.

I hear a rustle behind me, and it's Sunny Revere.

She wanders into the kitchen looking sleepy but satisfied, like a cat stretching in a warm spot. She smiles slowly at me, her energy quelled for once. I shove my head in the fridge, pretending to look for something.

"Wendybird," she says over a yawn. "How are things, sweetie? I feel like we haven't talked."

"Fine," I say to the inside of the fridge. "Exams went well." There's a pit in my stomach colder than the air on my face.

"Look at me, Wendybird!" My heart stops; I withdraw slightly, glance at her. She's hopped up on the counter, bony feet dangling with chips of old glitter polish winking from her big toes. "Long time no see!" She grins. "God, I'm famished. Got a workout last night!" She winks at me.

My stomach twists; I'm back inside the fridge like the crisper is full of fascination.

"You get that ten score on the AP?" she says, plucking a banana off its stem and tossing the skin in the sink.

"It's out of six. Not sure when I'll find out." I shove the door closed and turn to leave. I don't need her to see anything deep inside me.

"Come on, slow down!" she says through a mouthful of mush. "When'd you grow up so fast?" She grins at me, a bit of banana on her lip. "Shaye swears you have a crush on that Andrew—he says that play is just a ruse for you to hang with dudes. Is there something I need to know?"

She looks so pleased with herself, like she's on the cusp of my secret. My skin crawls with self-hate. Why has he invented that story? I do not want me discussed.

"There is nothing," I snap. And I stride quickly out of the house, hoping there's no awful truth left in my wake.

Outside the house, his bike is gone. I hope this means he left right after leaving me. Please tell me he didn't crawl back into bed with Sunny...but she looks...she looks like a woman who's been busy.

I shudder. My head spins, and my eyes refocus on feet pounding the asphalt toward the bus stop. Is he thinking of me right now, wishing I were with him—or is he really in love with her and just made a stupid mistake? Because I need to see him again. I need him to tell me what we did isn't twisted...

that he will leave Sunny, or figure this out somehow—that he can wait for me till I'm old enough, that we can do whatever the right thing is, though I don't know what that is anymore.

On the bus to school I tell myself maybe he sees her as a friend and me as something more. That though he has this weakness, though he kissed me—my stomach whirls—he said he couldn't help it. He's struggling. I'm struggling. But if we feel this, isn't it right? I can't stop shivering.

Or is it horribly wrong? I'm no child. I'm an old soul, people have always told me that, with a wry face like they don't know what to do with me, a girl mismatched for this space and time. But I don't know what to do with my body, either.

In AP Lit I am ravenously happy Deanna is absent. Though her minions buzz distractedly with her impending tour and CD release party, it's so good not to have her scanner eyes probe me with whorish wisdom. I know she could see I have what she wants.

As Tanay, Andrew, and I run our scenes again, memories of his kiss finally fade because I start to feel swimmy headed. Bile rises in my throat. Then my lower half starts to ache. Damn my period. My body invades my life.

I look at Tanay. "Can you come here a second?"

She walks a few feet away with me so Andrew can't hear. I hate to ask, but I think I just felt something drip. "You have a pad?"

She doesn't blink. "I got a tampon."

I have this thing about tampons; I refuse to use them. But I say, "Sure. Thanks," and walk off with her big black leather purse to the bathroom.

Tanay keeps a house in her purse, so it takes me a good minute to find the tampon in one of the side pouches. I stand inside the stall with the thing. It takes me another good minute unwrapping it, since I always start from the wrong end. The thing looks like a log. How will it go in?

When Sunny threw me a menses party back in the day, it was a real bust, because all of her friends forgot to come. And in all the drama of the empty house and food gathering bacteria, Sunny forgot to explain the facts of life. She did buy me every size of pad and tampon, though, so I acquired a hurricane survival kit of Thin, Regular, and Maxi.

I don't know if other girls are like me but for a long time, I guess ever since I can remember, there's been a no-fly zone policy regarding the nether regions. Let's just say we don't insert anything, we don't discuss, hell, we don't even look down there. Until we're forced to, as we are now. It is a place that is sometimes rubbed and that always comes alive, often to my disgrace. If Shaye knew all this, he wouldn't mess with me—he would let this Freak Girl be.

I stare at the plastic applicator. It looks like a freaking missile. The rounded part can't stay in: I do remember that. But what if the whole thing gets stuck in there?

I could wad up a huge amount of toilet paper instead and wear it around like a diaper. But such strategy has left me bleeding through jeans in the past, and that's not a scene I care to make.

I poke around and hit The Hole. The end goes in a bit, so I push. Nothing happens. I shove harder, and I hit something. A wall. It hurts just a little, a scraping. Is my angle wrong? I squat a little more and my sleeve brushes the toilet seat: gross! I position my hand at more of a 45-degree angle, and there's more movement.

The bathroom door bangs. "Girl, you okay?"

Tanay. I hope she can't see me through the too-wide slats of these stupid stalls.

I make my voice sound weak. "I'm kind of sick."

"I vomit every damn time. Now I got too many absences because I always have to stay home."

I hear what sounds like her sitting down on the counter. Shit. I wish she'd go away.

"You need me to hold your hair?" she says.

"No thanks." That's really sweet. I'd never think to offer that. But now, well, I guess I'd do it for her. Though her hair is stiff and doesn't go below her ears, so never mind.

"Tanay." I have to get her focus off me.

"What?"

"We're going to get an A, you know."

"Damn straight. I ain't worried. Yes, I am. But not about us. It's all the other Ds I got."

I stare at my underwear; I have no idea how I'll get out of this.

Then she says, "You can't get it in, can you?"

"What?" My heart stops.

"I saw your face when you took it."

"I'm not so good with these."

"You use pads?"

"Yeah, pretty much."

"That's like diapers. How do you walk?"

"I don't know!"

"Get in my wallet, give me fifty cents."

I hand her the change beneath the stall door. I hear the coins in a slot and a twist of a knob. Then a bulky little package appears under the door. "This school is old school."

"Thank God for that," I say, and take it. She laughs.

"You know, they don't have these in any other bathroom," I say, just to be chatty and get the focus off what I'm doing with the crackling and the clank of the bin. I hate she can hear my soundtrack of shame.

"That's because these fools tear them down. People don't respect nothing."

"So why don't they tear down this one? What's so sacred about it?"

"Your girl too busy trying to throw up or get pregnant."

"Oh, so she's my girl?"

"Yeah, she's your girl."

We're cracking up; I'm picturing anamarexic Miss Dee trying to tear a pad dispenser off the wall. I can't help but notice, Tanay sounds a lot more black with me now—like Mushi more than Andrew. I don't know why, but that kind of rocks.

When I come out, I try to walk normal so she doesn't see the Huggies bulking up my pants. Chafe, chafe, chafe. Her look reads more than she should. Like she knows I have something hidden.

I give her back the purse. I see my pale face in the mirror with the shroud still intact. "Tanay," I say. "Do you think it's weird if, I don't know, like…"

"Like what?" she says, scrabbling inside the outer pocket. "Dammit, I'm starving and this came unwrapped." She holds out a lint-covered breath mint. "What's weird?"

I don't know how to tell her. About what I've done lately— how I let a man touch me in the middle of the night, let his lips meet mine, and liked it.

I decide trying to explain makes me look even freakier than I am. She doesn't need my crazy when she's trying to pass this class.

"Nothing," I say.

"You ready to do this thing?" she says.

"Let's do this."

We head back to class.

CHAPTER 27

WHEN I GET HOME, SUNNY says Shaye will be gone for a few days because Deanna Faire, not the best of instrumentalists, requires massive amounts of band practice before her CD release tour begins. There's a rehearsal and party this Sunday night at The Shade.

He didn't tell me any of this; he just disappeared.

I text him—*Sup*—but there's no answer. I count 64 minutes till I text him again. This time—*Hey hope she's not working you too hard*—gets 128 minutes worth of wait, but only radio silence in return.

I don't even know where he lives, or where he's come from; I don't know how he spends his days when I'm at school, except that afternoons and nights he is probably with Deanna; and if I know Deanna and her bathroom antics, she is crawling all over him this very moment—perhaps just for the pure greed of acquiring every man in her path. Or perhaps because she senses I have something, someone, and she can't deal with that. I don't know, but my mind goes crazy inventing things that might be.

Friday, I check my phone on each quarter of each hour, then text Shaye once in the morning—*Hi, everything okay??*—but nothing comes back. I can't bring myself to try a fourth. I review what I sent to see if it's lamer than lame—but my words seem fine.

Maybe I did something really wrong that night. Or maybe he figured out he made a big mistake and he's running from these feelings. All I know is, this silence is heinous.

Tanay invites me over to her house for one last rehearsal before we go up Monday, but I say no. I need to be here in case he stops by.

Friday night Sunny tells me to call Grandma and see if she'll take me out, because she's headed to Shaye's.

"Where does he live?"

"In Steeple Mount," she says, grabbing her Guatemalan knit bag.

"I mean, like in a house, or what?"

"An apartment." She stops and looks at me. "Why do you care?"

"I don't know, just asking."

She rushes out and I don't hear from her for twenty-four hours. Only a strange message on our machine: "Hey, Wendybird. Listen, I'm coming back for a bit and I'll get you to go with me to the Deanna thing. Shaye keeps saying we don't need to go, that it's no big deal and won't be polished, but I don't care, we're going." She sounds defiant—pissed off, even. I know that grim voice; it's grim in the pursuit of him. Something's shifted; I bet he's backing off.

Because of me.

Shaye doesn't want us there. I did something wrong—I made him do something wrong—and here I am again, alone. I should have known. Things always end in darkness.

By Sunday afternoon, I'm a wreck, jittering, and a counting freak, but I pull myself together with a shower and my best '80s garb: the argyle sweater, leggings, ballet flats. He says he loves my '80s—that he loves my legs. His saying these things has been my chant, my prayer. But my hair goes severely awry. In the bathroom, I undo the braid done while it was wet this morning, and we have bad perm circa 1982. This is not retro; this is dorkus for any era. Shaye can't see this unsightly me next to the glossy perfection of Deanna. I will not cry.

I go sit on my bed with iPhone in hand. I seriously think about calling Tanay, until I remember she already gave me a tampon. That's more than enough help for one week. I wouldn't want to be clingy.

Plus what would I say: I want to look good for a man who's my mom's boyfriend?

The front door bangs and Sunny wanders in. She sees my panic, and says, "Hold on."

She comes back with a black fedora and we go back into the bathroom. She sticks it on my head, and damn if I don't look half-bad. The frizz looks playful peeking out, intentional and cool, and the black cloth and gray band make my eyes pop, all dark, as if MJ—who I haven't thought about in days—has blessed this look.

Our eyes meet in the mirror, and mine glance away. If she would just do little, right things like this once in a while...if only I had not done so many big things wrong.

"Why don't you ever wear this?" I break the awkward silence. If she hid that graying mane with cute hats when she refuses to color it, she wouldn't look half-bad.

"Oh, this is from a bygone era." She looks wistful a second, and in my mind's eye, she's young again with a Princess Di cut like her old photos, untouched by motherhood, a life of her own.

She wanders out and soon I hear her on the phone, trying to goad her latest girlfriends into coming with. "You don't think he's losing interest, do you?" I hear her say, frantic. "I've tried to be elusive and do my own thing, you know? I'm not lint on black pants, remember." She cackles over some joke she has with this particular BFF. "But I've never colored my hair for a guy. I'm a sell out, right? I am, I am!"

I count, count, count to push her words away, and stare at myself in the mirror 16 more seconds. Will Shaye like what he sees? Will I outshine Deanna? That's all that matters. My stomach flips, dips, and loop-de-loops as my head sails away with our last moments together. That kiss. That kiss.

The Shade is a dark, cavernous warehouse with shaky toothpick chairs. Instead of indie rockers and hippies, tonight it swarms with Mainstreamia—Deanna minions, prepster faces from school and country club venues. We're late, of course—Deanna's been rehearsing for at least an hour. I crane my neck for Shaye but can't find him. Sunny drags me to a spindly fold-out chair near the stage, as if all I might want to do is take in the Dee-va rehearsing with her band. People are milling everywhere paying half-attention, because the bar in back seems to be the biggest draw. Deanna looks miffed, but adjusts her face when she sees me. It's like she knows she's got the upper hand as all rays of light turn her head a halo of rosy gold. She's a vision in a tight pair of jeans, her hair pulled up in a jaunty ponytail, and a short-sleeved cowboy shirt—one that looks vaguely familiar, crimson with silver embroidery—and she's surrounded by men, of course—an upright bass, a banjo, two guitars, pedal steel. She tunes her mandolin and turns to the others. "BKG," she orders them.

I feel huge and dumpy—I am swimming in this sweater—and the hat is dorky whimsy—and my plain pale face and hair, a wreck.

Now Sunny and I are blasted with sound with the speakers right near us: "Bootstrap Kind of Gal" rattling our rib cages and drawing tipsy crowds near the stage, cheering and whistling. I glance at Sunny, grinning and slapping her knee with off-beat, white-people rhythm. Does she even know what these lyrics say? I am searching the crowd, walls, corners, every inch of the gloom for a sight of Shaye. That's when I see him—two rows back, hanging with several women, any one of whom looks like she could be Deanna's mother—taut, lacquered skin; smooth blond or jet-black hair; tight abs; and couture clothes. He's not looking at me. He's smiling only at them, or only at Deanna, giving her thumbs up, grinning crooked with a look of pleasure that's too familiar. A look—familiar, intimate, knowing—that he once gave me.

I whisper to Mother I'm getting a drink. She requests a Corona. I don't argue I'll be carded.

I walk past him to the bar like I don't see him, but I feel his eyes on me. Of course the bartender denies me Mother's beer. While he gets me two Pepsis, I lean forward like a casual, cute teen, kicking up a heel here on the rail, not a care in the world.

Suddenly I feel an arm slip around my waist and someone bump me. A quick squeeze of my side, like I am his. Shaye.

I turn and he pulls away immediately, grinning. His look says all is well, and there is no sorry anywhere.

"What's all this?" he says, scanning me up and down like I amuse him. "All covered up. Not sure I like it." Then he whispers in my ear, a breath that tickles: "Where are those legs, girl? Show what you got."

I duck my head, flushing all over. "Thanks."

The Pepsis slide in front of me and I grab them like a life raft. Behind us, "Bootstrap Kind of Gal" comes to a raucous end.

"Be right back, baby," Shaye says in my ear, and I'm left alone at the bar.

He didn't mention my hat.

I stay there and watch him climb on stage. "Thanks, y'all, for coming out!" he says, his voice booming from the mike—sounding way more Southern than I've ever heard him. "We're going to have ourselves a *good* time tonight." Cheers and whistles. "Because we've got some talent for you. This bootstrap kind of gal has a CD releasing soon, so y'all be sure to join us this July for a kick-ass party. Because after that, you may not see this girl 'round these parts again—she's headed to 'Nashville Star'!"

Whoops, cheers, and claps—the world loves Deanna Faire—who beams and gleams till she catches sight of me, and then it's a glare, straight my way in the light of the bar—like she's caught me fair and square—hopelessly in love with her manager.

I bolt for the bathroom.

There's a massive line of girls, so I'm stuck at the back. Behind me Shaye's voice rings out and on with Deanna praise while my head spins with hate. From this angle and distance, Shaye looks too perfect, sleek in his jeans, strong chest and arms—everything I want but somehow, I know, slipping farther and farther away. He doesn't want me, really, because I do not fit in this glossy world. He's saying, "We're going to give the talent a little break here, so y'all drink up and don't forget to tip your bartenders!"

My head roars with self-hate; I want to drop these Pepsis and run; I can't stay here—

"Hey!" shrieks someone behind me. "What's with the *tent*?"

It's Deanna several feet away, surrounded by Bethany, Ziona, and a pack of lookalike underlings, all giggling, but looking every which way like none of them said it. Her eyes laser me with the old, vicious hate.

She strolls up while my heart thunders in my throat. She yanks on my argyle sweater. "Wow, what a find," she says with a laugh. "Dumpster chic."

The crowd likes this and cackles.

I say, "What's this, cowboy concentration camp?" and yank the shirt on that skeletal frame.

"Ooooh," trills the posse of girls.

She leans in and mutters in my face, "Give it up, bitch. He doesn't want you."

"What, there's a competition?" I say. "Thought you were too busy with Koyt in the bathrooms!"

Squeals from every direction, because I've said it pretty loud.

Deanna says to everyone, "This one thinks she can sleep with my manager. So it's skank chic!"

"Oh my God!" Gasps and stray giggles.

"I'm not—" I croak, swallow hard "—it's not true!"

"Really?" Deanna folds her arms. In her eyes, there's supreme knowledge. "That's not what I heard." Back to the crowd. "Her and her mom. Special, huh?"

The blood burns my face. I am numb, my lips can't move, but my hands strike out, they cuff Deanna in the face, and we're slapping and grabbing and struggling till she falls back, hard, on the floor.

"You're lying!" I shriek. My voice scars my throat.

"Wendy!" Someone grabs me from behind with a vise grip. It's Sunny Revere. "What the hell!"

She's dragging me away, while Deanna picks herself off the floor, smiling. Her face says Shaye is all hers. Sunny has the force of a giant, she's hauling me straight through staring eyes, mutters, and catcalls till we come upon Shaye. He looks amused. His lips twist at the sight of me, like I'm a delicious, ridiculous thing. "Easy now, girl," he says as we pass. "Keep it together."

That smirk follows me home and drowns out Sunny's three-mile rant. The embarrassment. The horror. How could I do this, especially on Shaye's big night? How could I?

The next hours crawl inside my room, deep beneath my covers. What Deanna knows—how she knows—the tears run hot and fast while I see over and over the triumph in her eyes. And the shirt. Shaye was wearing that shirt the first day I met him. They've gone matchy-matchy—or it's his, tailored to her stick body—and every implication, every which way, is nothing but intimate. I just know it. He said something to her in the dark, about me—silly me—stupid me—for ever thinking he could care.

I can't leave this room ever again. I want to call Tanay and tell her everything—but I have no idea where to begin.

CHAPTER 28

H E FINDS ME UNDER THE covers asleep, tears dried on my face. He pulls the covers back and crawls in beside me. His body curves around me, insistent.

My eyes fill up again; they spill over. He turns me to face him, touching my cheek. He smells heavy with beer and I don't know why, it comforts me, it feels like home. "Tears, baby?" he whispers, wiping them off. "You and I both know she's a crazy bitch."

I blurt, "Your shirt. She had it on."

He laughs in my ear. "Oh, yeah. She insisted on taking it. Had it tailored to her little stick figure." He grabs my chin, makes our faces touch nose to nose, then pulls away, smiling. "She's obsessed with me, what can I say. Haven't you figured that out?"

"Sure, she's been a psycho bitch about you, but she acts like she knows about—"

"Come on, you really think I'd mess with that little sex machine?"

I laugh, but it's thin and shaky. I can't look him in the eye. "Did she try to seduce you?"

"Don't you all?" he says, and slides his hand up my leg.

I gasp—my body reels, and his mouth takes mine like it's his, sealing what I know—he wants me, not her, only me.

But the kisses taste too full of beer this time. And they're rushed, sloppy. But that's okay, he's with me—though it hurts when he grabs—there—and with a strong rush I don't want this, want to pry it off, feeling the pad in my pants chafe. I pull away. "I—I—"

"What?" A blast of air in my eye, his saliva too. He's yanking off my sweats.

"I—I have my period!"

"It's okay," he says, whipping the sweats onto the floor. "It'll be easier." His voice is distant, behind glass. He peels off my underwear; everything below freezes tight. He says, "You know I love you."

He wrests his jeans off and crawls on top of me—erect, ugly—pinning me and pushing my breath out of my chest. I don't know why he's doing it this way, it wasn't how I thought it would be, and though I am flat and frozen he inserts himself. It's rough, dryness and rasping, despite my blood. I don't know this man on top of me. The forever feel of him pounding, hurting, not caring. If I scream, yell, *Mom!*—if she finds us like this—this not him, this not me, she will scream and ask what I have done to turn things so twisted and dark.

When it's over, wet breath in my ear. "Nice, very nice."

He tosses the covers off and crawls off the bed. I think of a crab scuttling on a beach. He puts on his jeans. Now he is a man but I don't know who. He is standing over me, zipping up. "Don't even worry about Mean Taylor Swift," he says. "You've got all of me. Wasn't that proof?"

I fall backward inside my head.

"Come on, doll baby, talk to me. Tell me it was good." Rustles as he straightens his shirt.

I ache everywhere; if I open my mouth, I'll vomit black and blue.

He sits on the bed, and the vibration hurts me to my fingertips. He takes my hand. His sweat is slime. "First time, I know. But just you wait." He leans down and kisses my cheek. "It gets so much better, you won't believe it." Then he whispers in my ear. "So beautiful. Love it."

He walks to the door. I think he says, "Good night, pretty thing."

The soft click of the door is like another door I think I knew before, echoing back through years.

My body bounces up; my chest hits my knees. I hug them hard; my nails dig my skin, trying to stop the pain elsewhere. For minutes, or is it hours, I ask if there is anything left inside. I'm a dry husk curling, folding in.

Then I come awake to a buzz, in the back of my brain—a low, familiar drone; a machine on for ages, that I just now hear. Words form from the hum, demon chatter: *dirty little girl, dirty little girl.* I learned that phrase once upon a time like a song, the way you know multiplication tables or ABCs. The chatter, though horrible, it soothes me…my eyes close…I have to sleep, now, hard.

When I wake at 5:00 a.m. curled tight, I come to with a gasp. I race to the bathroom, ready to puke over every square inch.

I crouch over the toilet. Nothing but spit trickles up. My head wants to purge all its murk, shadows of a man who once took me to a park. All I know is I hate looking at swings too far away while a car stays firmly parked in the lot, and me, a prisoner there, strange hands in my hair. Saying after, *Remember, you wanted this.*

I shower for a long, long time, but it doesn't help. Water pours over and over unmoving stone. All I know is not to touch my hair. Something is wrong as hell with my hair.

Out of the shower, I stare at what's in the mirror. Then I stare at my towel. Maybe my face will imprint its bloody outlines there.

CHAPTER 29

TANAY FINDS ME SITTING IN the empty hall outside Teasdale's classroom at 7:00 a.m. "Hey, girl. You nervous like me?" she says with a grin.

I shake my head. I see her hands tremble. It appears that from now on, all movement will occur outside the stone I am.

"Look at that!" She whistles and jerks the skirt of the Chanel suit hanging from the door. "Girl, this is perfect!"

I can't speak to anything being right or perfect ever again.

She sits down, peering at me. "You all right?"

I look at my hands and shrug. What if I'm pregnant?

"You sorry now?"

My heart jumps. I croak, "About what?"

"That you took this part."

"No, no."

She shakes out her hands like there's something on them; I hear joints crack. "Times like these, see, I'm like, 'Why the hell am I doing this!'" She sighs and leans her head against the wall. "But that's just stage fright. I bet you don't get that."

I say to the floor, "Not really."

"Maybe not an A+, but I'm thinking we'll get an A. We're doing this real and honest. I feel Ruth, you know what I'm saying?" Her foot is tapping like a machine gun.

My stomach roils, nausea dancing up its sides. She glances at me, like, *What is up with you*, so I say quick, over bile in my throat, "Why Ruth?"

"I don't know—she's there for people, I guess."

I blurt, "Don't you ever want to get away from people?"

Tanay looks at me like I'm speaking Polish.

"I mean, travel." *Don't vomit,* I tell myself with every bit of strength I have. *Don't ruin her big day*—I swallow hard on saliva.

"Yeah, why not. Myrtle Beach, maybe. Disney World. Where would you go?"

"Bali. Lebanon. The front lines."

Tanay's eyes widen. "You're crazy. Why would I want to leave my family?"

She's right. I am crazy.

She jumps up. "I've got to change. You coming?"

"In a minute."

"That's right, get in the zone," Tanay says, looking pleased. "'Cause we're going to the Oscars."

She leaves to go to her locker, another wing over. *Must do well for her. Got to do this.* I put my head between my knees and try to breathe. I try to imagine going home this afternoon with news for Sunny Revere, begging she make him leave—the one who isn't what I thought he was—and every cell of my gut writhes with knowledge it won't happen.

My stomach revolts; I swallow hard; a memory shakes loose. The Man at the Park, it was Nelson, and I was ten. Sunny hugged me when I said, *He makes my tummy feel funny, he touches my hair, I don't like him.*

And she said, *Aw, he just likes you, sweetie. Don't worry about all these different boyfriends; I'll settle down soon.*

Nelson knocks. I open the door. He looks like he's starving, reeking of beer. Then he steps inside and closes the door.

There the film sputters on its reel, flapping in the wind. I can't remember; I start to shake—this is my fault—two horrible times says I must want this, ask for it!

There's no air! Count! Count! Linoleum, lockers, walls, too small for my expanding heart stretching its seams, threatening to blow—1, 2, 3, 4, 5, 6, 7, 8, 9, 10, 11, 12, 13, 14, 15, 16—I will die, please let me die—let it end—

"Wendy?"

I look up—mouth open, panting—at Andrew standing over me, his face startled. "You all right?"

I'm twitching so hard I'm palsied—my hand is on my chest—

"You got asthma? You need a doctor?"

I shake my head, gasp, "Can't—breathe!"

He kneels next to me. "Breathe. In. Count with me, breathe in, hold it, one, two!" I do it for 1, gasping against the heart that could bust a lung. "Push it out now, one, two. Again, in. One, two. I got you." His hand is on my shoulder.

After a minute I can do 1 and 2, then 3 and 4. The whole time he's saying, "One, two. It's cool, you're okay. One, two, three, four."

He sits back, and it's just me breathing in the silence. Finally he says: "Something happen?"

In my peripheral vision, I see his fingers lace together, his elbows propped up on his knees. *He is clean,* is all I can think. Untouched, like Tanay. Like everyone else.

He says, slowly, "When I'm going through some things, or my baby sister is—she gets the panic attacks, too—we got words we go to."

Words, words, words. Just words.

"There's this one line, works for her. 'Be of good courage.'"

A dull bell in my head. "Shakespeare?" My voice creaks.

"No, the Bible."

I would mock this if I could trust my breath wouldn't fail me.

"I know you're not religious, but hear me out now. It's about staying strong, waiting for the right path to open up."

I snap, "Did he talk about safety?"

"Who?"

"Jesus. Michael says no one will ever hurt you. Did Jesus ever say that?"

He eyes me to see if I'm being my old smart-ass self, but then he sees I'm deadly serious—flat with hate, nothing but trampled ground.

He says, "I'm sure He does, somewhere." I see his brain scrolling through Scriptures.

"Look where you live." My voice bounces off dull white walls and scratched lockers. "It's not like you can call Jesus and say, 'Move me out.'"

Andrew says, very quiet, "Trust me. I ask Him that all the time."

"So why bow to a god who only suffered one damn day?"

Andrew says nothing. His face has a look like he's someone from another century. Then he puts a hand on my arm. "Mind if I pray?"

I don't know if I mind—maybe because my head's not tethered to my body. I hear him say, "Father God. We come to you in Jesus's name. Help Wendy in this difficult time. Our Father, who art in heaven..." I can't move or speak while he recites his well-meaning hocus pocus. The praying player, the man who broke Tanay's heart, he seems to be trying, but it means nothing, empty words, breath gone right away, all of us tools of someone else or systems we can't see. His hand on my arm is a kind, strange weight.

When he's done, we look up and see Tanay walking toward us.

Her eyes are wild; they laser him, then me. Andrew retrieves his hand.

She stands over us where we sit. Then she says, coldly: "Someone stole my shit."

"What?" Andrew says.

"The costumes! Granmama's housecoat, my granddaddy's shirt and pants I had for you—" her voice is on the edge of tears, glaring at Andrew, "—and they took all the makeup, too—"

And I've forgotten the music. As has Shaye. He never did come through with the songs and a record player like he said he would.

Andrew stands and puts his arm out to Tanay to hug her. "It's all right, girl, we can—"

She slaps him away. "Don't," she says, with a look of death. "Don't you *ever*."

Then she gives me the same look.

No—she doesn't think—she can't think me and Andrew—?

She stalks off down the hall.

Andrew looks at me, panicked. I want to scream, "Fix this!" but my throat has closed.

He goes after her.

They come back after the first bell, walking miles apart. Tanay doesn't look at me.

Teasdale makes us go first. Andrew tries to tell Teasdale about the theft, but all she does is raise her eyebrows. We assemble in the front of the room, staring at the floor. I glance up and see Deanna smirk. I know I've found the thief.

We are passable, but with no costumes, no soundtrack, it's truly sad. Tanay is a cold wife in regular 2009 clothes, jawing without heat at Walter, and Walter in his regular 2009 garb takes his anger out on the white woman who is wearing a 1980s blue ruffle blouse and leggings, because why wear Chanel. She may as well be a robot.

Let's just say it: our play is busted.

We sit down, and I glance at Tanay, sunk down in her seat, unmoving. She won't look at me; I know it could be never again. Tanay has been unwise in her affiliation with me.

When Deanna gets up with Bethany to sing, she simpers at the class, "So I wrote an original just for our times. It's about the American way. I like to think it 'connects the dots' with *The Scarlet Letter*, you know, people calling people out for adultery. Some of you might enjoy this more than others." Then she looks at me.

She picks up her mandolin while Bethany strums a guitar. Deanna sings,

> *All-American girl I am*
> *House in the suburbs and a mini-van*
> *I'm not ashamed to swim mainstream*
> *It's all part of the American dream*
> *You over there, thinking you're cool*
> *Breakin' the law, breakin' the rules*
> *Hey, you hippie, goin' with the flow?*
> *You're a freak, and your mama's a ho!*

The class snickers, eyes cutting my way. I sink in my chair. Tanay won't look at me at all.

I remember more Shaye words while Deanna's mouth moves, bright-red with victory. I must say, the harmonies are divine though the lyrics are Nazi as these devils sing of Wendy Redbird Dancing and her descent. Of her the flat target, pinned to a chair. Pinned to a bed.

When class is over, I move to Tanay, ready to say, "We did okay," or "You'll pass, don't worry."

"Damn," she says, her voice like flint. "Didn't think that's how you played it."

"What?"

"All innocent, acting like *I ain't into him* shit."

"Tanay, nothing hap—"

"Just another one sampling the chocolate. That why you hung around, did this thing?"

My mouth falls open like a door.

"I wondered, should I trust you," she says. "Guess I get a D on that, too."

She turns on her heel and walks out of my worthless life.

I turn to Andrew, but he's gone. Only Deanna stands near.

"Go back to your cave, Osama," she says. "Where are your friends now?"

She leaves.

I walk alone into the hallway swarms, only one thing in my head: Tanay's house doesn't creak and moan like the Passive Solar. Instead, it hums with white, clean, and metallic things. People there understand locks, keys, and airtight closures. How odd, yet how normal for them. How sad I may never see that place again.

CHAPTER 30

I'M NOT SCARED WHEN HE enters my room at 2:00 a.m. Strange how the panic, when it hits, it's all-consuming and random, but outside those moments, it's as if fear has left my building.

He crawls in next to me and holds me tight. No smell of beer.

"I'm sorry," he's saying. "I know it wasn't what you thought it would be."

I feel pinpricks of life in my heart, on various skin surfaces, but they are very weak.

"Sometimes men—when we love someone, the way I love you—well, we want it so fast—and girls want it slow—and it takes awhile to get a rhythm, you know?"

A rhythm.

"Will you give me another chance?"

I open my mouth. I hear myself say, "Something happened to me when I was little."

He rises up on an elbow. I can feel him peer at me.

"What?"

If I tell him, maybe he will understand. Maybe the old Shaye is in there, and he will be gentle. He will forget these needs and be the other person I believed.

"Someone messed with me. When I was ten. It was bad, I think. It's like I'm just remembering now."

"Oh, shit." He grabs his head. "That's why you were like a dead thing." He laughs to himself, like, *Isn't this crazy*. Then from a distance I hear him say, "Baby, I'm so sorry." I want to have faith in it. "It sucks. Really does. But don't freak out on me now. I promise you, believe me, it gets better. Your body knows what it wants."

He starts to stroke my legs, inching up my thighs, and his breath is rasping on my face, more desperate than the night before. Instantly I become like board, flat, pasted to the bed. I'm that dead thing, and I wish he would just hold me.

He puts his tongue in my ear, he's sucking my neck, and there's a murmur: "Happens to everybody, baby. You just roll with it."

What happens? As he pushes in, I grit my teeth, feel the soreness but not as bad as yesterday, aches only down there, a particular zone, and I say *happens, happens, happens*, heard anew 16 times, till it sounds solid and distant, like a piece of furniture.

Now someone has airlifted me, and I see the scene with a director's eye, and watch my mind grow obsessed with details of the clean-up. It is quite unlike me to leave the bed of evidence here a day, as I have done, and blood streaked, but also quite like Sunny to not have noticed. I am thinking how after my next shower of all surfaces but no crevices and certainly no hair, how I will ball these sheets into a round, tight roll and separate myself from these dry, crusty streaks of memory.

When it's over, he's dressing himself and addressing me with words of what could be wisdom, or a lecture. His voice is low and musical. "We took a risk, baby. Isn't this what life is all about?"

When I say nothing, he adds, "Don't worry, I'll bring condoms next time. You can't get pregnant on your period."

He's gone.

There is no more sleep. I rise and I make the roll, then I clutch it like a person, and stay calm by watching the clock, as if that can prevent the advance of seconds, minutes, or days.

And when it's 4:16 a.m., and I can't take the next sullied second of my life, I jump up. I find my penknife. If I can just slice me awake and see that inner light...*Ah.*

In the bathroom afterward I scrub my wrists 16 times, and then let hydrogen peroxide sting across my wrist, dripping pink foam down into the sink. No staph for me, thank you.

I go back to bed and crawl back under the covers. Something sweet like juice rushes through me; my insides sing. Happy for the tiny little stings and throbs, reminding me there's blood, a pulse, and live cells in every bone.

CHAPTER 31

I WAKE AND IT'S TUESDAY, THE Day After Our Failed Play, the Day After Two Nights with Shaye, in the last week of school.

I wrap myself tight in a robe and creep around the dim house. Sunny's door is closed. A look out the window confirms the bike is gone. *Thank MJ.* I catch myself against the window. I am so tired, it's like every pore hums electric with dread.

I go back to my room. I sit on my bare mattress and stare at the sheets rolled in the corner, behind my trash can.

In school during AP, more presentations, all boring. All that matters is that Tanay has found a different seat a couple rows away. Deanna ignores me, glowing with smug victory. Andrew with his whiff of Christian Febreze is absent. Poor guy: can't he see here's the smell of the blood still? All the perfumes of his Hallmark card religion will not sweeten this little, dirty girl.

Teasdale smacks us with a B- for our project. I figure Tanay's grade hovers between a C+ and a D. I think up 16 ways she can talk to Ms. DeVries about this and explain the outcome. It's not because Tanay didn't try with every fiber of her being.

When the bell rings, I follow Tanay at 4, then 8, then 16 paces, the "sorry" on my lips fading. I don't know what sorry means anymore, except that it is me.

During lunch I go to the library and stroll the lane of computers looking at numbers: 14, 15, 16. 16 is free. As I sit, blood rushes my head with more story: Nelson did the night shift somewhere at least 4 nights a week. I clutch the side of the computer table, while my head reels. Yes, I used to wish with all my might that his workplace was far, far away, to up the chances he might be hit by a truck while driving back. After 3 days of blessed freedom at our apartment, he would return, and it would start again. I would keep a count, and usually he would find a way to be with me alone at least 16 times during his stay. Once it was 18, and another time, only 9, but again and again, like some sick quota, the average rang up 16.

Every week, by the time it got to 15, I knew the beautiful end was in sight. That—that is why I have seized 16 as my own.

I close my eyes, willing the nausea to pass, and finally it does.

I see now the magic I've tried to make all these years— OCD hocus pocus to soothe the crazy, control the aches. All I know is this: now the count is mine. I count harder as the years get further away. Sometimes it feels like I'm trapped in one of those number banners they stick to the walls of a kindergarten classroom.

It's very good Tanay did not get to know me better. What a burden all this would be.

I visit Wikipedia, which tells me about *unlawful acts, compulsion* and *coercion, assault,* and *lack of consent.* Am I *a person incapable of valid consent?*

I am supposedly a smart girl, an old soul. Smart girls know better.

"Wendy." A voice behind me, and I jump.

"Sorry." I turn to find Andrew, his face like a boy's.

"What?" I snap.

"Can you please talk to Tanay? Tell her it was nothing."

I stand and walk past him out of the library.

I hear footsteps coming after. I pick up the pace, make him trot. When he reaches my side in the hall, I stop dead.

"What do you want her to believe?" I hiss. "That you're not with me? Or you're not with Mushi? Because I'm losing count."

His face falls. It's drawn and flat, like someone smashed him. "No way," he says softly. "No way to convince y'all."

We stand there, my insides growing colder with knowledge that there is something I don't know about him—yet I don't want to hear it, and I cannot help his pain.

He pulls something out of his backpack. "Had this for you," he mutters.

The little book in his hand hangs there in the outer space between us for I don't know how long. Finally I take it because I need him to leave, before tears fall. The fake crimson leather is cool in my hand, the thickness a solid and frightening weight. Whatever, I will take this mini-Bible home and toss it on top of the pile of plastic rosaries and other Grandma swag. I go back to my station in the library and hide there the rest of the day, helmeted by my felt-pad headphones, trusting in the clicks and whirs that gets Michael, wiser than any supposed saint, to retell me about how people are, how they do you, how they leave you this way.

When I disembark from the EZ Rider bus, the air is thick as water and I part it with my body, heaving against it. I pass a dull procession of dying trees lining Oak Street from downtown Millboro toward the Passive Solar, hung with a green, bright, and curly killer, kudzu that suffocates the pine, birch, and oak beneath. Lumpy, monster trees trapped by cancerous masses. Wouldn't it be nice if a big net of suffocating vines would o'ertake me and let me sleep awhile.

Sunny Revere is waiting for me in my room when I get home.

She's gone through everything I own. Scattered all my CDs, rifled through my dresser drawers, ransacked my desk. Moved the bed away from the wall, and from the looks of the bedspread, gone under it. I glance at my trash can and the sheets there; they look unmolested. My hands twitch to get at everything, rectify the disarray.

"Shaye had to leave for a few days." She is sitting on the bed, her long hands locked together like she's praying, her long face grim and white. "He told me what happened."

My heart goes crazy. She's kicked him out. I never imagined it would be this easy.

I sit down at the end of the bed, since she's sitting near the pillow, her back to the wall where he lay. She sighs deeply. There are gray shadows under her eyes and a brown-gray lock of hair falls loose over her forehead.

"I don't know what to do with you, Wendy."

There's something dusty, ancient—the whiff of mold?—about this conversation. "With me?"

"Why would you do this?" Her eyes fill up with tears.

My mouth dries up. I stare at red-rimmed, pleading eyes.

"Do you hate me that much?" she wails.

"What—what did he say?"

She rubs her eyes and chokes on a sob. "You ask him to come see you in the middle of the night—and then—and then tell him you want to sleep with him? *Why would you do that?*"

I jump up. "He's lying!"

"He *cried*, Wendy."

"What—what does that have to d—"

"You never cry," Sunny says. She shakes her head in slow motion like this is enough proof I'm criminal; I can barely breathe. "I never wanted to think—though I've wondered—you'd be so manipulative." Then under her breath: "Bad as your grandmother."

"Mother, this isn't true—"

Tears roll down her face. "The one good man, and you mess with it!"

I stand there, trapped in her all-consuming pain. I have to dig up each word, like a knife pries it from my chest. "I never asked…he came in and he…" I can't say it; her look says I wanted it, all of it. That I deserve it. Even if she doesn't know the whole hell of it.

"Don't." She holds up a hand. "I really can't deal with this on top of everything else."

She swipes at her face and stands. "He says you've been coming on to him whenever you two are alone and how he just didn't know how to tell me."

She shudders like the air of this room is infected. She walks to the doorway, and I wish this was a horrible dream. She's saying, "I told him he can't come here anymore. I'll be at his place from now on."

She turns. Her eyes are dead as his. "You've always been troubled, but this? I guess I have to make some decisions."

I hear the wail like someone else's. "Mom! Listen, please! *Listen!*"

But Sunny Revere has left. She has slammed the door.

I throw myself down, knees slamming, elbows bruising. I'm beating the floor, screaming till I lose count, till there's something like blood in my throat. I'm screaming I don't know how long, but no one comes.

CHAPTER 32

THE NEXT TWO DAYS, I must sleep a little at night, because when I think my eyes are pried open, I'm actually dreaming over and over with eyes tight shut from horror: me performing *A Raisin in the Sun* in our school cafeteria on the ancient, tater tot-encrusted stage. In that shallow space of institutional white paint roiling with dust bunnies, I must do a one-woman, ludicrous show because Tanay and Andrew are nowhere to be found. I'm so upset I scrawl SORRY in black paint across the wall while the entire school laughs at me with fang-filled mouths.

Then Tanay is in the front row, weeping inconsolably. "You bully!" she wails. I look beyond her, unmoving, to the very back of the cafeteria where I sense the presence of an incredibly handsome man. I keep thinking it's Cy, only he's a full man, it's Shaye, and he bares his chest to me like MJ in the *You Are Not Alone* video. Though it's white as a cadaver and spider-webbed with cracks, I want him with every skin cell. I tingle all over, but then it starts to feel like a chemical burn, and my skin starts peeling.

Despite my burgeoning leprosy, I perform the scene for him, only him. Yet I can't ever get him to look me in the eye. Somehow, though, his hands cascade across me, extending from the blackness at the back of the room, broad as an oil slick, rolling over me in huge, suffocating waves—

There's little relief to find myself awake and know he's not coming through the door that won't lock, or crawling into my bed. Any respite is only minutes marked before he will eventually arrive.

By day at school, the last days of this useless year, I move through thick and viscous air. No one speaks to me, and I speak to none. But all horror is relative.

When I get home on the third day, Shaye is waiting and Sunny is nowhere to be found. He orders me to my room without a smile. He knows he's only got these rare afternoons, on her schedule that he must track, now that she insists on going to his place.

This time, with the air so glacial and his eyes so flat with need, I descend into myself. The stench of the condom's rubber, the clinical insistence of latex, tells me this is a test, this is only a test. When there's a danger I might feel, I stare at the closet door with its pine knots and burrow in; I cower inside the darkest one. Over and over, I tell myself a strange tale—that one day, inside that little den, the knife will carve things all away.

Then I come to with his slobber on my cheek. He is saying I'm beautiful and he's brought me a gift.

It's a cassette of Rick James with a song called "Super Freak."

I am frozen flat while he runs his hands here and there and tells me about his mental mother and how she hated Rick James with a passion, which is why he listens to this song nonstop now. How he doesn't speak to his mother anymore and that's a good thing, and that I'm a good girl who he loves, who gets all this. I'm like no one else. I'm not a whore like so many girls who beg for it. He knows I want it, but why don't I smile just a little bit more?

Deep in my head, the smart girl says, *This is crazy talk. If he has felt such pain, why does he do these things?* There could be an essay written on this subject.

"I had to tell a little story so we could be together," he says. "No love lost, right? You two hated each other anyway."

The words bounce off my taut, unfamiliar skin. "I don't see how it…helps."

"You don't?" He gives me a look like I'm stupid, then gets out of bed and yanks on his jeans. "Like I could keep coming in here at night. We had to get her out of the house. Now the nights are ours because she's dead asleep at my place. Out like a light. Meanwhile," he swats my leg, "you and I can be together."

He's grinning at me like this is an amazing thing.

I roll to my side, and the sheet feels strange beneath my hand. A covering for something else, maybe a cooling board.

He gives me a look while he zips up. "You need to loosen up, baby. Have some fun."

I guess because I am silent he glances over his shoulder at me, unsmiling with disappointment. The dark eyes are not what I thought they were, full of feeling. They are reflectors, processing emotion they must pretend to show.

The click of the door is soft as it was in '04, '05, '06, when Nelson ruled our roost, in the dead, endless middle of the Dark Ages of Nought.

He is gone. The house is dead. So are his insides. That is the black-and-white truth of it. I thought there was something real and warm there, but behind those eyes, only dust.

I lie there, barely breathing, but suddenly I'm alive, trembling with violence, imagining even though Sunny's nowhere near that he now curls his body like a scythe around her, whispering lies she wants to hear. No, he is gone, the roar of the bike in the driveway says so, and it rattles the foundations of the house.

So, so stupid I am to have trusted you.

Someone else has said something like this to me before. In a fog I try to think, head swimming outside my body: *Who?*

That why you hung around, did this thing?

The voice of Tanay Who No Longer Trusts Me.

I watch my arm dangle from my bed, inches away from the iPhone. I've dreamed picking it up several times in an attempt to call. But she who thinks I am after Andrew, she who knows I ruined her play, she will say along with everyone else, *You asked for it.*

Therefore I should not mourn Tanay. To her I am a liar; therefore it's worthless to present my evidence because Sunny thinks I'm one, too. But it is becoming clear to me, unfurling like a motherfucker, in fact, that no one, not a one, is who they say they are. Why should Tanay not think the same?

Shameful. I can never purge what's inside. Too much wrong for anyone to ever fix.

I put Michael on my stereo, and he tells me all about human nature, 128 times over.

I sleep, fitfully, and when I wake deep in darkness, I'm wise with the desperate and hopeless truth. My life the last six years has been one big retreat. Like the way the glaciers receded, dragging boulders that carved canyons, leaving behind a barren landscape. Like South Dakota, where the rocks suffer deep scratches and depressions. When I was twelve, Sunny dragged me there because she'd met some dude online. Her first rendezvous with this new prospect was to be at some prairie landmark.

We drove two days straight. As we pulled up to the site, a herd of bison stopped our car. We were trapped in a cloud of pawing, snorting, gnarled fur. Then I looked to my left and saw it: yellow, brown, black, gray, and orange striations lining what looked like the hugest rock quarry.

"What's that," I said.

And before Mother could answer, I thought, *That's me.*

Thirty seconds later, when she stopped gaping at the bison, she said, "The Badlands."

Memory says the guy didn't show. But the name stuck. I am always the Badlands. I am what the deep, cold horror left behind.

CHAPTER 33

THINK IT IS A THURSDAY, and that we are almost near July. I wander through the empty house, touching various dusty patches, writing my initials every place I can. WRD. Wendy Reported Dead. Wendy Runs Desperately. Wendy Rogue Daughter. I consider the fingers covered with dust, something outside me, some other girl's hands.

July will bring escape. That is how I know I can survive this. I have July 24, 2009. In London, there I'll speak. Across the sea, in the presence of Michael, I will know what to do. Refuse to go home and tell Grandma. On foreign soil, clutching passports, the Ugly Truth may be easier to take. Grandma hates things with blurry edges, and she's not too keen on sex. The Ugly Truth has both these elements. The Truth will show Grandma that the granddaughter lacks a personal border patrol. That she is tainted beyond words.

But if she does not believe—and if she cannot help—then I'll run. Live in Stratford-upon-Avon and serve as theater usher. Be a street waif, be a gamine for the glory of the Bard. My mind dances with crazy, roaming for possibility. *Outer space, Tanay. I did say outer space.*

I turn on the TV. I will seek a classic film, black-and-white coolness and cleanliness of a bygone era.

Sunny the news junkie has it set on CNN, where reporters salivate.

"Several media sources are reporting singer Michael Jackson has died. Jackson was rushed to the hospital this afternoon after going into cardiac arrest..."

It is about the sixth hour. There is a darkness over all the earth. Because the sun is blackened and the veil of all things I knew till now is rent.

I hit the floor, I peer up at a screen like my soothsayer. *Please tell me he is alive.*

He is not.

I sit for hours, sweating, watching the flashback montages—his chocolate-skinned '60s childhood, his '70s afro youth, and his '80s leather-clad adulthood—as networks strive to keep us there, singing his songs. I see his old self, slim and spinning, tight and twirling. *Michael!* My face—I cover it, hold it—it's been such stone of late, so if I weep, only the floor could say.

No London. No Michael. No London.

His body is in the morgue, about to be sealed in a coffin. And I am way past embalming here.

Each time I think of Shaye, of Cy, of Cindy, of Tanay, of Andrew, of Sunny, the ache dulls a little more, and the numbness takes hold. Each person is simply another in a long line of disappointers. This is what people do: lie, or leave.

And those who don't leave, they—Michael—are killed. The doctor he trusted, Murray, he did it. I know he looked at MJ's body, broken for us all, and said, "Put this man out of misery. Head him toward everlasting life." But the horror is, that while MJ slept, thinking himself safe to close his eyes, Murray got to make that call.

From where I lie flat on the floor, I hear myself say aloud, "Why, Michael, why?"

That's when I hear him speak.

Get on board, Wendy. Leave your worries behind.

The voice is breathless, high, and striving. Floating above, and meant only for me.

I answer:

O Michael, I'd catch that plane right now if I could. No more sleepless, no more empty. I hear you. And you hear me!

He says, *You've been waiting.*

Yes, I say, breathless.

Waiting for the question. Are you all right?

I nod. I could cry for joy. Yes, exactly: he knows!

Then he says: *I am with you, always.*

I rise to my knees. I bow my head.

O St. Michael: Your leaving this world has rocked mine. Your sacrifice has cleansed my soul.

And I hear him say, *Wendy, let me send him to the maws of Hell.*

I stand. Call me Crazytown, call me Wacko Wendy—really, please do. MJ's passing has got me understanding what really matters.

I must go to His land, and I must kneel at His grave.

CHAPTER 34

THAT NIGHT, AFTER I HAVE written all the Sorrowful Mysteries I can in honor of St. Michael, I hear Sunny and Shaye come in around 1:00 a.m. They are loud, and they are drunk. That's why she's forgotten her Very Important Rule.

With her asleep like the dead, Shaye comes in at 3:00 a.m. and unwraps a condom.

But now, this time, St. Michael is there. He hovers His huge rhinestone wings, tremors His sequined jacket, and flashes His silver epaulets over every horrific thing. He is plastered to the ceiling with a vast, eternal frown.

So as Shaye descends, I hear me speak. Small, thin voice, but it is there.

"No."

"Oh, so you want to play that game?" Voice unsmiling. The wrapper crackles while he leans on an elbow, ripping it open.

As he starts to straddle me, I ball up, elbows out, jabbing him in the face.

"Ow!" He sits up, rubbing his jaw. "What the hell?"

"St. Michael won't like this."

"What?"

"St. Michael. He's watching."

Shaye's head whips around, surveying the room. "What—who?"

"Sssh!" I say, voice stronger. "He hates demons."

"Jesus Christ." He peers at me in the gloom. "Michael Jackson?"

My voice echoes in my head like it's a vault. "My Lord and Savior."

"Wendy, what the fuck. Stop this shit."

"It's my doom. Bloodstains. Everywhere."

A silence pricked with rhinestone sharpness, with jagged, ice-pick glitter. "Wha-a-a-at?" He retreats an inch.

"Right here. In this bedroom." *Dadadadum, dadadadum—* St. Michael's heartbeat is with me always.

"You're a goddamn freak." But he doesn't sound too sure of himself. He crawls off the bed. "I'm too tired for this shit."

He is zipping up, he is going, he is at the door—

I call, "Farewell, smoothest of criminals."

He freezes in the doorway. But he doesn't turn. He starts up again, sure like a machine, moving through the frame, rounding the corner. Gone.

In the silence, my heart ticks to life. *Thud, thud, thud.* Slow and steady. Sure.

I rise and hit the floor, knees bruising with joy.

O St. Michael, prince of heavenly hosts,
thrust into hell this Satan...

Then in the dead of this house, I hear the front door slam, I hear the motorcycle roar to life, and I vomit all over the knotty pine floor.

CHAPTER 35

THE NEXT MORNING, WHEN I think I've scoured away the last of the stench, Sunny Revere busts into my room with a cat carrier. She is all chipper moving the cat box and water dish back into my room like she used to do back in San Francisco. She shuts the door and unzips the carrier.

Inside, cowering against the back end, is an orange kitten with two huge ears sprouting from a tiny head, crusty little nostrils, and yellow eyes big as moons. Suddenly, my throat is thick. The edges of my eyes hurt. Not yet another creature just passing through.

"He'll come out eventually." Sunny is in seventh heaven, perhaps chatting with a hovering cat angel, because she never looks at me. Not once. She's granted salvation to another of Gaia's critters, so her work here is done. She sails out. The first days of a kitten's confinement will once again be supervised by me.

"We're going to Asheville," she yells through the door, and then a minute later, I hear the front door slam.

I feel the cat's eyes boring into me. Then I hear a tubercular, wet sneeze. He shakes his head like it rearranged brain matter.

I sit down outside his carrier and place my fingertips at the threshold. After a minute, he approaches and sniffs. Then he darts back inside.

"Strike and retreat," I tell him. "Believe me, I understand."

He stays in his paranoid crouch so long, I give up. I pour him some organic, all-natural, chicken-and-cranberry-pea food in his dish and then seek my own fare from the kitchen. The cupboards are empty. In the fridge sits a decaying avocado and organic pomegranate juice past its due date. There are no longer signs of Shaye and his solicitousness—his invasive hospitality within this house. That is because as St. Michael says, *I work all things to the good.* He has taught me that if I say thanks 16 times every 16 minutes, goodness will be revealed. Like the remembrance that I have Grandma's cash stash. Food is forthcoming. *All things to the good.*

Asheville means they've left for the first leg of Deanna's tour, which could mean five or more days without them before her CD release part here in Millboro, on the Fourth. They have rented a van to haul all kinds of Deanna swag and have left the Mirage and the bike. But the people, the perishable and needless people they are gone. *All things to the good.*

I am starving, but I cannot leave the house yet. A slice of the knife brings clean, and now, now I have my sign from St. Michael, words breathing in my ear: *All is of the ether. There is naught but spirit, and I am That. Make the pilgrimage.* Therefore, we will make all things ready.

His funeral is Tuesday, July 7—enough time, depending on my mode of transport, to make it there—but I have no illusions I will be one of millions once again to secure a ticket. That is too much luck, even with the blessings of MJ. All that matters is the kneeling and time alone with Him. Far away from here. Therefore, make ready.

I inscribe The List That Giveth Consolation.

1) Maps

2) Money

3) Birth certificate, California provisional driver's permit, and Social Security card

4) Music

5) Duffel of retro clothes

6) Keys to the Mirage

A firm, cold weight in my hand. So much more surety there to two tons of metal than the silly Bible Andrew gave me. Two tons. That's a lot of metal hurtling in my hands down Highway 40, only MJ knows how many days, 2516.79 miles to be exact. Driving without a real license doesn't scare me. It's the driving alone.

It's times like these, heart-shaking times, that I smack my cheek. I knew yesterday—June 25, 2009—that I beheld a great quake, where the sun blackened like sackcloth of hair, when the moon became as blood. Names of past people, ones I thought Good, no longer are worth a mention. There is nothing but spirit and ether. Nevermore shall anything ever be solid or liquid again. I must go it alone, and I'll be safe with Michael. The lightning of his leonine heart will strike anytime—did not the other night prove it?—and drive away all serpents. He will carry me through all fires, wrap me in his healing salves, and blanket me in his light.

Now begins my first act of devotion. *A sacred purge as you pack,* He has said. *Leave no trace.* I nod. *In the Name of MJ...*I make the sign of the cross—X marks the spot on your heart, followed by a moonwalk slide across the throat—*Amen. O MJ, prince of heavenly hosts, turn the course of my life and thrust into hell this Satan, who prowls about the world seeking the ruin of souls.*

I press my back against the door and survey my dark little domain. The knotty pine, the hardwood floors, all 100 percent likely in 1982. But the rest, all my worldly goods? Nineties and Noughts.

Nothing new comes with. Everything must go. iPhone. Laptop. Dri-FIT workout shirts, TV/DVD player, Sour Patch

Kids Chillerz, Snickers Fun Size. Anything made in China. MJ must have it so.

I head to the kitchen and grab a bunch of garbage bags.

When they are full, and the room is empty save for my vintage clothes and CDs, I start to drag the bags out.

Wait: were CDs around in '82? Yes, but Mother's told me people didn't buy them en masse till the mid-'80s. So they're not vintage. They're not really real.

I stand up and grab every single CD. All these, save *Thriller* and *Off the Wall,* they must go. Purge yet again, then go forth and find the relics. I'm talking vinyl only, and 1982 or prior— or nothing. It's like Grandma says: *Sometimes you have to pull out the haircloth.* Sacrifices must be made for righteousness. Plus, any work MJ did post-*Thriller* is not his finest.

I haul the bags to Sunny Revere's room and block her door with detritus.

I hear His voice again.

Go downtown, my child, to Album Alley. Find the record and its player.

I take the EZ Rider to the doorstep of Album Alley. The window display is empty, laced with tendrils of dust. Only a handmade sign tilts there. GOING OUT OF BUSINESS.

Inside, The Curmudgeon hunches in the same position where I last left him.

I say, "Do you sell record players?"

"What's that?" He squints like I'm speaking Mandarin.

"Record players. Turntables. Do you sell them?"

He snaps, "Do I look like I sell them?"

I say, "You're the only one with LPs on a street gone straight to hell."

He snorts like I might have a speck of sense. "I've got something. Got to get rid of it anyway." He limps to the back of this place narrow as a closet and ducks through a short door.

A fairylike, ethereal voice soars above my head, like glistening dust pouring from those ancient speakers. A woman sings about silence swooping down, rays and gray, a kiss. About giving your heart away.

The Cur comes back with a small white suitcase. He slams it on his counter littered with receipts and trash.

Glory be to MJ. This little suitcase is a record player bearing a slick photo of my King, my Lord of Lords, circa 1984, sporting yellow satin vest, bow tie, and jeri curl! *Lo, the brown skin warm as liquid Godiva! There, the painted Egyptian eyes, solemn with buried pain! The red script of His name signed across His image like an oath! O my MJ, is this is a sign or what?* This is some serious vintage.

I pull bills from my jeans but The Cur waves me off. "Someone gave it to me as a joke. I was about to toss it."

"Thank you." I put my money back, then cradle the record player in my arms like a newborn. "Do you happen to have *Thriller* and *Off the Wall* on vinyl?"

He walks a few steps to the Rock & Pop section and pulls two LPs in crinkly plastic. "$3.99, but you can bet your ass I could charge you twenty instead." He shrugs. "Wish his music died with him."

He tosses the albums on top of the player; *Thriller* cuffs me in the chin, but it hurts so good.

I free a hand and pull out forty bucks. He refuses to take it. "The man is dead," he says. If craggy brows could look remorseful, his do.

I can't believe this fortune. MJ's truly in charge. How else could I be blessed with all these relics? I won't stop praying to Him—ever!

"So," he snaps, "why do you listen to this shit?"

"It's spiritual."

That freezes his sneer. "You want spiritual?" he snaps. "I'll show you spiritual."

He stomps around the store, slinging CDs into a box. After a while, he brings me a box full. I peer in: *#1 Record* by Big Star, *Pet Sounds* by The Beach Boys, *Road to Ruin* by the Ramones. More names I've never heard: Booker T and the MGs. Neil Diamond. Judee Sill. Queen. Marvin Gaye. Nick Drake. Vic Chestnutt. Joni Mitchell. Roky Erickson.

"There's your teenage symphonies to God," he says.

"Thank you." I don't know what he means. And how do I tell him I don't do CDs anymore?

"What's wrong?"

"I only do vinyl now."

"You have to pull them, then. I don't have but a few of these."

I hesitate, but he seems serious. So I wander around the store figuring out what genre the Ramones and Beach Boys are. It takes me a good while, because he won't help at all. I stack my stash of vinyl—12 LPs, since I can't find the rest.

When I come back to his counter, I say, "If you were to choose bluesy, romantic music for Southside Chicago, 1959, in an African-American neighborhood, would you suggest Motown? Supremes and Jackson 5?"

He looks disgusted. "1959? Hell no. The Supremes didn't have a record till '62 and the Jacksons, '69. Who the hell told you that?" He snorts. "You want Jesse Belvin. Rufus and Carla. Stax Records, all the way."

I glance down at MJ. *See? Every word Shaye ever said was a lie.*

MJ's eyes bore back into mine with great understanding.

I say, "Thank you very much." I start for the door, balancing my stash.

Behind me he says, "You still hang with that Shaye Tann?"

I turn, heart thudding. "No."

He snorts. "Smarter than you look. His client—her parents—they just jacked up my rent."

"The Faires?"

"Yeah, maybe this place will be her sweet sixteen gift. Hell, let her open another boutique. The whole damn world's gone digital; tweak her voice, put her out for sale." His face is getting red, which is a little scary. "I don't have time to shoot the shit."

I leave. I step outside into the dangerous world, where Dee's crew could still be lurking, where Dee's family of landlord wolves could be circling, while I carry these bona fide relics, precious as the finger of St. Thomas or the head of St. Catherine. Grandma says she saw it in Siena, Italy once—St. Catherine's head. When one lives life as a target, relics could be the first casualty.

The cars outside my bus are all from a past era. I see an '80s Camaro, an ancient VW Rabbit, a vintage '60s Mustang, a rusty old '70s Honda. I doze and daydream of me in a car, maybe a DeLorean, dark and sleek plus space-age door, popping open to admit Tanay when I cruise by her home. We race down a long highway, "Beat It" blasting from every speaker, shaking our lungs. We are headed only MJ knows where. Perhaps we'll drive ourselves right off the Florida Keys into azure oblivion.

I return to the Passive Solar, to my pristine room, scrubbed clean of filth, and place the record player near the outlet by my bed. Then I place the LPs carefully onto the bed.

I open the player. It's pristine and virginal: a warm cream-colored base with a plastic, raised disc where you set the LP. Like a place setting with the arm and its needle: the disc = plate; the arm, curved fork. A sacred meal. *This is my body, broken for you.*

All is well. I can't believe this providence. How He comes through every time. It's still a little scary when His spirit speaks to me.

I feel a cold wet nose on my ankle. I jump. A scrambling of nails on wood—Strike and Retreat dashing back to the safety of his carrier. I smile. "Dude, it's okay," I say. "MJ's in the house."

I unwind the long white cord and plug it into the wall. Then I unsheathe *Thriller* from its plastic. The gatefold cover opens to Michael of the angelic white suit, a tamed tiger cub scrambling over his shoulder. I show it to Strike, unblinking yellow eyes in his den, then prop the cover on my bed against the wall so MJ's grave visage can watch everything.

I slip the paper off the disc. I've never held a record before. I love the perfection of concentric rings expanding outward. I love the sweet, dry smell.

I place it delicately on the raised surface of the player. I twist the On/Off button, and the record starts to spin. My heart starts to thud. There's a dial on the base I can set to a mysterious 45 or 33 1/3. Which one? I remember Grandma showing me her Johnny Mathis collection of 45s and pulling out a stack of LPs the size of salad plates. This record is bigger, so why isn't there like a 55 or 65 setting? 33 1/3 it must be.

Now what? Won't it scratch to place a needle on a spinning disc? But it seems wrong to start it with the needle already on. For a second—but only a second—I wish Sunny Revere were here. I must do this alone and somehow not risk sacrilege.

I lift the arm, slowly, slowly, and set the needle down gently at the very edge of the spinning disc. Staticky sounds, like an old radio spitting out signals from another universe. The LP ripples, a wave while it spins. Then, the staccato beat of drums: St. Michael's "da-da-da-da-dum"—

I stand dead center in the room, letting this sound warm as syrup coat me. Everything that angers and singes, everything that panics and fears, now slows and cools like lava in the face of such beauty. There are no forgetful mothers and no forgettable daughters in this realm I enter. No boys or men where eyes are dull with need and numb to feeling. It's as if

MJ's voice melted, straight chocolate, right onto this disc. Sure, there's some crackling foil, the occasional nut to interrupt the smooth...but lo, this is His body!

I don't dance; in fact, I really can't. But St. MJ, he demands it.

Strike and Retreat peers up at me spinning madly. He keeps vigil through the mesh of his carrier, his snake eyes eclipsed with black.

CHAPTER 36

O N THE SECOND DAY AFTER, the Second Day of Freedom, and the Day I Depart, the doorbell rings at 9:00 a.m. I am woken from a blissful sleep, Strike nestled against my stomach, dreaming of the memorial service and St. Michael—His face incandescent and His robes so white, they hurt my eyes. I open the front door to Grandma, studded with pearls and fastened into a red silk suit.

She glides by me with raised eyebrows. You don't enter places wearing a $1,000 suit, looking like old Kate, and not get what you want. I stand in the hallway while she does a whirlwind inspection of the premises. Knowing her, she could be here five minutes, so might as well keep vigil by the door and act like nothing's wrong. I know my packed duffel with its small parcel of worldly goods sits safe beneath my bed, no doubt guarded by a cowering Strike.

Though I'm wearing naught but the black Keds, sweats, and hoodie I slept in, she comes back and grabs my elbow with a swift movement toward the Mercedes. Not a word, not a word till we're strapped into the leather front seats and zooming our way into downtown Steeple Mount toward The Rose Room, a ladies' lunch and tea place Grandma practically lives at when she's not hiding out in the tropics.

As we exit the car, Grandma snaps, "And where does your mother happen to be today?"

"You know how it goes." It's hard to speak, maybe because I'm still asleep, or maybe because the light of day outside my room brings nausea and fear one must fight with prayer and forcible will. "A new guy shows up, they tour the town, things happen—"

"Happen my foot. We're responsible for every breath."

Sometimes I think Grandma has more than a hunch what went down in my little life long ago. But remember, she doesn't do excuses. Certainly not the Shaye, can't-help-myself kind.

Inside The Rose Room, there's dark pink everywhere like decaying bubblegum and a scary preponderance of fluffy aprons and Victorian lace caps. I stand out like a big black thumb. But Grandma loves this old-lady speakeasy that lets matriarchs break the half-hearted smoking laws. We're silent over black tea and iced scones.

"So I suppose London is off," Grandma says, "now that your hero has departed this Earth."

I sip tea. It's bitter on my tongue but comforting—not unlike the presence of Grandma. I shall call her from L.A., from a stranger's cell or one of the last pay phones, and assure her that though I leave no trace, I am indeed safe.

"Terrible way to die," she's saying. "Elvis, Marilyn, all of them. Complete waste of talent." I feel The Stare. This look has followed me so long, seeking my insides like I need scrubbing with her Brillo pads and Clorox. I return the favor at the pink peonies on this tablecloth vomiting phallic innards.

She snaps, like I ought to give her tears: "Well, you must be sad!"

"Yes."

"I suppose St. Thomas wouldn't suit you," she says, fumbling with her cigarettes. "Warmer than London. Blasted place is always raining."

Her dry fingertips struggle with the extraction. What a

scene might it be should I, the teen, lean forward and assist with her extinction. Does she really want me with her in St. Thomas? No, of course not. Let's try to picture—try very hard—my pasty-white pelt turning the color of burnt toast on some Caribbean beach. The image fades immediately. There are too many marks, mostly on arms, but low enough on inner thighs that swimwear will never work. All my sick handiwork made visible. No: I will stroll L.A. beaches instead, fully clothed.

"No," I say. "But thank you very much."

She drops the pack and snaps, "Why have you purged your room?"

Heart thuds, several times hard. "I've gone retro."

Grandma grabs my wrist when I replace the cup. She shoves up my sleeve. "What is this?" She points to the three thick scratches on the inside of my wrist, pink around the edges, scabbing over.

Count to 16. Naught but a trinity of scars, Grandma. *This is my body, broken for you.* Grandma should understand, even if it's not for her skinny guy on a block of wood or a magic wafer held by an old man.

I say, "I was playing with one of Sunny's cats."

She lets me go, rolls her eyes, and says, "Mass time. Be ready Saturday at four-thirty. Wear a skirt. None of this *Addams Family* garb."

Sweet relief. She won't investigate further. Act like all is calm, all is bright, and our family is what it is—its normal level of unstated crazy. "Sure, but Sunny won't let me. She hates The Church."

"She hates commitment. You, on the other hand, have something of me in you."

"I know, right. The only thing Sunny commits to is garlic."

"You *are* my granddaughter." She looks pleased, pulls a

cigarette with ease, and finally lights up. I see the slow fade and bleed of lipstick into the lines around her lips as she inhales. I sip more tea; I've eluded the trap.

"Have you read that book I gave you?" she says.

"Yes, thank you." It, the rosaries, and Andrew's Bible have actually survived The Purge and sit at the bottom of my duffel. It is dangerous to destroy other cultures' sacred relics; it might bring bad juju, and I will risk nothing of the sort before the Great Journey. Then I remember something, and it swirls along in my head with Shaye and Nelson. I say idly, breaking the scone into gravelly fragments, "I remember you said it helped you, that you prayed every night to get out of that house." I think of the photo of the skinny '50s Grandma with the troubled expression.

Grandma gives me a sharp glance. "Drunks say a lot of things." A beat. "Thank God I'm not that anymore."

The scone is dust in my hands. I'm afraid to look up.

She says, "Wendy. I've quit drinking and I'm in AA."

Her face is open and unshielded in a way I've never seen before. And suddenly, from the depths, something surges, and I don't know why but I want to sob. Maybe because for a second I can see how Grandma might have been all these years—kinder, calmer. Clear. A grandmother soft with forgiving love.

"That's great," I croak. Thank MJ my face is a plaster cast, I'm waxen, I'm my beautiful MJ's embalmed body—"Congratulations."

"Good." She's nodding. "Knew you wouldn't make a fuss." She inhales her cigarette like tasting it for the first time.

Maybe if I'm good—dress demure, act normal—Grandma might agree to let me stay over a night, or two, even three. Maybe departure is stupid as hell, and I have right here in my own background a chance to be safe—

"God only gives out occasional miracles," she is saying.

"And believe me, they're random. For fifty-five years, booze was my best friend, and now God decides to give me willpower at seventy." She peers at me, and nerves ignite. "You have to hang on by your fingernails in this life, Wendy. Scratch, bite, and fight. There's no free lunch." Her look says she reads between my lines. "So you have a terrible mother. No reason to give up."

Coming to live with her would be construed as giving up. I see how it is. I manage to say, "I have not given up."

"Then what do you call this—this slicing yourself!"

"It's not—sometimes I—never mind!" I want to rip this tablecloth—now I want to send shards of pink crockery flying—

"Sometimes what?"

"It's hard to feel!"

"Hard to feel? You feel when life smacks you in the face."

I hide my sigh and count furiously every tendril of ivy writhing on the wall behind her head. Grandma sips her oolong, I pretend to finish my Earl Grey, and I ask MJ to please airlift me out of here. But He doesn't, so Grandma snaps, "Well, it's worse than I thought then. I have a zombie for a granddaughter." She destroys her cigarette in the teacup saucer. "Wear something presentable Saturday. And wash your hair."

Conversation over. For a split second, I thought she looked worried enough I could tell her things...But no. Grandma surely hates every one of Sunny's boyfriends, but all she's ever done is frown, growl, or snort, while the mad carousel of life with Sunny Revere spins faster and faster, till the calliope crashes to the ground. All I know is right at this moment, I'm having a lot of anxious thoughts about sharp, cold things that will split my seams to relief.

In the car, back home in the driveway, she seems remorseful. She makes me wait while she lights another cigarette.

"Has she run him off yet—the latest one?" she says, then has a coughing fit.

I say when she is done, "No." I open the door, my eyes counting the inches of the vole tunnels in our lawn. Our lawn looks like a surface about to rupture, a quake on its way.

"Wendy," she calls as I walk away. "Saturday!"

Funny how though it's summer, the ash and dust of ancient autumn still lingers here. This is a house that's never known a leaf blower, and Sunny will never rake. All I hear is the rustle of dry, dead leaves across our covered path, swirling near the scratched red door, scattered by the wind's invisible hand.

CHAPTER 37

Inside the Passive Solar, I see a message blinking on the machine.

"Wendy." It's Tanay. Her voice, light years away, sounds so very strange. "Hey. I looked your mom up since you don't answer your phone." Her voice sounds richer, in fact—perhaps tempered by the rarer air within this room—the presence of St. Michael, listening close. "Sorry about Michael Jackson, girl."

A prickle of life within the heart region.

"Oh, hey, I got a B+ on that paper. Best I ever got in that damn class. I got a C- overall, but it don't matter anymore. Okay, then. Bye."

My hand reaches for the landline—the wires, cables, poles shooting across the state that might ground us together. I snatch that hand back.

If I told her my truth, what could she do?

Only St. Michael could ever get it.

She'll think I'm crazy. I think of 16 ways to explain the events of the last weeks and the need for St. Michael. How do you explain The Voice that's always been in my head, that I used to think was half-Wendy, conscience and wisdom, but maybe always has been MJ, the Voice of Trust and Reason? Sometimes you just know when you're being spoken to; no doubt she's heard some Christian chatter about this very thing. She calls it Jesus; I call it MJ. We're all capable of losing our minds to a greater power.

I turn around and around, taking in all of the Passive Solar where He hovers now. All I see is a stagnant reign of furniture collecting dust and the corners, mold, while Mother's favorite channel plays on and on. *Michael, speak to me!* I'm spinning, whirling, speeding past light, but He is silent. He hates this place.

It rises up within me, sharp and sure and strong. *Leave, tonight.*

I descend on my room and retrieve my duffel. I split it open and count my worldly goods once again. *You can do this. Count your way to sure. Those 2516.79 miles must begin at night and stay mostly at night, when I won't be noticed and look underage to Shayes astride their Harleys and marauding men high up in trucks leering down. The horror.*

I put my head between my knees. This house has no air— it's a humid blanket, pressing down. And if I go outside—the kudzu trees still sleep, weighed down. Obscene, pendulous webs spun by some mysterious insect now droop from the trees, too, tangling up with the vines. Summer here, the cruel summer, will forever be the horror of his body, the daily threat of being pinned—

—Something slams my chest so hard I think my heart has stopped. I fall toward the bed. I'll never be touched by anyone again, I'll never breathe again. Because I will die right now. Breathe! Count! Breathe!

I hear a squeak. I feel Strike burrow into my side, like he's found the Ultimate Source of Warmth. He immediately goes to sleep. His deep, sunny orange is a small pulsing circle of light in this dim room. He smells like softness. His purring soothes, a chugging chant, a feline psalm to sleep. His sermon: when in doubt, take a nap.

We lie there till my breathing slows to 8 inhalations per minute.

When I'm calmer, I deposit Strike on my pillow and go straight to the record player. I open it to the find The List That Giveth Consolation. Check, check, check, check: all is ready, all is calm, all is bright.

I twist on my record player and *Thriller* starts to spin. "Wanna Be Startin' Somethin'" ba-da-da-da-dums, to be followed by "The Girl is Mine," to be followed by...Did you know, if you grab a needle off a record, it can leave a scratch? If you rip a CD from its case or drop it, there might be a scratch, but it's harder to do. But iTunes or other MP3s, you can stop and start anywhere. You can go off and do something else, you can be doing a thousand things at once and only half-listening. But if I put *Thriller* on the player, it's more of a commitment.

Suddenly, I see myself as if poised on an ethereal timeline, part of a chain of a million teens stretching back through the ages, at least fifty years. Sitting breathless before their record players, waiting, waiting, for the next song. Willing to listen again, as many times as needed.

Commitment is nice. I grab The List, and we count some more.

CHAPTER 38

A T THIS WITCHING HOUR OF 11:00 p.m., I drive slowly and wisely toward Tanay, my life stowed in the trunk. I hope it's too late, that I will see naught but a darkened house, because it's too hard to say goodbye.

Better to count my way there.

- Maps, money, ID? *1, 2, 3.*
- Duffel of retro clothes? *4.*
- Albums and record player? *5, 6.*
- Grandma's pink rosary, Andrew's Bible, and *Our Friends the Saints*? *7, 8, 9.*
- My journal and its body of evidence? *10.*
- Keys to the Mirage? *11.*
- Food and water set out in my room for Strike? *12 and 13...*

May Sunny not forget him while I am gone...may he be adopted out to a good family.

No.

At the next light, I make a U-turn and head back to the Passive Solar, just slightly over the speed limit.

I race back inside the house. I find him hiding beneath my comforter. *Squeak, squeak, squeak.* I bring him in his carrier, along with the bag of food, bowls, and on the second trip, his box and litter.

Strike and Retreat? *14.*

When I get back in the driver's seat, I grip the steering wheel. 15 is the car. But I can't get to 16. Now I'm going to be sick. I make myself look back at the house again.

When Joe Jackson got into financial trouble, he needed a buyer for the Encino estate. His son stepped up. And what did MJ do? Demolished the thing. Reduced each horrific memory to dust and ash. Erected a delightful Tudor mansion in its stead.

Perhaps some day with Tony or Pulitzer in hand, I'll return to this abode, and do the very same. Erect in the two front windows of the Passive Solar a sign. It will be my first act of demolition. One poster for each window, mammoth words to be read from hundreds of feet.

A GIRL WAS MOLESTED HERE!

Let that dream serve as 16.

As I drive, senses flooded by the garlic and patchouli scent of this car that Sunny Revere doesn't know is in motion, St. Michael sings from the 1991 cassette player of the Mirage Colt how something has begun, how I myself have started it. Dark and empty streets open before me. St. Michael makes all my paths straight.

I pull up in front of Tanay's house. And there she is, sitting on her front step in a black silk robe, her hair standing on end, wrapped with a red bandanna.

It's yet another sign.

I park behind a rust-colored Cadillac in the driveway. I cut the engine and get out. The metallic chatter of cicadas hits my ears in a roar; everywhere, nothing but that fortress of securing trees.

We contemplate each other. All the way here, I've been working up the courage to face Ms. Sadie. But here sits Tanay by herself, like a gift.

She eyes me, top to bottom—black pants, white shirt, red jacket. She says, "Something tells me you're leaving and not coming back."

My throat chokes with solid tears; I will them away. I can't meet those eyes, the open door I saw the day we first talked. I tell the ground, "Perhaps."

"Hmm." She scans me for crazy. "Hold on. Let me get my cigarettes."

She disappears inside and comes back with her cigarettes. We sit on her front step.

She lights up. She smokes. I think of 1, 2, 3, 100 ways to say what else has happened since we last spoke, but nothing comes out.

"Where you going?" she says.

"California."

She gestures at the car. "Your mom's cool with it?"

"Sunny is…extremely busy right now." I turn my face from Tanay's stare. "I doubt she'll miss me."

Several beats; I can feel her wheels turn with too much knowing. Damn that third eye. "Wendy. That time in the hall: was Andrew praying over you?"

I nod.

"Why? Did something bad happen?"

Time has slowed to long, cold seconds—funny how ice cold in this thick heat—and I can't feel my body anymore. My hands in front of me look like someone else's.

"He—the guy," I begin, and my throat clogs. "The boyfriend. Things got—crazy."

In the quiet I can feel her listening close, every inch of her present. And on my numb body, a slight reflection of that warmth, like sun. Like some day I might throb again with heat, nerve, feeling.

Her voice is very still as she says, "Crazy like…he hits you?"

"Worse," I croak.

Around us the crickets surge, struck with alarm.

I say, "She won't listen." I shrug—light and casual, like my body's a loose thing. "This always happens."

"Always?" I can see Tanay's hand without the cigarette clutch her knee; I don't dare look at her face. Long silence. I look up. She's frowning. "I don't get it."

"She doesn't...I don't know, she can't...But I mean, I didn't—I guess I didn't try very hard."

"To do what?"

"I don't know. Stop it?"

Tanay inhales deeply, shaking her head. She expels a long, hard stream of smoke. "It's not about you trying. It's about him not trying anything."

She casts her cigarette away, a jerk of anger, and we watch the red end glow and throb on the ground. She says, "The way I see it, you've got to go."

My heart rings with this endorsement, and my head spins.

She stands up. "All right then. Give me a minute."

She disappears inside the house.

Um, did she just say she was coming?

It's a whole fifteen minutes of waiting, and I'm getting more than anxious. Ms. Sadie is too close, and Sunny and Shaye, not far enough away. On a whim, they could be driving home this very second, raiding the house for evidence, noting the car's MIA. Informing authorities.

But finally Tanay comes out with a huge suitcase. She drags it down the walk and opens the trunk of the Cadillac.

I hiss, "What're you doing?"

"We ain't taking that," she says, jerking her head at the Mirage. "P.O.S."

"What do you call this?" I point at hers.

"Yeah, it's a hoop-dee, but it's a damn tank. Nobody's going to kill us while we're up in here." She grunts as she lifts and shoves her case in. "They took Granmama's license anyway." Then she glares at me with a fierce mama look. "You're still fifteen, right? Meanwhile, I got my license."

I don't mention that they'll probably take hers, too, for this little stunt. Instead I pull my duffel out of the Mirage and put it into Tanay's trunk. Then I bring out Strike.

"Awwww." Tanay grabs him. He scrambles for a second, but she's rubbing him right, and now he's got orange fur all over her tank top. His eyes get sleepy with the joy of being scratched. I load his box, litter, and cat food in the trunk. Strike in his carrier gets the back seat.

Tanay tells me to park the Mirage a ways down the street, near an empty house for sale. I do so and leave the keys in the Mirage's ignition. For a brief second I see Sunny Revere run screaming through the streets how her car's been stolen. Funny I can't see the same scene when it comes to me.

I come back to her in the driveway, and we open the doors of the Caddy. And freeze when the front door bangs behind us.

"Who that?" It's Granmama, on the front step, peering across the yard.

Tanay puts a finger on her lips, then calls, "Me, Granmama. I got to go to the Wal-Mart."

"All right, then. Don't stop for nobody."

"Yes, ma'am."

That was easy. I want to ask Tanay how often she takes off at 11:00 p.m. solo for some shopping, how she is daring to defy that matriarchy within, but no time to plumb this mystery. I get in the passenger seat, Tanay gets in the driver's, and holds her hand up to stop me shutting the door. She cranks up the tank. We ease down the driveway, my door hanging open. Once the engine roars like a 747, I close it.

She says, "You got a map? Gas money?"

I look at her. "I've got everything I need."

We pull off into the night.

CHAPTER 39

As we merge onto Highway 40, Tanay says, "What's the plan?"

"L.A. in three days."

"Girl, are you serious? Isn't it like halfway across the world?"

"37 hours, 59 minutes, 2516.79 miles."

"Shoot, three days? You're crazy."

"Okay, five, then. The service is Tuesday the 7th." Being anywhere near Michael to honor Him, even hovering outside the Staples Center, the beauty of it grips me like a vise.

She grabs the map from my hand, a crackle of paper, and waves it in the air. "What's this?" She laughs. "I got GPS on my phone."

I snatch the map back and recite cities like pearls on a string—a beautiful itinerary toward MJ. "Asheville, Knoxville, Nashville, Memphis—"

"—Damn, Texas? I always wanted to eat me a big-ass steak."

"We're not sight seeing this round."

Tanay punches the map and it crumples on me. "We got to stop sometime! Let's have some fun!"

I smooth out the map. "I'm not sure how one defines fun."

Tanay laughs. "Girl, can we pleeeease put some miles between you and the nerd?"

"I'll do my best." I smile. Tanay is with me. I don't have to do this alone, thanks to St. Michael, all good and deserving of all my love.

"He sure is quiet," Tanay says, glancing over her shoulder at Strike who cowers in his carrier.

"He knows how to go underground."

She is silent a full minute, which makes me look up. She says: "Is that a metaphor?"

Over heart thuds, I say, "Maybe."

More quiet. Then: "Wonder how long till Mama puts the police on us."

"Huh?"

"What, you think she's going to sit around? Her ass'll go Amber Alert on us. We got a cousin who's police—"

"What—she can't call anybody!"

"You try telling her what to do."

I pound the dash. "If she'll call the police, why'd you come? Pull over!"

"Don't worry, I'll calm her down—"

"I said pull over!"

"Damn." Tanay speeds up. "You need to calm your shit."

"No police!" I yell. "They'll drag me home and—" The fear slams my chest so hard this time, I'm choking, my head and chest will explode, and Tanay's voice comes like a thin cry far away—"Wendy, you okay, Wendy?"—while blackness seeps in.

When I come to, Tanay's got my head pressed between my legs and thumps my back. "Come on, girl, stay with me!"

I sit up, chest heaving. She stares at me with relief. "You scared the shit out of me."

"Sorry," I gasp.

I see we're parked on the shoulder. An occasional car whizzes by in the darkness.

"Listen," she says. "I'll call her when she gets up. I'll explain everything. It's not like I'm not coming back. She'll whup my ass, but long as she knows where I am, it'll be all right."

I shake my head. Everything has changed now. "We have

to get through Tennessee in the next ten," I say. I rip open my travel wallet and hand her a twenty. "We're low on gas."

Tanay doesn't argue and turns the key. In the ensuing silence, I make a million guesses as to what she's thinking: how I'm beyond Mushi crazy, or maybe how pitiful it is Wendy is scared to go home.

We pull off on the next exit and into the parking lot of a BP. At the pump I hand her a second twenty, but she shakes her head, keeping her palm open, and I fish out another. Half my cash stash will get guzzled by this '90s relic.

No one looks twice at us as we wander through the convenience store and buy turkey jerky (me), pork rinds (Tanay), Chex Mix (me), and York Peppermint Patties (Tanay). I purchase a bright red wrinkled hot dog that's no doubt been a resident of its rotisserie more than a year. *Take that, Mother; to hell with my health.* It tastes heavenly to me.

Back inside the car, I know I must make this fun: Tanay says I need to have some fun. I dive into the back seat and find *Thriller* in my stash. Tanay speeds us out of the station at a dangerous clip. She squeals around the corner onto the bypass, then takes the ramp onto 40 like Nascar. I slip the CD into the stereo; track 5—we need track 5.

Gongs blast our ears, sonorous and deadly; drums kick in; sirens wail. We are invincible. Guitars churn, slam our brains—two of them, bass and lead doubling the riff. *Get out—get lost—beat it—don't you demons ever come near again.* St. Michael's army, on the march—

"So what he found was," –Tanay yells over the music, cutting into my thoughts as the speedometer hits 70, "—was, you know, some snobby Miss Thing from a New York prep school. Just moved down here looking all Halle Berry high and mighty." She sighs. "Mushi gave me a call and said get your ass over to the movies, you got to see who he's with. So I drive over and what do I see but the two of them walking inside."

A moment of silence for the betrayals of men. "Is she a Christian?"

Tanay sighs. "Who the hell knows. With her color, she could walk the streets and he won't care."

"Now he's got somebody to save."

"Ha! True that."

The memory of Andrew speaking prayers over me and handing me a Bible beats in my head like a kick drum. I want so very bad to call him a Christian creeper, toss his Bible out the window, but his apologetic face returns, hovering in my head. I say, "You know, he tracked me down because he wanted me to tell you—"

"There's nothing to tell," she snaps, that cold Tanay I do not want to see again. She glares through the windshield. "He can beg till kingdom come, I won't listen. He and his goddamn purity ring ain't worth shit."

I shrug like I could care less, but I don't know why, something still eats at me. I'm not sure why a high-and-mighty prep school girl would go around with a boy from the 'hood— or why Mushi's word would be worth two cents.

"Another reason to get the hell out." Tanay presses the gas, and we lurch forward. "You showed up at the right time."

"If Andrew's reason number one, what's number two?"

"Mama. She's got the wrath of God since my grades came. Bs, Cs, and a D. Now that AP score's coming and it won't be pretty." She dives a hand into her purse and taps a cigarette out into her lap. "Mushi was right. My ass will never measure up."

"Your ass won't live long with that habit."

"Don't you preach." She lights up.

"Why do you listen to Mushi?"

Silence. A long drag, and the car fills with a fog of smoke, acrid but somehow comforting. "Her and most of my friends since kindergarten— now they got babies, they're in summer school, or they're in juvie or on their way there. But I don't fit in your world, either—the AP professor shit you and Andrew do."

"You fit," I say. "That paper you did—"

"Yeah, but I had to sweat my ass off for a damn B+," Tanay says. "It doesn't come natural like it does for y'all."

"My grandma says have to scratch and bite and fight to survive. No free lunch."

"Damn, she could be Granmama's twin."

There's a very sore lump in my throat. Grandma lives by her advice, to the letter; otherwise, I'd be asleep in one of her four bedrooms in Manor's Club this very minute.

"No, your grandma's different," I say. "She lives with you. She wants to."

"Whatever. She's the bouncer and Mama's the warden."

I snap, "So here's your choice as I see it: give in to Mushi, who gives you hell and wants you to go to hell. Or, do what your mom wants, who wants you in heaven. Sweating your ass off at a desk doesn't seem like a raw deal to me."

Tanay takes another drag, then coughs harshly in our silence. Then she rolls down the window, a crank that takes some doing. She tosses the burning cigarette into the dark roar of highway.

She glances at me. "Well, good for you, Miss Thing. Guess you got a third eye, too."

"We're twins, motherfucker."

Her look is so startled I bust out with a laugh. Creaky, rusty, but you might say it's there.

She grins. "Damn, Dancing. Maybe you can have a good time."

CHAPTER 40

I think I've fallen asleep because I wake up to road signs saying Asheville, and Tanay crowing, "Hey, girl, rise and shine, it's Hippie Land!"

I sink low in my seat even though I know Shaye and Sunny have left this town, trailing Deanna elsewhere. I growl, "Wake me when it's over."

She chuckles. "Naw, you wake up because your ass is about to chauffeur mine."

We pull over and switch, and the steering wheel feels amazing in my hands. Maybe because this car is a schooner, too solid to go astray; or maybe because for once I emerged from a dead sleep with no demons; or maybe because I didn't realize driving is such power when you have a partner. I start telling Tanay how I have Grandma to thank for my first spin one summer visit when I was twelve and particularly morose and monosyllabic, hair dripping with grease. I reminisce about how damn good I was that very first time behind the wheel.

I glance over; Tanay is looking at me funny. "You're a trip, Dancing," she says. Like she wants to give me a hug.

I bite my lips to keep more chatter inside. Freak Girl can't alarm her copilot; there are too many miles till Tennessee.

She says, "Why was your hair all greasy?"

"What?"

"You said you didn't wash your hair."

"Oh." I run my hands up and down, up and down the cracked leather of the steering wheel. "I guess I needed lessons in personal hygiene."

A beat. "Wendy. Don't lie to me." Her eyes are steady. "Us on the run like this, and you're still telling stories?"

I turn to the windshield and reveal in a hundred words or less the rough outlines of Nelson. I don't tell her what I'm afraid I don't know anymore—what got shoved deep down for centuries, maybe never to come out—yet might well torture me forever.

For a while the wheels roll beneath us, catching on occasional potholes, thumping out a rhythm louder than fear in my head. Sweat pools beneath my hands and I wipe my palms on my legs. I see Shaye's face before me like a stone façade, caught in a sneer, cracking in key places, but no threat to shatter. I hear Tanay take a deep breath.

"I'm telling you what. Granmama says, *All sin's the same.* True that. But then there was this one day when she said this one thing, and I can't ever forget it. She said, 'Listen to me, girl. You watch who you let in your world. Jesus said, 'And whosoever shall offend one of these little ones that believe in me, it is better for him that a millstone were hanged about his neck, and he were cast into the sea.'" I had to look it up, because it kind of freaked me. It was like I had to know, right then."

I wish I could understand the fear in her face, the chill she's feeling. I say, "You'll have to translate."

"What it means is, *There's a special place in hell for those who mess with kids.*"

My heart stops, takes this in, pushes it out.

"But I'm not a kid."

She gives me a very strange look. "What's that supposed to mean?"

"I don't know." My throat is so dry. "I'm almost sixteen. I take APs. I should know better."

A swift shake of her head. "No. Somebody's ass needs to go to jail."

"I must be made of stupid to have ever trusted him."

"I don't care if you did a pole dance—it's on him!"

I'm nodding, just to get her quiet. I can't tell her—or anyone—the worst truth of all, piercing my insides, condemning me to stocks in the public square like a capital-W Whore: wouldn't my body not want him if it's wrong? Wouldn't it just shut down at the beginning of things?

We can't burden her with such questions.

Tanay taps the window, hard, again and again. "No, see, that's how they work. They reel you in. They make you feel like you're the only one in the world."

We roll on, and Tanay preaches on, about *To Catch a Predator*, how dudes like Shaye, they can't ever grow up, they have a disease, they need to be locked up. I listen, I know I do, but it keeps bouncing against a rubber wall deep inside. My mind wanders, traveling all over this numb body, counting days since he last entered me. I recall my disloyal body, igniting in its nether regions when he told me I wanted it, that he always knew, and the shudder I force myself to have to cleanse myself of him, followed by the cuts...I can see the neon warning signs of sex ed books: condom failure rate at 15%. I drive on, counting breaths, seeking calm, fighting vomit, and for some strange reason, it quiets me to watch the white lines down the black road like a timeline of history, and dwell on men of old, rapists all, when women were chattel, men in Shakespeare's day using linen sheaths, fish bladders, animal guts, whatever methods with their 13-, 14-, and 15-year-old girls imprisoned on louse-filled beds. Those girls were whores, wives, mothers at my age and younger; maybe this magnetic horror of mine is wired into problem, primitive genes, the fault of a shiftless Daddy and clueless Mommy. Maybe like these white lines in the black road, that I have heard are not two but ten feet long, my trauma isn't what it appears. It's not so very tragic, something Tanay should mourn, just typical, a history that I must swallow and take as destiny.

"You're real quiet," she says. "You okay?"

"I'm great." I give her a big smile, a fun smile. She doesn't know I'm never coming home again, that this isn't just a joyride, and that no amount of Child Protective Services can help me against the Sunny and Shaye lies.

She yawns. "How long till sleep?"

"It's 85 miles, or 136.77 kilometers, to Knoxville," I tell her. "Want to stop there?"

"Please." She also wants Mickey D's, so we find one within the next ten minutes and stop at the drive through for Cokes and Big Macs and extra fries. I insist on paying, and she doesn't argue. We eat for a few minutes in the parking lot, and she says she wants the wheel back. Fine by me.

We get settled, and I see her Droid glinting at me from inside her huge purse splayed open by my feet on the floor. "You have 3G?" I ask.

She snorts. "Course. Why else have a phone?"

I grab it and go on Facebook. I must go to Sunny Revere's page. I know I am weak, but I must. I've never been away from her more than two days in my life. She told me once she slept with me every day when I was a baby. That she didn't let go of me even to eat. That I became an "asshole" of a toddler at the age of two, and she had to let me go. How it killed her soul. Is she hurting now, like a limb's been hacked? Is she?

I think of Katherine, Michael's grieving mother, who stood by while Michael's life spun faster and faster. She is a black-and-white still, like Auntie Em, crying to the air, searching for her son. Though I hate Mother, I hate worse to see her cry.

She's changed her profile picture. To a picture of me—

Wendy with the bowl cut, circa age ten. I see that at 2:00 a.m., Mother posted:

I am a terrible mother. I've been too busy doing so much work on myself, to make up for the sins of my mother. And in so doing, I've forced my baby away. Wendy, my little redbird, I am so sorry.

25 people already like this.

So she has come home. She found the empty room.

Flutter of wings deep down, beating at all my doors. Does she understand what's happened? Does she really know what to be sorry for? Does she really not blame me for Shaye—for what happened?

I read the post again and again.

Mother. Tell me he's gone. Come get me.

I open the Comments field to say this. I watch the white box, and it stares back at me.

I go back to my picture. What I didn't know then at ten. What I was about to know soon.

I could ask Tanay. "What would you think," I begin, "if I were to write—?" I stop, because I see I have a message in the Inbox. I never have messages. I panic it's Shaye.

It's not. Deanna Faire has sent me a message.

I effed up. Sorry.

I'm stunned, her English like Greek to me, until I realize Tanay is saying to me, "If you were to write what?"

She knows I'm on, so she writes, *are we good?*

I write, *Are you with him?*

Who?

The devil.

A long pause, then: *I have to be.*

Then don't write me. Ever.

Where are you

I take a deep breath and write back, *Going to meet my King*

She IMs back, *What king?*

I laugh aloud. She thinks I'm so stupid as to tell her—
him—where I am. I don't trust the timing of this missive.
Tanay glances at me. I text, *why do u care*

22 seconds of silence. Then: *I care. I'm really sorry*

Yeah right

Are you alone

With tanay

There's no response for a full minute.

Seriously I'm sorry

I put the phone down. Then I pick it back up. I write,
A change of heart huh. Stone can't change.

"I don't know who you're texting, but it better not be my
mama or yours," Tanay says.

Long pause before Deanna writes, *Sometimes you have to do
the right thing*

I hear a snort. Tanay is leaning, looking over my shoulder.
"Deanna? Are you crazy?"

"She's sorry. Says she wants to 'do the right thing.'"

"What's she mean, the right thing? That bitch ain't right.
She was a snake way back in the third grade. Leopards don't
change their spots."

"You're mixing metaphors."

"Metaphors can't help your ass handle a copperhead."

"What's a copperhead?" I say.

"See what I'm saying?" Tanay asks the road. "Lord, she's
walking into the woods barefoot."

I see Deanna's IM'd in the meantime: *You there? THE
KING like MJ? Are you in LA?*

Tanay mutters to herself, "Third eye says someone's trying
to reel your ass in."

I read the text a second time, and now it chills me. I'm
dealing with the devil's strumpet. His words caress her ear,
hover over her shoulder, piping in music to get me, the prey, to
stay logged on. Get my coordinates. Get me home.

I tell Tanay, but my voice is weak: "I'm not stupid. I'm just enjoying her suffering."

Tanay glares. "Wendy. There are two types of people in this world. No, make it three. Those who tell the truth all the time. That would be my Granmama and Jesus. Those who tell the truth some of the time. That'd be you and me. Those who tell the truth none of the time. As in Deanna Faire."

As in Shaye Tann. Evil does exist. Sunny has always said there's no such thing, that everything is gray.

We stare at each other several seconds till I get chills, all over my body. Then I see we're drifting. "Watch out," I say.

She rights the wheel, a little too quick, and the car shakes back and forth till we're straight again.

"Well, I'll say this." I turn off her phone. "The Bible According to Tanay makes a hell of a lot of sense."

She snorts. "If I'm so smart, why am I running scared?" She yawns. "Find a hotel before I drive us off the road."

The Motel 6 just south of Knoxville looks like heaven to us, and there we land.

CHAPTER 41

I WAKE CLUTCHING MY NECK AND screaming, screaming over a voice saying, "Girl, Wendy, it's okay! It's okay!"

Tanay's arms are wrapped around me. I'm in a musty single bed sitting up, strangling myself, rocking back and forth. It dawns on me where I am: Motel 6 somewhere just inside Knoxville. The room is gray with filtered light from heavy drapes. What day is it? My throat is raw.

Someone pounds on the wall next to us and cusses. "Sorry," I croak. "There was this boa constrictor—"

"Yeah, you were dreaming something fierce," Tanay says. "Gave me a heart attack!"

My head spins and my chest is tight. There was a horrible snake and spider talking to me, and they were funneling information back to Shaye so he could track me here. The copper taste in my mouth says Dirty Deanna was, is, and ever shall be Shaye's tool. She needs him for her filthy lucre. He's pulling her strings.

I'm trembling all over. The residue of this dream will stay on me like a slime. Whisper count to 16, then recite the prayer that saves:

> *O St. Michael,*
> *as it was in 1982,*
> *was then, and ever shall be,*
> *world without end,*
> *Amen.*

I take a deep breath so I can scratch, bite, fight. "What time is it?"

"I don't know, lunchtime?" Tanay yawns and gets off the bed. She collapses onto hers and checks her phone. "Noon."

"Can you see if the funeral's still the same day, same time? Because they could change it!"

Tanay hands me the phone like I might be one of those Scientology freaks. I get on Google and search for news of the day and the place I will be near his casket. I shiver; tears prick my eyes; it hasn't changed.

"We have to keep moving." I jump up. "It's what, how many—" I fumble for the map and uncrinkle it "—six hours from Knoxville to Memphis. We get there by six tonight, eat, switch drivers, one of us can sleep and then we keep switching—we still have twenty-five hours left—"

Tanay snatches the phone from my hand. "Why're you tripping? We have plenty of time to get to Cali. First I got to call Mama. Then we are going to see some sights." She walks to the door and steps outside into too-bright light.

While she paces outside our door, her voice rising and falling, I search for Strike. We let him loose when we went to sleep about 6:00 a.m. My little hollering episode probably sent him packing. I find him in the farthest, darkest back corner beneath the bed. He's not a happy camper, his fur covered in dust as I drag him out, but he forgives me and snuggles into my stomach, one eye on the door and the sounds Tanay makes. Motel 6, chosen for its pet-friendliness, doesn't take issue with his cat box, but dear Strike takes issue with cleaning ladies and loud sounds such as engines backfiring, motorcycles, and whooping rednecks. I count folds in the drapes, brown spots on the walls, and cigarette stains in the carpet. Outside, Tanay's voice rises. And rises. I realize my hoodie smells like her cigarettes.

When she comes back in, Strike cowers. The look on her face could strike someone dead.

She slings her phone on the nightstand and throws herself on the bed. She rolls away from me to face the window.

I say after a minute, "What happened?"

"Angelique DeVries says come home right now. Or she'll put my ass in juvie herself." She pounds the bed. "She's taking my goddamn license. Says my ass will never amount to anything."

"She's angry," I tell her. "She wants you home. People who want you home will use any tactic." How nice must that be.

Tanay pulls the covers over her head. I get a sick feeling in my gut. I can't have Tanay go fetal. I need somebody to pretend to wear big-girl pants. We can't both be crying for our mommies.

Her phone chirps. And chirps.

I say, "Want me to get that?"

A shrug.

I pick up the phone. Maybe I can reason with Ms. DeVries, blame it all on me—but it's a text from a number I don't know.

Miss you. I will keep trying. Day 37. I'm just sayin.

Could it be?

I text back

Who dis

The Unknown texts

Oh that's cold. You know me. Drew

So he has been texting her incessantly and keeping track. By my count, he's accurate; 37 would indeed take us back to a fateful day in May when it all fell apart.

I cradle the phone in my hands, and I know what I must do. Maybe it's the memory of his sad face; or maybe I'm just a sucker for sob stories, but I want to trust him. Mushi was and is a snake, and I was a false alarm. This New Girl, the

America's Next Top Model of High-Yellow Skin? Something seems quite shady about the story.

"What do you really know about this New Girl?" I say to Tanay's back.

She grunts.

"What evidence do you have of their dating?"

Long pause, then a growl. "Back up off me."

"Tanay." I go over and shake her shoulder. "Do you have anything more than Mushi's testimony?"

She rolls over and glares at me. "What, are you the DA now? I don't know! She said, go on to the movies, see what you got to see, and when my ass got there, I saw plenty of evidence!"

"What, exactly? Andrew walking into the theater with a girl?"

"Yes!" she hollers.

"Holding hands?"

"No!"

"Kissing?"

"If you don't shut up..." She turns away and pounds the comforter. "I saw him with my own eyes!"

I pick up the phone and step outside into the glare of noonday sun, severe against the paint-peeling walls of the Motel 6 balcony. I text

So who is she

Not five seconds later

Who

New girl! Movies!!

Whaaaaat....

Then a few seconds later: *Are you for real? That's my cuz.*

Your cuz. For real...

You didn't think now...

Oh yes I did.

She's visiting from Baltimore. You can meet her. Go ahead and come see for yourself

My heart pounds for Tanay. *Ok. When.*
Today?
Can't. In Knoxville.
A long startled pause. *Why*
On the run
What? With who?
With Wendy
Are you ok???
I guess Freak Girl as a traveling companion freaks him somewhat.
We are fine but stay tuned.
You can't drive that far
Yes we can
Stubborn
You know me
Then I panic. He can't text Tanay out of the blue anymore—she'll know what I've done. I write
Do me a favor don't write back till I write you
Why
Just promise ok
What about your moms
JUST PROMISE
OK I PROMISE
I'll hit you up soon
I snap the phone shut, my breath tight, and lean against the scabby wall. I can't believe what I just did: Tanay will kill me. I keep breathing, deep, over the cold pit in my stomach: have I taken her on the same ride, having her fall—or me, her proxy, fall—for a lie? I believe Andrew, I don't know why, but what if I'm still designed stupid, taking in his story is like a certain sob story of a mental mother? Of another hurting man whose tale is that he has a "cousin"? A man can make you think he needs you for something else, not what he actually gets.

I need something very sharp. The only thing that keeps me from scrabbling through my duffel for my knife is the presence of Tanay in that room.

I go back inside and lie on the bed, fighting nausea. I pray to MJ I'm not a curse on my only friend in the world.

CHAPTER 42

I WAKE FROM WHAT MUST BE dozing to Tanay saying, "Hell with all the damn DeVries; let's do this."

"How many are there?" I say sleepily, but get no answer. We get back on the road, me behind the wheel, jittery from plotting her love life and fearing Angelique DeVries will call law enforcement. Never mind Sunny is now home and no doubt missing her Mirage too much, or plotting with Shaye who's nervous I've gone rogue and might tell a tale. A change of Sunny's chameleon heart and suddenly they could track me rather than sit on that couch; it's hard to know what emotion will move her next. We must drive fast, but safely. I maintain a legit 67 miles per hour.

Tanay's researching Memphis on her phone. "There's a hell of a lot more there than Elvis. National Civil Rights Museum. Stax Museum. Rock and Soul Museum. Sun Records. We got to stop *one* of these places." She gives me a pleading look. "Come on, now. I'm not trying to spend all your money. I got some, too—how about a day in Memphis?"

"On the way back," I say. "Please understand, I have to get to L.A."

She looks out the window. She chews on something, I don't know what, maybe the danger of Mama and weighing it versus Wendy's Crazy, versus The Pursuit of Fun.

She slips in a Billie Holiday CD without comment. I'm

grateful for the warbles and the wails: just the right amount of dark to reflect our mood. When it's done, I put in The Beach Boys.

"Oh, yeah, some psychedelic shit now!" Tanay starts grooving in her seat to "Wouldn't It Be Nice." My heart lifts; she seems fine.

"Actually, they look like clean-cut white boys, not hippie-trippy." I show her the cover.

"White boys," Tanay muses. She puts her feet up on the dash and cackles, but it's bitter. "There's my whole damn problem. Maybe I need to find me a white boy instead."

"Uh, no," I say. "I know for a fact they suck."

A sharp glance my way while I send vibes to MJ that Andrew not break his promise to me, I mean, her.

On cue, the phone chirps, and I jump in my seat.

I freeze staring straight ahead. She checks her phone. Then a grumble: "Mama trying to break through. Oh hell no. She can freak till she finds me."

I swallow a sigh of relief and urge the pedal to 68.

The Beach Boys still sing their song full of wishing and hoping and praying, for a day when a boy and girl can wake up together in wedded bliss. I can't help it, but my thoughts go to him. If only he had kept us in this romantic limbo—my babyish, freakish hoping for more touches, but not consummation, not knowing what kills you on The Other Side. It is twisted, but if, only if we could have rested in a kiss—never gone where he had to take it—wouldn't it be nice—but no. Wouldn't it be nice if everything were not what it is.

By the time we pull into Memphis city limits, we're so hungry we can't see straight. Now Tanay is driving and I realize from the state of my gut that this plan is more than a bit manic.

"Any kind of food," Tanay moans over the steering wheel.

"Another Mickey D's, I do not care." Then she looks panicked at the bridge ahead. "Shit, that's water—I don't want to go over water!"

"It's just the Mississippi River," I say. "Yeah, let's stop. I guess take this one here—Exit 1," I say. I'm fumbling with the map but it's hard to get bearings.

"Well, I'm on the damn ramp, tell me where to go!"

"Calm down. I don't know, merge and—"

"Get me away from this water!"

"Uh, Riverwalk Avenue—I don't know, turn left here!" We're passing Jefferson Davis Park. Andrew and I recently reviewed details about his Confederate ass in AP History—but now that seems like eons ago—

"Where are we?" Tanay yells. "This is ghetto! Watch us get mugged!" Things are looking sleepy, rough, and abandoned.

"I don't know—"

"Ah, National Civil Rights Museum!" Tanay sings out, shrill. "All right, all right, we're okay—" She takes a left on GW Carver and we're in what looks like a warehouse district, but sketchy ghetto, too. A rusty red building to our left, a yellowing green sign posted, looking very 1950s: Clementine and Hattie's Sundry Store.

"Thank you, Jesus, they got food." Tanay screeches into a spot on the street across from the rusty sandwich board confirming this truth.

"Fine, whatever, but we better be quick," I say. "Wherever we stop tonight, I'd say it better be no more than six hours of sleep, because we have to get back on the r—"

Tanay's fist slams the steering wheel, and I jump. "You need to *stop—this—shit*!" Her face contorts with disgust. "You're obsessed! Get off this crazy train."

"I'm not crazy!"

"Then what the hell is it?"

"You—you don't know St. Michael!" I scream.

Silence.

"Did you just say, 'St. Michael'?" She stares. "Do you, like, worship him?"

After several seconds, I manage, "I told you it was a pilgrimage." My voice shakes.

The silence ticks with threat.

"I thought you were joking," she says, voice like ice. "Damn. I mean, I know you're sad and all, but that is some crazy shit right there."

"You came with me." My voice is colder. "This is my trip, and I make the rules." Her face blurs and I see minutes flying from me, I see the Staples Center filled with undeserving hordes who drove St. Michael to distraction, gloved fools mimicking a man they never truly knew. I see Shaye, Sunny, and police advancing.

"Oh, is that how it is?" Tanay snaps. "After all that's gone down, what you been through, you care this much about a pedophile motherfucker? Please."

She opens the door, gets out, and slams the door so hard my bones hurt.

I watch her go, and I'm falling back, disappearing, knotholes waiting, and at their end, frigid rock walls.

I sit there a long time staring through the windshield, without seeing. I prepare a speech to deliver—how Michael, broken by a tormented home life and toxicity of American celebrity—floated too high in the ether to understand you can't pat kids and serve them milk and cookies in a Neverland bedtime story dream. No one understands a boy whose father abandoned him early and needs to redream his childhood.

But the words I think to speak are hollow, they bounce off these windows, and I am sitting alone with these bizarre thoughts on a strange Memphis street corner.

I enter Clementine's & Hattie's.

Inside it's dark—a dive bar—and the air is thick with heat. There's a grill in the middle of the bar where someone's frying up burgers for two frat-looking boys. In the corner are three ancient black men playing cards and gumming burgers. But it smells greasy good and the sight of a mint-green, hand-painted sign makes me feel better.

NO SMOKIN DOPE
NO CURSIN GOD
NO BEGGIN MONEY
SHUT UP AND EAT UP
C. & H.

Tanay is sitting right next to the frat boys at the bar and talking to them. An old jukebox blasts a black woman's strong voice about being alive again, a rockin' bass and tight drum—serious old school—just loud enough over the hiss of the grill.

Tanay glances at me when I sit down next to her. She tells the bartender with the long hair and goatee, "She'll have what I got."

The boys lean around Tanay to check me out. Their eyes glaze over at the sight of the matted hair and hoodie.

"That one's Lowell and the other's Grayson," Tanay says.

"Naw, get it right now: the Cap'n and Crunch," says the guy closest to her. He's pudgy with a round moon face, piggy eyes, and a backward baseball cap. I get a gross vibe, loud and clear, like his sickly sweet cologne already clogging my throat.

"Yeah, whatever," Tanay says with a grin. "He's got to be the Cap'n and the other one is the sidekick."

The other one tips a bottle of Pabst Blue Ribbon to his lips; thick lips in a sleepy face that should be handsome. He's blond with fine cheekbones but the narrow slits for eyes and plump pink lips that match the pink polo. They give me a Shaye vibe, though they don't look a thing alike, so strong in my gut, I have to hold on to the counter.

He says: "He couldn't captain shit."

"So y'all ain't Batman and Robin then?" Tanay grins.

The Cap'n checks out her cleavage and says, "Naw, dude, then it'd be a gay-ass thing." They crack up and clink bottles. I'm floored by the brilliance of this conversation.

I can't place their accents. They're not Southern or Northern or Midwestern. Their voices are flat and careless, that is all.

The Cap'n leans into Tanay. "Where y'all staying?"

"We don't know," I say loudly.

Tanay glares at me. The jukebox woman sings how she's a woman again, how she'll never stop loving her dude. I watch the bartender wipe down the grill with pickle juice.

"They play soccer," Tanay says. "They said we got to see them scrimmage tomorrow."

"As opposed to the Civil Rights Museum?" I say.

"If y'all don't want to see us play, then meet us at Graceland," the Cap'n says. "We're going there tomorrow before we take off." He swills his beer.

Tanay gets her burger and Coke. I get my Coke.

"Soul Burger," the Cap'n says. I hate how he pushes his shoulder into Tanay and I hate how she giggles. What the hell is she doing? I stare at the white bun, the machine patty, the wax paper around it, cuddled in the basket with a bag of potato chips. It looks ridiculously American mainstream, full of processed crap, but it smells like heaven. He says proudly, "I had four."

Tanay says, "Damn, boy. You're a bottomless pit." She bites into her burger and closes her eyes. "Hell yeah, this mug is good."

"Interesting how your cussing has accelerated," I say to her.

"Who made you mama?"

She hasn't looked at me directly since I came in here.

"This used to be a whorehouse," Crunch says to the Cap'n. "There's a bathtub upstairs."

The Cap'n looks at us and cracks up. A new record drops in the jukebox, courtesy of the black gentlemen in the corner, and the same woman sings about how losing her is losing a good thing.

"Who's singing?" I say to the bartender as he serves me my burger.

"Carla Thomas."

"Of Rufus and Carla?" I say.

"That's right, Stax goddess," he says. He looks at me like I might be a little smart.

The Cap'n burps like a beast and stands up. He tosses two twenties on the counter and says too loud to the bartender, "I got this." He jerks his thumb at me and Tanay.

Tanay beams at him. "Y'all didn't have to do that."

"Y'all," the Cap'n says, looking at Crunch. "Southern girls. Now that's cute."

Crunch rolls his eyes and says, "I want a tour of the whorehouse."

The Cap'n looks at Tanay like she's another burger to gobble, then runs his hand across her back like he's known her forever. "Bye, *y'all*," he says with a grin. I hate him. I can't eat this burger. The onions, greasy and sautéed, sauce dripping—I can't.

Tanay eats with gusto while I swallow saliva and nausea. I work on my Coke instead.

When she's done, she turns away from me slightly while she checks something on her phone. I see she's got something she's looking at in her contacts. She got the damn dude's phone number.

Has she lost her mind?

She glances at me. "Don't you judge. I don't do Christian anymore."

"But you do sleazy frat boy?"

After that Tanay and I do not speak. She asks the bartender for a decent place to stay and he tells her where the Welcome Inn is.

I don't dispute her decision. All I know is two gross white boys have come between us and she won't let go of that phone. And in fewer than four days, the light of my life will be buried, without me there.

CHAPTER 43

I T's 3:00 A.M. I SIT up in bed, listening to Tanay snore. The sounds of a stranger. It's for these and many reasons I can't sleep. My stomach gnaws with hunger since I left most of the burger at Clementine's & Hattie's. Strike does a yoga stretch like he hasn't a care in the world and pads around the comforter, pleased I keep his nocturnal schedule.

I grab him and hug him hard. He purrs. He's so real and soft. My heart starts revving. I am homeless and I am stupid. Tanay will go home eventually, but I can't. I bury my face in his fur; Strike smells like vanilla mixed with cotton fluff.

And even if I get to L.A. and I do see the grave site, what then? I can weep kneeling before the flowers and the candles, eyes streaming as I take in the light of the stained glass, and cry my agonies to him, but what after that? I can't hug St. Michael's stone or his crypt. Where then?

Scratch, bite, fight. *St. Michael! What now?*

He is silent. A sudden, ugly sight in my mind of God and the angels barring the door to children's heavenly bedrooms, having heard the horrific rumors of my MJ here on Earth.

Strike squirms with all the force of Satan and rakes my hand. Blood bubbles up. I drop him on the bed. Heart slams, but I can't panic. I grab Tanay's phone off the nightstand and step into the urine-yellow light of the Welcome Inn hallway.

I leave a voicemail on the landline of the Passive Solar.

"Sunny. Mother. If you…if you want to make it up to me, please…Make sure Shaye is gone when I get back."

I hit END. I want to throw the phone, slam a receiver that does not exist. I sink to the hallway carpet, clutching it instead. Maybe it will chirp or vibrate when she sees my call. But it's like a stone in my hand. *Sunny. Mother. Mom. Please.*

Millstone. I look it up. A grinding stone, one of a pair, and heavy as hell. Driven by wind, water, people, or livestock. I see Shaye of the stone face bow his head before me like an Olympic gold medalist; I hang this thing around his neck, and his spine sags. His sneer snuffs out; he is startled by the weight. But instead of the sea appearing like a tsunami, the ground cracks beneath him. Everywhere, the earth quakes, and he is swallowed by magma to the ninth circle of hell.

I wonder if Tanay would help me with the hanging now. Her snoring body in the bed behind this door feels foreign, not someone who would quote scripture of revenge for my sake anymore.

Why did she flirt with those fools? I do not want to hook up with them later; the thought makes me sick.

I start to text Andrew; I will tell him Tanay is going off the deep end toward bad-news boys. I stop once, twice, three times. What can he do? He's in Millboro and we're in Memphis. She feels full-blown hate for him and now for me.

I think I fall asleep because my eyes get fuzzy, for I don't know how long, and then suddenly, my neck is sore and cramped from flopping forward.

I go inside the room and lie on the bed, breathing slow as I can. When Tanay finally wakes at 9:00, she announces, "We're going to Graceland."

I snap, "Why? To see Elvis or the Cap'n?"

She doesn't even look at me. "To see if there's going to be any fun on this mug."

Huge surge of anger. I do not want to go to Graceland. There are a million other meaningful things to see!

I bark, "Why would you want to see a gaudy, overblown estate? A white man that was no hero—just made black music palatable for racists? When you can see the place where Otis Redding and The Staple Singers recorded?" Tanay's eyes narrow, but I can't stop. "When you can stand on the balcony where King was shot?"

Her eyes burn holes in me. "Don't you talk about Dr. King."

Every inch of me turns hot pink. I shut my mouth and turn away, hating all of this, fed by ugly memories of a certain man's lecture about originals, number-one singles, Grammys, never mind white men who dance black. An encyclopedic brain like mine was yet another mirage that he and I had a "connection," the false belief that he "got" me—that he cared. The truth burns.

All I can do now is keep eyes and ears on the whereabouts of her phone and wait for a sign.

We check out, and the chirps continue—followed by a ton of texting, with little smiles of satisfaction. I know it's that crass Cap'n and his Shaye-like first mate.

She uses her GPS app to get us to the neighborhood near Graceland, a sketchy area if there ever was one. We drive past homeless men looking cracked out and then a cluster of police cars roping off a crime scene, a body under a blanket. I know she's alarmed but she says nothing, just slows her driving and fumbles for cigarettes.

We park across from the mansion and I buy us tickets for the Platinum Tour. Tanay doesn't say a word when I hand her one. I notice that despite the fumbles, she hasn't actually lit a cigarette since she got up. She glances here, there, through the crowds, I know seeking the Cap'n and his sidekick, but no frat boys emerge from touristy crowds to claim us. Instead a group of shuffling, overweight geezers follows us onto the bus headed to the mansion.

As the bus grinds us closer, we see people signing the fieldstone wall, grinning and snapping photos. I would never sully a relic at St. Michael's—and I don't care what she thinks of that thought.

We pass through wrought-iron gates graced with music notes and chug up the hill toward the two-story mansion of tan limestone and tall white columns. "Damn," Tanay says to a black woman across the aisle. "This mug is tiny. Not even as big as *Teen Cribs*."

"You got that right," the woman says.

I feel very small and white, like Elvis's house. And petty with my small anger, as Tanay texts way too much, to that stupid, obtuse, dim-witted Cap'n.

The audio tour gives us Elvis's voice and Lisa Marie's voice explaining each room. St. Michael's bride, I think dully, our guide, but this thought barely breaks through my fog. I must count hard as hell to not think of early conversations a month ago before darkness descended; times when I thought he could school me with wisdom, when I wanted all he could give without knowing what it was.

Tanay doesn't listen at all. Her eyes are on her phone.

Fine. 1, 2, 3, 4, 5, 6, 7, 8, 9, 10, 11, 12, 13, 14, 15, 16. I will open wide my X-ray eyes; I will commit this all to memory, memory of how she hated on me this day. Then I will cut her out of my life. How dare she drag me here and not even pay attention?

I see gaudy but pristine white of a living room, the royal-blue drapes, and the fifteen-foot custom couch. I see green shag floor and ceiling and the gleaming Polynesian woods, and I see counters where banana pudding was to be made fresh nightly and three packs each of Spearmint, Doublemint, and

Juicy Fruit gum on hand at all times. And here, the three TVs that Elvis watched at once. There, the rip in the pool table where they think someone danced. The piano where he played hymns.

We stroll, then stop when we are told, crowds bumping us from behind, people pressing everywhere in this small space. That touch on my arm, that brush of my shoulder, it could be another Shaye in the making—a lewd man in my space, someone after me from behind. The press of human flesh tells me this is no shrine, it's a hollow shell funneling voyeurs, too many of them sick men who want a piece of something.

In the Meditation Garden, bright sun hurts my eyes. There the fountains burble and splash in the crystal-blue pond; the heat presses our skin. Tanay and I stand a few feet apart before the gravestones of Elvis, Gladys, and Vernon, and his grandmother, and a memorial stone for his twin brother Jesse Garon. She texts on and on.

I squat, think about kneeling, anything to keep her image from my peripheral vision. My hands look long and bony, poking out of my red jacket, all white skin clutched before me. How can she...doesn't she get all is dust? She is texting through the morbid truth of things? I don't know her at all.

"Damn you," I say. My voice sounds crusty, from a deep quarry. "Have some respect!"

She turns slowly, staring down at me. Then, to my surprise, she pockets her phone and looks at the gravestones.

"It was the drugs, right?" she says. "He'd be what, seventy-four?"

I nod.

"Michael was fifty," she says. "Drugs again."

The loss—it's so great, I sway, and catch myself with a hand on the hot ground. I'm sweating through my shirt. Michael held his arm out to Dr. Murray and said, "Hit me." Neverland,

I can't go there—it's No Land. No one will tour the premises, ever—especially not the bedrooms. Empty, cobwebs, covered places. I feel flush with nausea. *Noughts Land.*

"Wendy, you okay?"

I swallow hard, then say: "Elvis died on a toilet but that is no comparison to what people think happened in MJ's bed."

A careful look. "You mean, that stuff with the doctor?"

"I mean the bed with the kids."

A long piece of quiet. We let some tourists waddle past. Then she nods. "Okay, Dancing. You passed."

"Passed?"

"You're not as crazy as I thought. Let's go to L.A."

We leave. We pass numerous outbuildings stuffed full of gold, platinum, and double-platinum records unseen. We see no sparkling jumpsuits, private planes, or fancy cars. As we board the bus to return to the other side of the road, an obese woman with a Texas drawl complains, "Man, long live Elvis and his gift shops."

Tanay and I glance at each other.

She cracks up. I hear myself laugh, again, so weird and rusty, but undeniably there.

CHAPTER 44

I AM DRIVING AND FEELING GROOVY. Tanay still likes me, and I like her. In California, there are so many places to go. We'll try San Francisco first—I can show her the Palace of Fine Arts by a shimmering Bay—then take her to laugh at some for-realz hippies in the Haight—and maybe call Cindy from Japantown and say, "'Sup—want to meet us for sushi?" Surprise the hell out of Cindy—and say after that, "I'm on the move." No needless interdependencies here. I am perpetual motion.

I hear Tanay say through my fog of happy, "We're almost out of gas. Stop at that BP right there."

We pull up to the pump and as I move to get out of the hoop-dee, I feel her hand on my arm. She's staring at my wrist.

"Does it hurt?" she says.

Her grip isn't tight, just calm—warmth shooting through me. It keeps my heart from going crazy.

"Does what hurt?"

"Cutting yourself."

She saw the scars when I squatted by the grave: skinny white wrists, laced with pink. Damn them.

"It's more like when you hit your funny bone," I say. "I mean, it hurts like the devil—but then it doesn't."

She flips my wrist, stares at the marks. "Think you can stop?" she says.

"I don't know."

She sighs and lets go. "Well, least you're straight with me. You got that knife on you now?"

"Yeah."

"Give it."

I want to say, *I'm not your kid*, but I pull it from my jacket pocket and hand it over anyway.

We gas up. I stand at the pump while Tanay swipes at her phone, laughing.

"What's so funny?" I say. "Surely your mother is not amusing you."

"The Cap'n showed me this new app. I just downloaded it. Foursquare." She laughs, then texts something. "Guess they'll be here in a minute."

My heart sinks south, fast. "What is it—a tracking device?"

"It posts to Facebook where you are. Like, 'Tanay is at Graceland.'" She shrugs, a swift glance at me, defensive. "I mean, Mama's not on Facebook, and I'm not friends with Deanna or your crazy-ass clan, so we're safe—"

"They're coming here?" I demand. "But we're going to California!"

"We are! Damn, girl, what's wrong with lunch or something? That's all I'm thinking—"

Right then, a gleaming blue Mustang convertible pulls up alongside our pump.

"Well, hey, Cap'n, hey, Crunch," Tanay calls, with too big a smile.

They're grinning back at her, smug, faces shiny with sunburn and hair wet, slicked back.

"Ladies, ladies, ladies." The Cap'n eases his girth out of the driver's seat, saunters over, and slaps hands with Tanay.

"Found you," Crunch says, tapping his phone. His glance is dead-eyed, like we're objects to clock by Google Earth.

"Y'all blew us off," Tanay says, pretending irritation. "You missed the King!"

The Cap'n shrugs. "But hey, we got here, right?" He's looking straight at her boobs in her lacy tank top and not even trying to hide it. "We've been stalking you."

Before I can say anything, he adds, "What y'all want? Beer? Wine? *Chocolate?*"

Crunch throws his head back and laughs—a high-pitched, eerie cackle. Tanay gives them a second look but smiles, a little tight. "Naw, we're good." I can tell she's flattered, because now Crunch is looking at her in a way he didn't yesterday—seeing her boobs like the New World. His eyes are pretty, but eyes and mouth don't match.

"You can come with," the Cap'n orders, thumbing at the convenience store. "Pretty thing can pick out whatever you want."

Pretty thing. I swallow a gag. Tanay looks at me—guilty, like it's uncool they don't see me. She says to Crunch, "I've got to go to the bathroom. Meet you in there." She walks away.

I catch the Cap'n looking at me like I'm dirt.

"What?" I say. My hand tightens on the pump, sweaty.

"Why do you hold her back?" he says.

I say, "Why should she waste her time with you?"

Crunch hops out of the car without opening the door and walks fast toward Tanay who is heading behind the station.

Cap'n glances their way, smiles, and stops gassing up. Leaves the nozzle in his car and goes right after Crunch.

"What the hell?" I call after him.

I replace the handle at the pump. I wait a minute, staring at that corner where they disappeared, heart rattling. Something deep inside says: Go get Tanay, *now.*

I walk fast at the corner of the building. When I get around it, there's nothing but a grimy unisex bathroom door.

Behind it, someone is yelling—Tanay.

I try the door. Locked. Scuffles inside.

"Come on, just a kiss," I hear the Cap'n say.

"No! Get off!"

"Tanay!" I scream.

"Wendy!" she yells.

I hear the guys laughing. I pound on the door. "Let her out!"

Crunch cackles. "What, you want in?"

"Nah, she's got a flat ass," I hear Cap'n say.

"Wendy, come on!" Tanay screams.

I yell, "I'm calling the police!"

The guys laugh.

"I said, get off me!" Her voice is shrill, beyond fear.

I run back to the car, but halfway there, I realize Tanay has her phone. Jesus.

I run inside the convenience store. I yell at the cashier—a large woman with straw hair and heavy lids—"These guys locked my friend in the bathroom!"

She and a few dead-eyed patrons stare.

"Call 911!" I yell. "They're hurting her!"

Straw says, "You kids stop messing around."

"Please! I'm serious!"

"Don't pay 'em no mind," Straw tells the zombie crowd. "Trash, all these kids."

"It's the truth!"

I'm sobbing as I run outside back around the corner.

"Wendy, please!" Tanay is screaming.

"Hold her still, dammit!" Crunch yells.

"I got her, I got her!"

I scream at the door, "Let her out! Or I'm destroying your car!"

Quiet.

"What the fuck?" Crunch says.

"She don't have the balls," says the Cap'n.

I pound the door so hard I could break my hand. "Watch me!"

I run back to the hoop-dee and grab Strike's carrier off the back seat, putting him on the concrete between the gas pumps. I throw myself into the driver's seat. I pull away from the pump with a roar. I burn a sharp U. Then I head straight for the back of the shiny convertible and ram it with the wrath of St. Michael the archangel and all his heavenly hosts.

The hoop-dee shudders; my head snaps forward. My chest hits the steering wheel.

The bumper in front of me is crushed.

I back up, then surge forward. I hit it again. The convertible moves a good foot this time, the Mustang's bumper is a wreck, and a taillight shatters like flying chips of blood and urine.

Straw and a crowd of dead-eyed rednecks have gathered outside, silently taking in this scene.

I back up, hear hollers. In my rearview, I see Cap'n and Crunch race from around the corner, mouths open, screaming at me. I don't see Tanay.

Three's a charm, but four is godly. One more time, and then another. Bam, bam! The hoop-dee wins. I win.

As I back up for a fifth, the Cap'n has come upon me, he's pounding the hoop-dee with his fist, his fat red face is screaming through the windshield.

I switch gears. I close my eyes and drive straight at him.

CHAPTER 45

A T THE LAST SECOND HE jumps out of the way. Another hard hit. My bones jolt, the cars groan, and the crinkle of shattered lights.

Trembling, I shift to park, the two cars touching like nose-to-nose fighters, and get out of the car.

I walk a few feet toward that seething red face. He's only an inch taller. I raise Tanay's phone to his face.

"Now I will call the police," I say. "And tell them how you tried to rape my friend."

Behind us, people snap shots with their cells. The Cap'n runs at his car like a little boy, cussing. He guns the engine and screams out the window at Crunch, strolling up without any rush, "Get in!"

Crunch gives me a flatline glance, like it's just another day at the sociopath races, and walks slowly at the car. He gets in, and neither look at me again. A screech of wheels, a roar, and they're gone.

I race to the bathroom. Tanay is crumpled in the dark corner, her tank top ripped and face streaked with mascara. I fall to the floor next to her, grab her hard.

Straw finds us there, clinging to each other, crying.

The woman's face awakens at the sight of us; her eyes ignite and her triple chin trembles. She says, "Y'all need me to call the police?"

We shake our heads, and stand up, shaking. Straw waddles behind us, mumbling something about how she oughta call if boys were messing with us. Ought to do something, ain't somebody going to do something?

I walk Tanay around to the passenger side of the scratched hoop-dee, its front end wrinkled but not caved.

"Sorry," I say hoarsely after I get into the car with Strike. I turn and move him to the back seat; he cries piteously. "Sorry I fucked up your granmama's car."

Tanay says with a sob, "Can we go home?"

She turns to the window and buries her face in her hands.

"Yes," I say. This time, I have to be strong. I stretch my arm around the back of my seat, stick my finger through the holes in the carrier netting, and let Strike sniff. His cold nose dances along my finger and I close my eyes. *Sorry, sweet boy.*

I point us toward the highway, looking over a hood that is worse for wear but tough as hell. In the passenger seat is a girl fragile like an egg; in the driver's seat, a girl tough as nails, wrought from stone.

Quiet, just rumble of wheels, until the fourth mile. Then Tanay mumbles something, again and again, into her hands. I start listening.

"The Lord is my light and my salvation; whom shall I fear?" This she repeats many times. Then she gets more expansive. "The Lord is the strength of my life; of whom shall I be afraid? When the wicked, even mine enemies and my foes, came upon me to eat up my flesh, they stumbled and fell."

After several rounds of this, I say, "Did they—"

"No."

I find my breath again.

"They didn't get nowhere." Her hands have loosened a bit but haven't let up from her face. Then, finally, one drops, sinks to the seat, while the other cradles her face against the window.

All I can do is take her hand. She doesn't resist. We ride like this for I don't know how long.

It's an hour later when we stop at a rest area. Tanay walks like a zombie away from the car toward the bathroom, leaving her phone.

I grab it and text Andrew.

Now. We need u now.

It takes him only five seconds.

Where are you?

Memphis

I'll meet you—where?

My breath catches. He would come all this way? How? He doesn't have a car—

No it's ok we're coming home

Pause. *Ok*

I add, *Meet me at my house. Tonight.*

I startle, as Tanay is back at the car, peering at me at work on her phone, face hard with questions.

"Here," I say, extending the phone. "It's Drew. He wants to help."

A frozen moment where I wonder what she'll do. But then, she takes the phone.

I leave to use the bathroom. When I come back, she is no longer texting but talking. And crying.

I back away from the car and go sit on a bench outside the rest area. In the swamp heat of this sun, I feel rays penetrate and soothe my jitters inside. There is cleansing.

Many minutes later, she comes and joins me on the bench. She says, "Well. Guess we got it all worked out."

"That's good."

"It's his cousin."

"Is that so?"

She glances at me. "You sneaky bitch. You knew all that?"

I smile. "I might have sent a text or two."

A pause. "You did that for me?"

I shrug. "I had to know the truth."

"Me, too," she says. "Me, too."

We sit in the heat, feel sweat coat us, but neither of us move.

Then she says, "I told him what happened."

"Good. Bet he could kick their—"

"I mean, to you."

Flutters inside. How kind of them. But Tanay does not know what plans I already make, what I've devised sitting in this sun, once I see that she is safe and sound. She doesn't know there's a Greyhound to take me back West, that I do not need to stay more than a minute in Millboro, ever again—somehow, my money can last—till Grandma hears me out and maybe gives me a chance.

"He thinks—and you know, this is what I've been thinking all along—we got to tell my mom. You understand? About your situation. See what she can do."

I'm so cold despite the sweat. "There's nothing she can do."

"Yes there is. There is." Tanay's voice is clear and clean, like a shining knife. "Girl, this is what it is: you've been raped, and it's for the police now. I don't care what your sorry mama says; I don't care what his pedophile ass tries to say. We're taking care of this."

The wind kicks up, out of nowhere. It ruffles my hair, and I get a huge, body-shaking chill. Painful, it's so much like a hard hug, and I feel moisture at the edges of my eyes. I listen, hard as I can—*St. Michael, are You there?*—and no voice, just wind. As if Something nods at Tanay's voice, massive energy moving air, saying, *Go on.*

"Wendy, don't you go on the run again."

I bow my head, blinded by tears.

She takes my hand, like she can hear my silent yes.

CHAPTER 46

ELEVEN HOURS OF DRIVING GETS us into Millboro at 11:00 p.m. The town is bright with lights and wandering citizens, hipsters everywhere, making merry. I am not scared, strangely, should I see his scanning eyes or ravenous face. The dust inside him, I could poke holes right through. I could drive a car through his very frame.

We pass the Coexist Café; we pass Nature Fare; and we see a glut of posters on every light pole. That's right: tonight it's Deanna Faire, in concert.

CD RELEASE PARTY

7/04/09

THE SHADE

Happy Fourth of July. Bootstrap Kinda Gal—just what the Founding Fathers had in mind when they wrote that Declaration and formed this perfect union.

"Sunny and Shaye will be there," I remark, as we pass another pole. "They won't be on the lookout for me tonight."

"They sure as hell don't know where I live, so you're safe." Tanay is driving now, and she looks like captain of our ship no one will ever mess with.

Coming right up is The Shade. Shaye smirks inside, looking up at the Dee serenade; Sunny sidles up to him, right now, believing each word he says—

Tanay's phone chirps, and she tells me to check it. I tell her, "Drew says he's at your house, talking to your mom."

"Oh, shit—ohhhh, shit," Tanay moans. "I can't do this, I can't do this—"

"You have me and my drama as a distraction," I tell her. "Think about it, how mad can she get when poor little Wendy is there?"

Tanay gives me a sharp glance; perhaps she doesn't like my clinical tone, but I can't get too upset about my pitiful circumstance—I'm more tired than I have ever been in my life. "Oh, no, you don't know. She'll beat my ass and be glad there's a crowd." She leans over the steering wheel, like she's willing her mother to disappear.

"How about this," I say, and the voice sounds like someone else's. "How about we stop at that old Shade."

We're at a light. She turns to me. "What? Why?"

"Can Drew meet us?" I say. I am numb, but I am sure.

I feel her stare, third eye in full gear. "You want to say your piece?"

I nod.

"Text him," she says. "We got your back."

He writes back within seconds. *On my way.*

I don't tell her that after this, in the crowd at The Shade, I can and will disappear. That after speaking to Sunny and Shaye for the last time in my life, I can and will board the bus that stops off by The Shade. In a very few minutes, and she won't have to worry again. I will be okay. Her family can't take on my mess, and the police sure as hell won't take the testimony of friends. We're all better off with me way out of state.

Sunny will have no surprises for me—no matter what I tell her. Yet I'm pulled. The tug won't stop. Perhaps the two-year-old in me must say her piece. Or confirm that Sunny Revere has always been flat as a paper doll, not wired for motherhood, dancing only for herself.

We park in an illegal zone, since every space is full—the

place packed in honor of one Deanna Faire. "Give me a damn ticket," Tanay says fiercely. "We ain't straying far from this car, in case he pulls some shit."

We approach The Shade and Tanay hangs back, searching over her shoulder for Andrew.

"We'll be fine," I tell her. "What can a man do to me in the public square?"

"Nothing, not with me around," Tanay says. "I need to kick some ass."

I see Mushi written all over her, and it's a little scary.

We walk at the door and I fish in my travel wallet for cash.

"We're sold out," smirks the bouncer. "Biggest thing in town tonight." He looks Tanay up and down; he's a black man who does not fit this country gig. "But I might sneak you in, sweetness."

"Fuck you," Tanay says, without rancor.

We hear a door bang to our left. It's a stage door, a few yards down, where one of Dee's musicians stands in a leather jacket, smoking.

"Hey!" Tanay hollers at him, walking fast his way. "You got a light?" She's pulling out her cigarettes as I trail her.

"Wait a minute, beautiful, where you going?" the bouncer croons behind us. "Don't you try to sneak in now—"

The musician, a twenty-something white dude with a goatee, is the bass player who I saw backing up Dee at that rehearsal it seems eons ago. He considers us while he inhales, then touches his cigarette to Tanay's, unsmiling.

"Get us in?" Tanay says, low.

"Why not?" the dude says, and lets us in under his arm.

"Hey!" Shouts behind us from the bouncer. "Come on, man!"

"Thank you," Tanay tells the goatee guy. "Listen, I need one more favor. My friend, Drew Burrell, we need him to get in, too."

"Aw, come on," Goatee Guy says. "Y'all, maybe. But I'm not going to let in a whole posse of underage."

Tanay puts her hand on his arm and gives him big, sweet eyes. "We're not here to drink. We need protection," she says. "Dudes are messing with us all the time, and we need him."

You can see the guy melting at too-cute Tanay.

As we dart down the narrow dark hall, I hear the dude tell the hollering bouncer, "Let it go, man. You see the women that like this music? Need all the help we can get!"

The little hallway opens into the very back of The Shade, behind the bar and near the restrooms where a long line of either too-plump or too-skinny white girls snakes around the corner, chittering and twittering and dancing on their toes with waiting. We're standing at the end next to an unlabeled door, covered in graffiti.

A chirp of the phone. I hand it to Tanay. "Drew. He's here."

She grabs it and says, "Be right back." She grabs my arm. "Stay right here—I'll come right back." She runs down the hallway to the stage door.

A burble of rumor comes down the line to the bathroom— grumbles and girly rants. "I thought she was supposed to be out here signing CDs."

"Well, she's kind of a diva."

"Ha! You think?"

"Where the hell is she?"

A girl in front of me jerks her thumb over her shoulder, at the door I'm standing near.

My heart has slowed to one beat a minute. I'm walking through thick oil, I'm swimming, as I turn, then turn the knob, opening onto the face of a snarling Bethany, standing guard behind the door. "What are you doing here, bitch?" She grabs my arm.

I shake her off and barge past her.

I'm inside the tiny dressing room with a scarred mirror, and a few feet away Deanna stands in front of it, biting her lip. In the mirror she looks cadaverously beautiful, her skin almost translucent. The sky-blue, empire-waist dress, when she leans, catches against a stomach. Right there, I see more than skin and bones beneath—a soft swell that rises.

Bethany's still screeching. "Get *out!*"

Deanna looks at Bethany like a zombie. "It's cool. Wait outside."

Bethany retires like a good minion, snarling at me. I come stand behind Dee.

"What do you want?" Deanna says to the mirror, her voice weak. We stare at each other in the glass, till she does an automatic check of her face. Her hands tremble.

I say, "When are you due?"

And before she can hit me, I say, "I know who it is."

"What?" Her eyes glaze over like she's about to faint. She sways, then steadies herself on the counter. I reach for her, but she swats me away. "I'm fine." She swallows hard.

Why do I want to take her in my arms and tell her it's okay?

Through perfectly sculpted, white teeth, she says, "Don't you tell. What do you want, money?"

"Deanna," I say, "you really think that's why I'm here?"

Her eyes brim with tears. "Fine, do whatever, then."

"You asked what I want—I want everything to end."

"Jesus." She looks back at the mirror, at herself. "Is that why you ran away, like an emo bitch? What, because you were bullied?"

"Because I was raped."

Her stunned look lasts forever. "You're crazy. He's always with me."

"So you knew," I say slowly. "Did I say it was him? Yet you knew."

A telling moment of silence while she composes her face. "What are you talking about—"

"Why did you text me?"

"I was worried about you!"

I search her face and it's a mirror, it's too glassy with composure to know whether this is true. Does she even know her own thoughts?

"You were worried? Or did he say, 'Get the bitch back so I can handle this'?"

My voice is not my own—or maybe it is. Maybe it is me who sounds so clear and resolute. Deanna grips the scabby counter littered with hair spray cans, powders, and lipstick. I add, "When you texted me, he was whispering in your ear, wasn't he. Trying to track me, and you never wondered why?"

"He's serious about *me!*" Her voice is shrill. "Not you, not your crazy mother."

"Serious enough to ruin you," I say. "Your career. Are you going to keep the—"

"No!" she hisses. "Why would I keep it? He's taking care of things."

"I'm sure he is." Just like he was using her to find my whereabouts, maybe wondering how to take care of a wandering Wendy, perhaps another little problem. How much I want to tell her that every night since May I've prayed a thousand times to St. Michael, *Just don't let me have a baby.* But her face is not the kind you tell this sort of thing.

She smooths her hair in the mirror. "I said I don't care what you do," she says coolly, grabbing a lipstick. She unscrews the cap, and it looks like a finger of blood. "Make a scene, tell everybody." Her hand jitters with palsy, and the cap hits the floor.

Our eyes meet in the mirror. I want to hate her, call her sociopath again, but unlike Shaye, she has fear glistening from her eyes, sweating out her pores. Beneath that terror, she still wants him, like a scared little girl. I can feel it like my own heartbeat.

"Deanna," I say, "don't you want it to stop?"

Her face opens for just a second, rippling with hurt and hate. Her eyes get wet. Then her face congeals like she stepped into a freezer. "Like anyone would believe a word you say."

She charges by me and the door bangs behind her.

After a few moments, I leave. I look down the hallway to the side door, and see Tanay at the end, craning her neck—calling, "There you are! He's here!"

We walk to the stage door toward the only boy I could ever trust. Thank MJ he came.

CHAPTER 47

ANDREW LOOKS HANDSOMER THAN I'VE ever seen him—a feat if there ever was one. He wears a long but fitted dark blue polo, Yankees ball cap, and crisp blue jeans with boxers hanging out just a peep, printed with a fox hunt scene. His eyes are big behind huge black-frame glasses.

"Aren't you the hipster," I say. I glance around. "Where's your entourage?"

"Easy now," he says. He throws his arm around Tanay, squeezes her, and she doesn't resist. Her face shines with happiness as she leans into him. "You going to mess with the peace we've got?"

I hold up my hands. "Oh, no sir."

"You all right?" he says, his face serious. I almost want to take his hand, clutch it, shake it, and say sorry—but his look tells me all is forgiven.

We all consider one another, sober as grown-ass folk, till Tanay nods. "Okay, we ready?"

I start to text Sunny Revere. Then I look up and say, "I think I'll text The Devil."

This guarantees both will show.

Tanay nods with understanding. Andrew looks disturbed, but I trust him to tackle Shaye to the ground if I need it.

Perhaps someday I will forget this number. I type it into Tanay's phone, then tap a message. Funny how easy the words come. *I'm outside waiting for you.*

After a minute: *Who is this*

PYT, I tap.

LOL who is this???

Wouldn't you like to know

Silence while the sound of bass, banjo, and guitar suddenly blasts from inside The Shade, rattling the flimsy walls.

I would

Outside. By the stage door, I text.

I give the phone to Tanay. He would be glad to come meet a stranger, PYT, in a dark parking lot, sight unseen. Who would have thought it would be so simple—and yet it's always been this way. I just couldn't see.

Tanay steps out of Andrew's embrace and walks away with the phone, tapping something. She starts speaking to someone—I can't hear who—and I turn to see Shaye come through the stage door.

From this short distance, I see a puffed-up barrel chest. I see too-skinny legs. That he's crammed into his tight jeans, boots, and a pearl button shirt. Like a linebacker stuffed into a flower vase. Like a centaur with cloven hoofs.

His face falls with disgust. "What do you want?" he says. He glances at Tanay, then Andrew. "Your mother's worried sick. Nice how you just disappeared."

The words hang with the humid air, a whiff of mold like the Passive Solar. I feel someone link an arm through mine—Tanay.

Behind him the door bangs, and a whirl of too-brown hair and a full gauzy skirt, mauve with jingling little bells. Sunny Revere.

"Wendy!" she screams. She knocks Tanay aside and collapses on me. The hug is boa constrictor, patchouli scented, and I'm holding her up. Tears leap to my eyes. She does miss me.

"Oh my God, we've got everyone looking!"

We. He grins behind her, smug. Victorious.

I am almost sixteen. I am full of the holy spirit of something saintly. Its lightning strikes from above all the cruel and ancient serpents who would destroy me. I pull away, and Tanay reclaims my arm.

"Oh my God, this has been a nightmare," Sunny blubbers, her lips wet with tears. "But you're back, Wendybird, you're back!"

A cold behind my shoulders pulses like a mass, like a front has just moved in. But inside I rage hot as magma, compared to that deep freeze swarming all around.

Sunny's voice regains its calm, tears like pearls disconnected from her eyes. "Sweetie, I know you've been so upset. Now where's the car?"

"Mother." I say the word, then breathe. "I'm leaving."

"What? Oh, no." She smiles over her shoulder at Shaye. "You're just pissed right now. We'll get through this."

"I'm leaving. For good."

"Why?" she whines, glancing everywhere, gauging the crowd's reaction, the eyes of Tanay and Drew more important than mine.

Somehow liquid legs stay standing. I swallow hard. "He raped me."

She's still smiling on five-second delay. Shaye's face is a wall; his eyes, chips of mirror. No one moves.

"Honey." Her look pleads. "I know you're emotional, but why go *there*?"

"Because I thought you wouldn't let him."

The silence is flat and thick, pressing all of us down. Sunny shakes her head once, twice, three times, refusing to look at Shaye.

And then I hear Tanay.

"Ma'am, you'll be getting a call," she says. "From Social Services." The leaden beats of Deanna's music pulse behind us; the crowd cheers, shrill and drunk.

Sunny looks at Shaye. Not a ripple in the granite face, his smirk like a slash in rock. He shrugs. "Kids. You know she's crazy, Sunny. She lies like a rug."

Her face melts with agreement. I sway, weak as she. But suddenly I hear, loudly, inside my head: *Wendy Redbird Dancing, no demon can touch you now.*

"I don't care what you believe, Mother," I say. "I will never stop telling the truth."

The words whisper around my ears, my temples, behind my back. It's not the trumpet sound I thought it would be but the sound of dry, dead leaves scattered by the wind's invisible hand. It could be the soundtrack of my life, that dusty sound of something brittle scurrying through the rock quarry.

Sunny's eyes are large discs wiped clear. They're afraid of me. I lose my breath—I don't know what is on my face right now, but somehow, she knows.

"Shaye?" she wails. "Tell me she's exaggerating. Or it was just flirting—a mistake!"

Shaye doesn't flinch. "She's lying," he says. "The bitch is lying."

You can call people a lot of things. But you do not call the daughter of a feminist hippie a bitch. Her face goes white as a scar. "What did you say?" The voice could be Grandma's.

Shaye wheedles, "Baby, I didn't mean it that way—"

"You meant it," Mother snaps. Her naked eyes skewer him. *"Did you touch my daughter?"*

"Baby." The eyes lie, but the mouth smiles. "I never did shit."

Mother fumbles for her phone, scrabbling in her woven bag. "I'm calling 911."

Tanay says, "I already did."

Right then, we hear sirens, far away.

Shaye's face looks blank and stupid for a long second. Then it contorts. "You goddamn fucking bitches! There wasn't anything here worth messing with, never was!"

His look gives me the death sentence. Only a shudder as it glances off my grown body. He bolts through the parking lot, straight at his Harley. He's kicking downward, desperate to get in gear, rocking the bike back and forth, cussing, as sirens scream nearer. Then a crank, growl, and roar of his machine. Skidding tires around cars, squeals out of the lot and a roar down the street.

The blood racing in my head almost knocks me off my feet. I turn, and Sunny weeps before me. The tears spilling over her lids are for once not for her. It's a waterfall unlike no other. I blink, but the image doesn't waver. "Wendy, oh God, I am so sorry."

There's not enough water inside her to clean this up but that's okay, it's okay, I don't know what to do now that she sees. I wonder what I look like to her with veils from her eyes ripped away, the way one wonders how a baby bird might see the world brand new.

I fight for words over my rattling heart. "I have to go." The sirens are closer.

Tanay has come near, Andrew right behind. I feel her cheek against mine and her arms tight as steel around me. That dusty sound of something brittle still roars through my quarry, but a different hum. Something—life—stirs in the empty shell, wakening, wanting out, needing air and sun. They walk me toward the car.

"Wendy!" The screams begin. "Wendy, where are you going?"

I get in the back seat next to Strike in his carrier. He mews. Through the window I lock eyes with Mother who's stumbling close. She looks stricken with a wasting disease, her face gray as the streaks in her hair. She turns and stares stupidly at the squad car screeching into the parking lot.

Tanay gets into the driver's seat, and Andrew gets in beside her. Outside, there's a wail.

"Wendy, don't leave! I love you, sweetheart! Don't you love me?"

"I'll always be your daughter, Sunny," I tell Strike, as I pull him free. He looks solemnly sad for a lightning second, as if he knows what I mean.

CHAPTER 48

GRANDMA HAS RETRIEVED ME AT the DeVrieses' house, and now we are together, driving to Manor's Club. There is no conversation because clearly she wants to commune with her cigarette.

The scene at the DeVrieses' was surreal. Ms. Sadie—who started talking to herself ever since we stepped out of the battered hoop-dee, a litany of "I told you to lock her in that room"—stood on the doorstep with her hands on Tanay's shoulders like she would never let go. Ms. DeVries stared at Tanay with a look that could freeze her in place. Tanay looked out into the night, just beyond where Andrew and I waited awkwardly together on the lawn, silent.

When Grandma's tank pulled into the driveway, it hovered there, humming, as if Grandma wasn't sure whether taking the key out of the ignition was a good idea. But I refused to make this easy for her. I stood as close to Andrew as I could without freaking him out—and hoping I was giving Grandma palpitations in the process.

Finally, Grandma stalked slowly up the driveway and flagstone path to Ms. DeVries, Ms. Sadie, and Tanay. Standing at the bottom step, she was still taller than Ms. Sadie.

"Geraldine DeVries," Grandma said stiffly. "It's been years."

A brusque nod from Ms. Sadie. "Yes, it has."

Tanay and I looked at each other, utterly confused. I still

can't digest that my grandmother has ever lived anything but a whites-only life.

"We co-chaired that community yard sale in the early '70s," Grandma said—and though her back was to me, I knew the loud explanation was for my surprise and benefit. "Both of our churches sponsored it."

"We made a lot on that thing," Ms. Sadie said. "We fed some hungry people."

Uncomfortable silence. Then Grandma said, "I suppose I need to take her off your hands, after this little stunt."

Ms. DeVries said, "Humpf!" and turned away from us, arms folded—but Ms. Sadie stood grim and unfazed. "I don't know if we'll let this one keep her license," she told Grandma, smacking Tanay on the head. Tanay didn't flinch. "The Good Lord saw fit to take mine away."

For a second Grandma looked guilty, like she knew she should have had hers taken years ago.

Clearly, the grandmothers didn't wish to spank us publicly, nor did Ms. DeVries trust herself not to beat me and Tanay senseless. Add to that Grandma's incredible discomfort around black people, and you have many reasons to depart. So after a hug from Tanay, I left with Grandma and Strike.

"Call me tomorrow!" Tanay yelled. "Okay?"

"I will!" I yelled back. Our eyes—first, second, third—met and agreed that nothing would stop us from talking, ever again. I was very glad I left her with Andrew still there, keeping things civil. He nodded at me like, *You'll be all right.*

Now rolling along toward Manor's Club, Grandma and I don't discuss what I couldn't tell her that day in The Rose Room or any of the years before. We don't discuss why she never asked me the right questions. All I know is, I am very happy to be her chauffeur in this tank of a Mercedes.

I have Grandma to thank for my very first spin one summer

visit when I was twelve. After one Saturday Mass she took the morose and monosyllabic me back to Manor's Club. She ordered me out and put me behind the wheel. She knew I'd watched her every move a long time, so she talked only in terms of pedals. I believe I drove at .000016 miles per hour along the perfectly groomed roads with nary a pothole nor false move on the part of shrubs, trees, or rocks. The silent houses, foreboding with white brick and sculpted shrubbery, bury their people so deep they could never know the crime of underage driving going down on their streets. And I did superbly that hot summer day. In a nanosecond, I learned the art of how to float my foot just a hair above the pedal. Hovering, just shy of contact.

Now as I take a curve at exactly 48 miles per hour, I'm thinking, *Now I will live in this strange locale—this Disney landscape, built by elves and mice for hidden old people who hate noise.* For a girl who likes to hide, it seems more than safe. It will be a quiet place where one can think. Dream. Sleep.

In this silence, when I get there, maybe it's time we mapped the Badlands. Got acquainted with the minuscule ZIP codes and locales frequented by others. Forgive all those miles of scarred rock. As we pass through the security gate, Grandma nodding at the sleepy guard, I begin counting the zones of me, broken into regions by dotted lines, flat like a wood puzzle, maybe someday to be found like Mars, teeming with buried life.

Grandma breaks into my thoughts. "You understand this will be a big fight."

"Yes. Epic," I say.

"Don't joke. And don't underestimate your mother." Her face is grimmer than usual and sucking the life out of that Virginia Slim. "She is, after all, my daughter."

"A daughter who never darkens your door."

My comment hangs in the silence, nothing but the hum of

wheels at less than 16 miles per hour. Then Grandma barks with what I think is a laugh. "Well, let's count that blessing, then."

I think back on Tanay, her strong and broad frame like a sentry next to Andrew who is tall and regal like a Queen's soldier. I think of Ms. DeVries and Ms. Sadie, somber as they hand me off to Grandma, with looks of *Handle With Care*. I have four—no, five—people who want my news, who wonder where I'll be tomorrow. This is so strange my heart surges with a queer little leap. Whom should I fear?

We are passing the Manor's Club "meadow"—a park where a few well-groomed elderly walk expensive, inbred dogs past fake stone sheep. It would be just about the opposite of the hippie Nature Fare green. A memory hits me of that place, of me and the one I once called Mom. It was back in the early Oughts, one summer visit to Grandma, when Sunny said we must escape—flee!—that "damn Manor's Club" so we could hang with her BFFs on that dusty patch of dying grass where Millboro kids run wild, dancing on the edges of traffic.

I was eight, and innocent. Some dude was playing bongos and another, a scratchy mandolin. I wanted to spring like a jumping bean, screech like a banshee, and tell the world I am here, here, here.

Mom has bought me a mango smoothie, and it tastes sweeter than sweet. I have on my favorite turquoise, beaded twirly skirt, and red cowboy boots. I am cute, and I know it.

I jump off our blanket and start to whirl. Joy surges through me like fire. The crowd starts clapping, some people cheering. I laugh and stomp my feet in time to the bongos. And around me I hear someone, the newest BFF from Mother's tribe, yelling, "Look at Wendy Redbird—she's dancing!"

Mother smiles, like she's designed me just for this moment. And the friend does not stop, she keeps calling the joyful refrain: "Look at Wendy Redbird *dancing!*"

HOTLINES AND WEBSITES

Phone calls won't cost you anything. Your school counselor or an adult you trust can also help you consult listings online in your region so that you can find centers that provide counseling, hotlines, crisis support, or clinics.

RAINN (Rape, Abuse, and Incest National Network). 24-hour phone/online hotline connecting you to the nearest crisis center. Calls and chats are confidential. Calls will not show up on your phone bill, and the site advises how you can protect online exchanges.

- 1-800-656-HOPE (4673)
- www.rainn.org
- https://ohl.rainn.org/online/ (online chatroom)
- http://centers.rainn.org/ (search for a local crisis center)

National Suicide Prevention Lifeline. 24-hour hotline.

- 1-800-273-TALK (8255)
- 1-888-628-9454 (Spanish)
- 1-800-799-4TTY (4889) (TTY)
- www.suicidepreventionlifeline.org
- http://www.suicidepreventionlifeline.org/ GetInvolved/Locator (crisis center locator)

Childhelp National Child Abuse Hotline. 24-hour crisis intervention and resources for child and adult survivors.

- 1-800-4-A-CHILD (1-800-422-4453)
- www.childhelp.org

National Runaway Switchboard. 24-hour hotline and website for runaway and homeless youth, and their family members.

- 1-800-RUNAWAY (1-800-786-2929)
- http://www.1800runaway.org

Al-Anon and Alateen. Local meetings for support for others dealing with alcoholism of family or friends.

- 1-888-4AL-ANON (1-888-425-2666)

READERS' CORNER: A GUIDE FOR READING GROUPS

- What is Wendy's attitude toward life when the story begins? What accounts for her mind-set?
- What does Wendy believe about Michael Jackson? Why?
- Is Deanna Faire a stereotypical bully, or does she move beyond caricature? What does Wendy gain from dealing with her?
- Why does Wendy and Tanay's friendship develop? What do they give to one another?
- How do various characters see race—or not—and what consequences do such attitudes have?
- Compare Wendy's family with Tanay's family. What is revealed in the comparison?
- What does the relationship between Shaye and Wendy reveal? What are adult readers to make of this relationship? Teen readers?
- Whose fault is it that Wendy suffers her trauma? Why does Wendy blame herself?
- A mother like Sunny is hard to explain to a child. Explain Sunny Revere.
- How do you characterize Wendy's relationship with her grandmother? Does it change?
- How does Wendy's faith in Michael Jackson evolve,

and why do you think it takes this particular direction?

- By the end of the story, what has happened to that faith?
- Does Wendy end up in the right place?
- What do you think will happen next? If you could write a sequel, what would be the first events?
- There are many instances of doubling. For example, Sunny and Wendy obsess over a musical artist; Deanna and Wendy love the same person. What other instances of doubling do you find, and what effect do they have on your perception of the characters and story?
- The book is framed by car travel, and Shaye lives by his motorcycle. What do the various modes of transport indicate—for Sunny, Wendy, Grandma, and Tanay?
- The narrative breaks from the present tense to past tense only a few times. Why might the change occur where it does?
- Epigraphs can serve as an introduction, a summary, or even as a counter-example of a story's themes. Why does the Camus quotation preface this story?

For more detailed chapter and scene questions, visit the Readers' Corner at www.lynhawks.com. For outtakes and musings of the pain and joy of revision, visit the Writers' Corner.

Please feel free to share your discoveries and analysis of the novel with Lyn.

ABOUT THE AUTHOR

How Wendy Redbird Dancing Survived the Dark Ages of Nought (formerly titled *St. Michael, Pray for Us*) is the first book of the Girls Outside series, stories about young women who are gifted, weird, and wise. It was the first runner-up for the 2011 James Jones First Novel Fellowship.

Lyn Fairchild Hawks is also the author of *The Flat and Weightless Tang-Filled Future*, a collection of short stories, which includes "My Grandma is a Racist," a prequel story of Wendy as a child. She is a member of the True North Writers & Publishers Co-operative.

As an educator, Lyn has written books for teachers, including *The Compassionate Classroom: Lessons that Nurture Wisdom and Empathy* (co-authored with Jane Dalton); *Teaching Romeo and Juliet: A Differentiated Approach* (co-authored with Delia DeCourcy and Robin Follet); and *Teaching Julius Caesar: A Differentiated Approach.*

Lyn lives with her husband, Greg Hawks, a musician; her stepson, Henry; and Sonny, an orange tabby, in Chapel Hill, North Carolina.

Contact Lyn at www.lynhawks.com.

A member of True North Writers and Publishers Co-operative Authentic Writing for the New South. *Scribere quam videri scribere.*

truenorthwriters.com

Made in the USA
Middletown, DE
16 July 2015